Logan Belle's first visit to a burlesque club on her birthday inspired her to write the erotic trilogy *Blue Angel*. Her latest novel is the erotic romance *Bettie Page Presents: The Librarian*. Her short fiction has been published in the anthology *Obsessed: Erotic Romance for Women* and the upcoming *Twice the Pleasure: Bisexual Erotic*. Logan Belle lives in New York City, where she is working on her next erotic novel. To read more about Logan Belle and her books, visit www.loganbelle.com.

D0552772

Also by Logan Belle:

Blue Angel
Naked Angel

Fallen Angel

LOGAN BELLE

Canvas

Constable & Robinson Ltd
55–56 Russell Square
London WC1B 4HP
www.constablerobinson.com

First published in the US by Kensington Publishing Corp., 2011

First published in the UK by Canvas,
an imprint of Constable & Robinson Ltd, 2012

A copy of the British Library Cataloguing in
Publication data is available from the British Library

ISBN: 978-1-47210-615-5
ISBN: 978-1-47210-618-6 (ebook edition)

Printed and bound in the UK

3 5 7 9 10 8 6 4 2

MIX
Paper from
responsible sources
FSC
www.fsc.org   FSC® C018072

Acknowledgments

In writing this book, I was tremendously inspired by Courtney Cruz's July 2010 production, *The Fempire Strikes Back,* at LA's The Music Box. During that show, the performer Sin Fisted put on a spectacle that pushed the boundaries of what burlesque can be.

Thanks once again to Alicia Condon, my talented editor. I'm grateful for your support. I'd also like to thank the artist Wendi Koontz, creator of the fabulous Blue Angel tattoo. And, most importantly, thank you to Adam Chromy, who continues to surprise and amaze me with reminders that romance doesn't just exist in fiction.

Sometimes it is harder to deprive oneself
of a pain than of a pleasure.
—F. Scott Fitzgerald

1

Mallory Dale glanced out the twenty-first-floor conference room window of the law firm. Park Avenue was still lined with traffic, but rush hour was technically over. She was looking at Friday night, out-on-the-town traffic, and this meant she was late. Extremely late.

Across the table, her boss flipped through the files she had spent all week painstakingly organizing.

She fidgeted with the handbag in her lap. Inside, her Black-Berry vibrated every few minutes. It had been like that all day, text after text:

I love you.

Or: *don't be mad.*

She imagined now the messages were more likely along the lines of:

Where the fuck are you?

"I think we're in good shape," her boss said, moving the color-coded manila folders into a box. The top button of his blue oxford shirt was undone, his tie loose. Not for the first time, Mallory thought how lucky she was to have a hot boss.

Paralegal work was boring, and working late sucked, but at least she had something nice to look at across the conference room. Although on a night like this, when she was seriously late for her night job, her real job—her real life, actually—Gavin Stone's considerable attractiveness was small consolation.

"We're done?" She jumped up, pulling her bag onto her shoulder.

Gavin smiled at her, shaking his head.

"Am I making you late for clubbing...or whatever it is you kids do on a Friday night?"

"Yeah. Something like that." Let him think she was clubbing. Or drinking. Or just running out to get laid. Anything but the truth. The thought of her day-job boss knowing about her night gig made her stomach knot up like a rope. She wondered how she would ever reconcile the two halves of her life—the two halves of herself, actually: Mallory, the responsible person who wanted to earn a decent salary, save for retirement, and have a solid, committed relationship with her boyfriend, and "Moxie," the burlesque performer who loved her boyfriend so much she used to let him talk her into stretching the definition of the word *monogamy*.

As for her boss, he always called her a kid, but was himself only about seven years older. Although with his big lawyer job—he was one of the top divorce attorneys in Manhattan with his own boutique firm—it seemed like there was a generation between them. And his unflappable, Manhattan born-and-bred cool also made her feel like he was a real "adult" and she was just barely passing as one.

Mallory looked down at her hands. She noticed a chip in her Chanel Noir nail polish. Did she have more in her bag? It was getting harder and harder to find the color—a metallic black with the most subtle flecks of silver and gold. Thank God for eBay, or she would have run out a year ago.

"All right—get lost." He smiled and winked at her, professionally of course. She was sure she wasn't his type. She'd seen the photos of his preppy blond girlfriend on his desk.

She checked the time on her BlackBerry—7:45. And on the screen, the latest text from her boyfriend, Alec:

I know you're still pissed at me, but the show must go on. Where are you?

The cab sat in traffic around Union Square. Mallory leaned her face near the open window, trying to catch street lighting as she smoothed gold glitter over her eyelids and a dark smear of MAC's Russian Red on her lips. She pulled on her garter belt and thigh-high stockings underneath her ugly (but functional) khaki Gap work skirt. The cab driver didn't seem to notice the shuffle in the backseat. Next came the four-inch white stilettos. And that was about all she could manage without the rest of her costume, which was waiting for her at the Blue Angel.

She pressed play on her iPod, and the Yeah Yeah Yeahs "Heads Will Roll" started. She was performing to that tonight. She'd been inspired watching Sofia Coppola's film, *Marie Antoinette,* and she'd convinced her boss, Agnes, to make her a French Revolution corset dress—with a seam down the back for easy removal, of course. Her pasties were in the form of the French flag. Agnes made those, too. When she'd planned the French Revolution–themed number, she'd anticipated that part of the fun would be sharing a wink with her boyfriend, Alec. They would laugh about it after, and maybe she would even keep her towering, blond Marie Antoinette wig on while he fucked her. One of his favorite sayings was the rallying cry of the youth revolt in France in the spring of 1968: *vivre sans contrainte et jouir sans entrave.* Live without limit and enjoy without restraint—with the word *enjoy* serving as a double entendre for *come.* And for a while—three years into their relationship, in fact—this philosophy had worked for them. The perfect open relationship. It wasn't easy, but they had wanted each other badly enough to try. So they were monogamous, except when she gave the green light for him to bring another woman into the bed. It didn't happen that often, and it was usually just some random, attractive stranger they both ended up chatting up at a bar and never saw again. They typically never even exchanged real names, and it was never someone they knew. That had been the unspoken rule. Until last night.

"Late, late! Late, late, late," Agnes yelled, ushering Mallory in the side door that circumvented the front of the club. "I've been asking everyone, where's Moxie? Where's Moxie. And no one knows!"

Moxie was her stage name—they all had one. Alec said her choice in name was sexy and spunky, just like she was.

She could hear him already on stage, the host of the evening, warming up the crowd with his usual biting pop commentary laced with double entendres. He was a great writer—the Bill Maher of burlesque, Mallory always said. Back when she was speaking to him.

Last year, his "day job," *Gruff* magazine, had assigned him a story about the growing burlesque scene in New York. He had become fascinated with the subculture and brought Mallory to her first show on her birthday. Before she could say "shake your ass," she had abandoned her plans to practice law and, instead, auditioned for a place on the Blue Angel stage. Now, a year later, she was one of the top draws at the club. And Alec had made a place for himself as occasional MC.

"Sorry—I'm half-dressed." Mallory pointed feebly to her stockings.

"What does that mean?" Agnes said, her Polish accent thick and her attitude even thicker. "Half-dressed, undressed, late is late. You have to try costume on and what if it doesn't fit?"

Agnes drew fitfully on her cigarette, the no-smoking ordinances be damned.

"You've been making costumes for me for a year—when has anything not fit? You're a genius!" Flattery got you everywhere with Agnes.

"Yes, this is true."

A corner of the backstage area, wood-planked and poorly lit, was the makeshift dressing room. It looked like the chaotic backstage of a fashion show; clothes were scattered everywhere, along with compacts and stray lipstick tubes and stockings of every color, and no one had any privacy. In one corner was a black sheet, thumbtacked diagonally to make a closed space, but no one bothered to use it. Next to it was a signed copy of a photo from this season's Dolce & Gabbana ad campaign that was plastered all over New York, a campaign featuring Bette Noir. Last year, Bette had been just another girl performing on the Blue Angel stage. But then she started dating a pop star, *Us Weekly* featured her on the cover twice, and the next thing everyone knew she had an agent, a cameo in an indie film, and then the national Dolce & Gabbana print campaign. Needless to say, she hadn't been back to the Angel since the first *Us* cover.

Mallory shed her skirt and tank top, avoiding Agnes's disapproving gaze. "You know, Christian Louboutin made a pair of limited edition Marie Antoinette heels," Mallory said. "They were incredible—only thirty-six pairs, and they were all sold. Six thousand dollars for a pair of shoes."

"What color?"

"Yellow, I think."

Agnes waved her hand in dismissal. "I wouldn't pay six dollars for yellow shoes. I make your dress a proper color!"

Behind her, Agnes removed a pouf of the palest blue satin

from her garment bag. She shook it out in front of Mallory with a flourish.

"Oh, my God. It's gorgeous!" Louboutin shoes be damned—Agnes's dress was the greatest homage to the queen she could imagine. The bustier was baby blue satin threaded with white lace and five delicate, pink velvet bows from the décolletage to the waist. The back of the dress was nearly floor length, and supported by the mini-corset it would be full in the back, with a shorter bustle in the front that would brush her mid-thigh. She would pair the dress with a baby blue garter belt and white thigh-high stockings.

"It's perfect," Mallory breathed, stepping inside the dress.

"Pull this side seam, off it comes," Agnes said, appraising her clinically. "It fits. You find someone to lace up the back. I can't be bothered when you show up so late."

She shuffled away, on the lookout for any girls who might be goofing off with a smoke outside or one too many pre-show shots of vodka instead of getting ready to perform. She was like a bizarro-world dorm mother.

Mallory was happy to have the dressing room to herself—a rarity. The universe was rewarding her for being late.

"That dress is worth losing your head over. And I don't mean the one on my shoulders."

Mallory turned around, searching for the French phrase for fuck off. But she could only come up with *merde*. That was the thing about Alec—when he was close to her, she couldn't think for shit.

"I know, I know—where's the guillotine when you need it, right?" He grinned at her, his sexy smile with the slight gap between his front teeth, the dimple on the right, and two days worth of scruff that she couldn't look at without imagining how it would feel between her legs.

It was difficult for her not to smile back at him. But she didn't.

"I'm late, so just...go."

"I'll help you with the back. Come over here where there's more light."

He steered her to the back of the room where it was obviously darker.

"Stop it, Alec. I don't have time for joking around."

He pulled the corset tight with the first band of ribbon in the back, then traced the line of her spine with his finger. "I'm not joking."

He pressed her forward to the black sheet, the makeshift dressing room.

From the stage, she heard the first chords of "Mercy" by Duffy. That meant Cookies 'n' Cream was on stage—a petite, pretty redhead with the hips of a ten-year-old boy and the double-D breasts she bought when she still worked at Goldman Sachs.

Only two performances to go before it was her turn.

"Finish tying this thing," Mallory said. But Alec's fingers moved away from the dress to her ribcage and forward still until he cupped her breasts with both hands. His index fingers played gently with her nipples, and her breath quickened despite herself.

"I need to get dressed," she said feebly, her body automatically arching back to meet his erection pressing against her ass. He rubbed it against her, and she reached behind to press her palm against the length of him. He pushed her hand away, maneuvering her slightly off balance, so she was forced to reach forward and steady herself on a wooden stool covered with weeks' worth of odds and ends of discarded clothes.

He traced the edge of her panties, then slipped a finger inside her, perfectly slowly.

"Yes," she breathed, and he moved it in and out, in and out, the pressure growing slightly with each stroke.

"I don't know why you're so upset with me," he breathed,

his face against her own. "Regardless of what you think, I only have eyes for you. And I definitely only have this for you." He took her hand and pressed it against his cock, hard in his pants.

"Sometimes you make that very difficult to believe," she said.

"You're crazy." He pressed a finger against her clit, barely rubbing her. She felt her heart racing, her mind entering that fugue state that only he could send her to. She arched herself against him, and he dipped his finger inside her again. She knew she was going to come, but didn't want to—didn't want to give him the satisfaction. She made a feeble attempt to pull his hand away.

"Sometimes I think you like fighting just so we can make up," he said, and then she came, her pussy shuddering against him in waves that made her moan much too loudly.

He pulled up her underwear and kissed her neck.

"Come here." He turned her around and cupped her face in his hands. Her mind was already switching back to logic mode, worrying about the cum on her costume, the time she had left before going on stage, whether anyone had heard them.

"I have to get ready," she said.

"Look at me," he said. She did. His eyes were so beautiful, green and gold and blue. She loved his eyes, and nothing made her feel sexier than having his eyes focused on her. The gaze of a thrilled audience was nothing compared to a single look from Alec.

"Alec…"

"We are great," he said. "That's all you need to think about."

He kissed her, and she opened her mouth to him, her stomach doing the little flip it always did, still, five years into their relationship.

He smacked her playfully on the ass.

"Are we cool?" he said.

"It's not that simple."

"I think it should be."

The first chords of "Heads Will Roll" played over the sound system: showtime.

The thirty seconds before she stepped onto the stage were always the same for her: sheer, unmitigated terror. And then the music kicked in, and the darkness gave way to a stage light, and she tugged off a glove or a stocking, and the crowd met her gesture with applause or catcalls or whistles—the usual give-and-take between burlesque performer and audience that was as much a part of the show as the exposure of any body part.

Tonight, she stepped out in her slutty Marie Antoinette garb (complete with towering blond wig), and the Yeah Yeah Yeahs filled the room with the opening refrain: "Off with your head... off with your head..." The crowd erupted in laughter and applause. *They get it,* she thought, and that initial connection to the crowd fueled her through the first minute of her act.

She slowly draped herself over a chair, pulling up her dress to reveal her garter. The crowd screamed and clapped, and she turned to flash her ass. She felt the heat of the stage lights on her skin, and she realized her pussy was still throbbing slightly from Alec's touch.

The song pulsed toward the middle, and she had to fight the urge to race through her act. The foreplay with Alec had left her oddly unsatisfied, and the only thing that would make her feel better now was the rush that came with baring her body to the eyes of dozens of strangers. But going too quickly wouldn't be fair to the audience, and when she was on stage, they were the most important part of the show. It wasn't really about her at all, and her recognition of that fact made her a better performer than most.

When it was finally time, the tempo high and the song peaking, Mallory tugged on the dress's easy-off seam—and she turned in front of the crowd with bare breasts, her nipples covered with sequined French flag pasties (which elicited yet another round of frenzied applause and shrieks). Her pussy was barely concealed by her white lace Belabumbum thong, and her legs stretched long and invitingly thanks to four-inch Celine heels (thank you, paralegal paycheck).

She circled to the rear of the stage, then up toward the front. She cupped her breasts as if offering them to the audience, and the crescendo of applause was almost as good as the pressure of Alec's fingers inside of her. She slowly eased out of her thong and felt the surge of adrenaline that always came with the knowledge that forty strangers were staring at her shaved pussy. She moved back to the chair, crouched with her bare ass to the audience, and rested her head as if in a guillotine.

Stage to black.

2

Mallory made her exit as a striking blonde rushed to the stage: Violet Offender. She was Agnes's latest discovery, a performer who put punk before pussy, with tattoos above her crotch and ass to prove it. The first time Mallory saw Violet take off her clothes to reveal the words inscribed below her navel and on her lower back, she couldn't believe her eyes: on Violet's front, the tattoo read *Merci*; on the rear, a centimeter above her ass, it read *No Mercy*.

Mallory tried to make a quick getaway. The sight of Violet killed her post-performance buzz.

"Hey—that was very cool," Violet said, grabbing Mallory's arm. Mallory pulled back as if touched by something hot.

"Thanks."

"You're not still upset about last night, are you?"

"I wasn't upset. I was just tired."

"Okay, cool. Listen, I'll do the tip jar tonight."

"Really?" Mallory waited for the catch. The tip jar was everyone's least favorite job at the Angel. At the end of the show, someone had to stand at the door in all of her naked glory and hold a can to collect tips. Tonight was her turn.

"Yes. Absolutely."

"Okay. Whatever."

Was this her way of apologizing for crashing Mallory's night out with Alec? Alec insisted he mentioned offhand where they were going, that he had no idea she would show up. But Mallory couldn't help but wonder if he was falling back to old bad habits.

There was a time—a brief, chaotic time—when they had tested the boundaries of their relationship with the occasional three-way. It had started as Alec's idea, and she had gone along with it. Alec would argue that she *more* than went along with it—that she had enjoyed it as much as he did. But the truth was, she had always had mixed feelings about it. Her girlfriends thought she was crazy, that she was asking for trouble. And then a few months ago, she and Alec had both agreed that the adventurousness of it wasn't worth the tricky emotional terrain. But her best friend, Julie, had told her it wouldn't be that simple.

"It's like what Chris Rock says in the HBO special.... Once something is 'on the menu' for a guy sexually, it's impossible to take it off."

"It's off," Mallory had insisted. But last night, when Violet had showed up at their dinner date at the Stone Rose, she had to wonder.

Alec was almost finished with his MC segue between acts, and Violet squeezed Mallory's arm with a wink before slinking onstage.

"Hey, Mal. Great costume," said Poppy LaRue, her arms full of discarded clothes. Usually they had a designated "stage kitten" to clear the stage after each performance. It was the stage kitten's job to clean up the stage after each act, to clear it for the next performer, while she waited for the day when she would get the nod from Agnes to take the stage herself. But this natural order had been disrupted when their stage kitten was poached by the rival club, the Slit. "I love Cinderella," she said.

"Cinderella? Oh—no, Poppy...It was Marie Antoinette."

Seeing no flicker of recognition, Mallory told her, "Never mind."

Her friendship with Poppy had come a long way. Poppy LaRue was a tall, pretty blonde straight from the cornfields of Arkansas who had started at the Blue Angel a year before Mallory. She had been so threatened by Mallory's appearance on the scene and the attention Mallory got from Bette Noir—the object of Poppy's excruciating crush—that Poppy tried to sabotage Mallory at the club and even, Mallory suspected, made a play for Alec. But Poppy had mellowed once she fell into a great relationship with Patricia Loomis, Mallory's former boss at her old law firm. Mallory and Poppy had become genuine friends lately. Poppy had even confided in her one night, over strong mixed drinks at a bar after a show two months ago, that while she loved Patricia and had never had a relationship like the one they shared, it bothered her that Patricia wasn't pretty.

"Can you believe Ryan Ellison is in the audience tonight?" Poppy said, stretching her long legs like a colt after a run. "I've never seen a movie star here before. There was that musician once....What's his name?"

"Ryan Ellison is in the audience?" Mind clicking, Mallory looked back at the stage curtain, where Violet was doing her thing. "Who else knows about this?"

"I don't know. I just heard Agnes telling Violet."

The tip jar. Standing at the exit after the show: the perfect way to meet Ryan Ellison.

That *bitch*. What an operator. And she was trying to operate her way right into Alec's bed.

* * *

Violet squinted at the audience, trying to single him out while she moved through her performance to the Faint song, "Erection." It was impossible to see with the stage light in her eyes. Some of the girls liked that—made it easier to show their pussies without looking someone in the eye. Violet thought *they* were pussies. But not her. That's why Agnes had told her that Ryan Ellison was in the audience. She knew Violet wouldn't fold under pressure—unlike Mallory. No way could Mallory handle performing in front of the hottest actor in Hollywood. Hell—she couldn't even handle the suggestion of a threesome with her own boyfriend! What was that about? The way she looked at Alec and her last night...It was like they were suggesting making a sacrifice to a demonic cult, not some harmless fucking.

She'd have to work on her.

In the meantime, she would be working on Mr. Ryan Ellison.

Violet exited the stage to applause, foot stomping, and whistling. She loved being the showstopper—the final performer. She knew she would be the one the guys were thinking about later that night as they fondled their still-hard dicks. And hopefully she was the performer the girls thought about when they ate each other out. They were the ones she was really performing for—all those cute lesbians who came to the show every Friday night as a warm-up to their own lovemaking.

Like that couple who came every Friday night last month, a redhead and an Asian who sat in the front row. On the last night, the Asian came up to her and said her friend was going back to Ireland. Did she want to come to the going away party?

Yes. She did.

The next night, Violet followed the directions from the Asian girl's text to a shitty apartment off of Avenue A. She climbed six flights of stairs to a small room filled with drunken undergrads dancing to bad house music and drinking cheap booze and flat beer from a keg. Violet hadn't hung out at parties like that even when she was in college, so she certainly wasn't going to start now that she was three years free of that scene. She was just about to hightail it out of there when the Asian girl appeared by her side, taking her by the elbow.

"The real party's in the back. Wait here a sec—don't leave, okay?"

Violet nodded, watching her slip back in the crowd. Jay-Z's "99 Problems" played off the iDock. She began a mental countdown from twenty and resolved to leave at one.

She had reached three when she spotted the Asian girl weaving back to her through the crowd. The Asian girl grabbed her hand and led her to the bedroom. It was dark—only a desk lamp was on, and a black T-shirt was tossed over the lampshade—and smelled like cigarette smoke. Violet had hated cigarettes ever since she quit three months ago.

The Irish girl was on the bed. She was naked and blindfolded, her arms tied to the headboard.

"Your going away present has arrived," the Asian girl said to Irish, taking a seat at the foot of the bed.

Violet was about to give her a piece of her mind—tell her she was a performer, not a call girl. Then she looked more closely at the girl on the bed. With her dark hair and pale, cream-colored skin, she reminded Violet of someone else she knew. Someone she had fantasized about getting in this exact same position.

She moved to the edge of the bed, peering at the girl. She reached out and cupped her breasts. The girl stirred only slightly, mouth open and nearly breathless. She hadn't made a sound since Violet had entered the room.

Her breasts were bigger than those of the woman Violet really wanted—but that woman's body was an impossible standard. This girl was close enough—close enough for Violet to close her eyes and take a nipple into her mouth. Close enough for her to slide her mouth down the length of the redhead's lean torso, pausing at her hips.

Violet sat back on her knees, and lifted off her tank top. The girl shifted her hips impatiently. Violet turned back to her, placing her hands on her thighs and gently spreading her legs.

"Take off your jeans," breathed the Asian girl from behind. Violet considered telling her to fuck off, but then thought better of it. As long as she was here, she might as well increase her chances of getting off as well. She hopped off the bed, easing off her white jeans. She kept on her black thong, and turned back to Irish, who had spread her legs wider. Violet got on her knees, ass in the air, and flicked her tongue against Irish's pussy. She wondered what Asian thought of the view.

She pressed her tongue deeply into Irish's cunt, and the girl finally emitted a sound—a short, breathy gasp. Violet felt a stirring between her own legs and was happy to sense Asian moving around behind her. She didn't know what the woman was going to do, but anticipated it would feel good.

She focused on Irish, moving her mouth to her inner thigh and slipping her finger in her. The girl clenched her thighs against Violet's hand, and Violet made her motions quicker.

Asian moved behind her, grinding her slippery cunt against Violet and reaching around to feel her breasts. Violet just wanted her to finger fuck her and get her off quickly.

Violet put her mouth on Irish's clit, and the girl yelled out, "Don't stop," in her thick accent. It jarred Violet, breaking her fantasy that she was sucking off the woman she dreamed about, reminding her that she was instead with an exchange student in a crappy apartment building filled with people chugging beer. The woman she wanted would never be in this situation.

And because of this, even when Asian moved her fingers expertly inside her, even when she tasted Irish coming, even when they were finished and both women gazed at her with adoration and told her she was the most beautiful thing they'd ever seen, Violet felt nothing.

And she was tired of it.

Sometime between the end of her set and the time she got to the door with the tip jar, the crowd discovered there was a celebrity in the house. Ryan Ellison was surrounded by audience members, although this was New York, so they were all busy pretending not to notice him.

Violet stood by the door, wearing only combat boots and a black thong. A few people filed out, stuffing singles and the occasional five in the jar. Cheap bastards, she thought. She didn't know how the other girls tolerated this job. It wasn't that she thought it was demeaning—she just wanted to punch these people who spent an hour watching them flash their pussies and then couldn't part with a few bucks on the way out the door to go drinking.

Which brought her to a momentary dilemma: What if Ryan Ellison didn't fork over some cash? Could she still go through with it if he fell into the "cheap bastard" category? It was one thing to be a starfucker (literally), but another to be with someone who exhibited her pet peeve of behavior: cheapness.

Did Bette Noir worry about things like this? No, of course not. If she got hung up on the details, she wouldn't have managed to fuck her way to a six-figure Dolce & Gabbana contract.

But Violet had nothing to worry about. By the time Ryan Ellison reached the door, he was holding a fistful of twenties.

"Great show," he said to her. It was surreal talking to him—she had to remind herself it wasn't the character from the last movie she had seen him in. The one about the six college kids trapped on a beach along with a drug cartel. The press made fun of it, but it was number one at the box office all summer. Ryan looked gorgeous in it, but even better in person. He wasn't just cute or sexy. He was handsome in the way most movie stars weren't, not really. And he was tall. Much taller than her, which always got her a little hot.

"Thanks," she said, meeting his eyes. To his credit, they were looking at her face.

"We're going to catch another show—wanna come with?"

"I don't know," she said. "I have to change...."

"I'll wait for you out front. Black Escalade. Take your time."

She pretended to think about it for a beat. Thirty seconds. Then she said okay.

Mallory found Alec waiting for her by the front door. She was carrying her beat-up Danskin duffel bag over her shoulder, and he took it from her.

"Is that what you're wearing?" he said.

"What do you mean?" She looked down at her jeans and UGGs. Perfectly suitable for the car ride home. And she couldn't wait to trade in her jeans for sweats. She was exhausted. Her post-performance high had evaporated like cheap perfume.

"We have the Baxter party tonight."

"Oh, my God, I totally forgot!" She shook her head. "I can't go. I'm just—I'm not dressed for it, and I'm not in the mood for a party. There will be so many people there...."

"We can't be no-shows, Mal. Not for them."

Mallory had met Justin Baxter and Martha Pike through Bette Noir. The couple was well-known on both coasts for their lavish parties and connections in media and the arts. The Baxters were multibillionaires, thanks to Martha's sex toy and accessory empire. Most famously—and lucratively—she'd invented the Pike Kegel Ball, a device to strengthen and tighten the vagina. While Martha didn't invent Kegel exercises, she made them cool, sexy, and fun with accessories. And she was living very well because of it. Her handsome husband, Justin, was a huge fan of burlesque. Their private parties were notorious for performances by the best up-and-coming artists in New York and LA. Rumor had it that on more than a few occasions, movie stars and models had spontaneously tried their hands at burlesque at the parties, getting on stage and shedding their clothes.

The Baxters had, in a sense, given Mallory her start in burlesque; she had done her first performance at Justin's birthday party in LA last year, when Bette met her girlfriend, Zebra, and bowed out of the lineup at his party so she could join Zebra on the start of her world tour. That was around the time when Bette quit the Blue Angel, and Mallory had only seen her a few times since.

She liked the Baxters, and she would always feel somewhat indebted to them for the chance they gave her to become Moxie. Alec was right—they couldn't bail on the party.

"Okay, you're right. But what should I do about my clothes? Should I go home and change?"

"We can't go all the way back uptown and then turn around to go to Bond Street. It's already eleven o'clock. You know what? Put your costume back on. They'll love it."

It sounded crazy, but he was right. If there was any place she could walk into on a random Friday night wearing a Marie Antoinette costume, it was the Baxters' house.

"Okay. Give me ten minutes to get dressed again."

Even though Violet took a half hour to clean off some of her body glitter and put on jeans and a simple black tank top, the Cadillac Escalade was parked outside, just as Ryan had promised.

He opened the door from inside the backseat, and she climbed in beside him. The driver was a beefy guy with a crew cut. He wore sunglasses even though it was close to midnight.

"Hey," Ryan said. He was smoking a joint and offered it to her.

"No, thanks. So where are we going?"

"Well," he said, taking a hit. "The Blue Angel was sort of the preshow for us. I'm meeting some buddies at the Slit."

The Slit was a club on the edge of the East Village. It was a much trendier and more high-profile scene than the relatively underground Blue Angel, complete with velvet rope front door, bouncers, and a dress code. It called itself burlesque, but it was really just a high-end sex club. Violet had gone a few times. Most of the acts were borderline misogynist: girls sticking knives in their pussies or getting tied up and whipped by guys calling them whores.

But that wasn't why she was going to say no tonight. Even when she was out with friends for a casual night, she had very little patience for sitting in an audience while other women were the center of attention. And that dynamic was out of the question for her night with Ryan Ellison.

"I'll pass," she said.

"What?" He looked at her like she had just sprouted a second head.

"I'm not interested."

Ryan told the driver to pull over.

"What's wrong? Are you offended or something?"

"No—not at all. In fact, if you want another show tonight, I can suggest a better one. Very exclusive. Very, very exclusive."

They exchanged a look. It took a minute, but Ryan's million dollar movie star eyes clicked with comprehension.

"Back to the Rivington," he told the driver.

3

A man dressed in a white tuxedo showed Mallory and Alec into the Baxter's infamous art deco apartment at 40 Bond Street.

"Please remove your shoes," he said. Mallory looked at where the man was pointing, and sure enough, there were racks of expensive heels by the door. It looked like the shoe department at Bergdorf's.

Mallory and Alec removed their shoes and placed them on one of the racks. She felt strange in just her stockings, but was distracted from her discomfort by the sight of the giant "fishtank" hanging in the foyer. Bette had told her about this, but still, it was startling: it wasn't actually a fishtank; it was a giant glass cube that housed a constant rotation of gorgeous young women. They lounged around inside, doing their nails or their undergrad homework or talking on their cell phones. Mallory found the concept incredibly offensive, but Bette had told her how much the Baxters paid the girls, and suddenly they seemed a lot less exploited. Tonight's exhibit was a busty redhead wearing black yoga pants and an off-the-shoulder T-shirt from

Barking Dog café. She was either watching a video or reading something off of her iPhone.

"Interesting," Alec said.

Mallory shot him a look.

"What? Is it not interesting? I'm just stating the obvious. Jeez."

Mallory looked around the room, taking note of the bold-faced names. Marc Jacobs. Jessica Szohr. Arianna Huffington. Graydon Carter.

And Billy Barton.

"Ugh, Billy is here," Mallory said. Billy Barton was an affected, twenty-seven-year-old Manhattan trust fund kid who owned and published the men's lifestyle magazine *Gruff*. Which made him Alec's boss. "I knew we shouldn't have come."

"Please—just relax. I need to talk to him anyway. He left me four messages today that he has a great assignment for me, and every time I called him back his assistant said he was in a meeting. So let's just make the rounds, I'll talk to Billy, and then we can go."

Justin Baxter, dressed in an impeccably tailored dark suit, noticed them from across the room. He excused himself from his conversation with a handsome, dark-skinned man she recognized as Dominick Monde, head of Tout Le Monde Films.

"Ah, let them eat cake!" Justin said, hugging her warmly. "Amazing outfit! Did you two come straight from the club, or are we lucky enough to be getting a surprise performance from the great Moxie, the Burlesque Ballerina?

"No performance tonight, Justin." She couldn't help but smile. He was handsome and charming and seeing him always reminded her of when burlesque was new and mysterious and unattainable to her.

"Come say hi to Martha—I know she'll change your mind."

"You guys did miss an inspired performance tonight," Alec said.

"I have to get out more. Martha has kept me tied up." Mallory and Alec exchanged a look. From what they'd heard about the couple from Bette, Justin might have been speaking literally.

"You go say hi to Martha—I'm going to catch Billy," said Alec. Mallory nodded. Fine, let him deal with Billy. She couldn't stand the way he talked down to them, like he was New York royalty and they were serfs in his kingdom.

Justin took her by the hand and led her through a crowded room toward the bar, where a petite blond woman was mixing pink cocktails and pouring them into champagne flutes. Waitresses flanked her with trays at the ready. Justin snapped a glass up and handed it to her.

"What is it?"

"Red velvet champagne cocktail. You'll love it."

She took a sip. It was extremely sweet. He was right—as she was someone who loved dessert more than drinks, it was perfect for her.

Martha spotted them and waved them over. She was stationed on a chair next to a long table covered with what appeared to be gift bags stuffed with pink tissue paper and tied with wide pink ribbons.

"You look gorgeous, as always," Martha said to Mallory when she bent down to kiss her on the cheek. Unfortunately, Mallory could not return the compliment, as much as she would have liked to. The woman looked as unappealing as ever, with her overweight, pear-shaped figure, and stringy, brown hair, her sausage feet stuffed into orthopedic shoes. The contrast to her model-hot husband was always jarring. When Mallory had first met them, she'd assumed their relationship was purely a business transaction: he lived off her fortune, and she was squired around town by a hot piece of man-candy. But the more she saw of them, the more she realized they truly enjoyed each other's company and shared a love of fine art, food, partying, and subversive sexuality.

"I love, love, love your costume!" Martha effused. "Please tell me you're going to perform? We threw this little gathering together last minute, and I feel terrible we have no entertainment."

"Oh, no, not tonight, Martha. I'm exhausted. I came straight from the Blue Angel."

"Just a quickie—it will only take five minutes and will make the whole night! Justin, find her some music."

"Guys, really, I appreciate the enthusiasm, but I'm just not in the right headspace tonight."

Justin and Martha exchanged a look.

"No pressure, doll. We just thought it might be fun," said Martha.

"Okay," Mallory said, eager to change the subject. "So what's new in the world of vaginal optimization?"

"I'm glad you asked! Your party favor will answer that," Martha said, reaching over and handing her a bag.

It was surprisingly heavy.

"What is this?"

"Open it," Martha said, with unabashed glee.

Mallory lifted a weighty cardboard box out of the bag and opened it to find a wide glass pot filled with what appeared to be pink jelly.

"Strawberry jam?" she said.

"No! It's for your vagina," Martha said.

Mallory looked at her blankly and then examined the pot. The label on it read HONEYMOON TWO.

"You coat the inside of your vagina with it, and the gel makes it slick and tight—and presto, you're a honeymoon virgin again." Justin said.

"Wow. This is really ... inventive," Mallory said.

"Not everyone makes the effort to Kegel," Martha explained. "Or their muscles are so far gone, it doesn't work. Regardless, I've come up with a quick fix. It's not even on the market yet. I'm giving my guests tonight a preview. Or, a pre-slather."

"Um, thanks," Mallory said.

"I'm going to bring some by the Blue Angel for the girls," Martha said.

"Okay—great," Mallory said. Because what else was there to say?

She looked around for Alec, but the room was filling up with women, one more beautiful than the next. And, surprisingly, her outfit wasn't the most bizarre in the room.

"Some interesting fashion choices around here," Mallory commented.

Martha sighed. "I find it tedious, Honestly, Moxie, you can get away with it. You're a performer. But most of these girls? Posers. They're absolutely unoriginal. It's Lady Gaga chic, and it's so yesterday. But my husband finds them entertaining, don't you, dear?"

"I have to admit, I do," he said, kissing Martha on the cheek.

Mallory saw Dominick Monde heading their way with a pale, freckled brunette in tow. She knew it was time to make her exit.

"Well, it was great to see you guys. I'm going to find Alec and head out soon. It's been a long night."

They kissed her good-bye, made sure she had her gift bag, and told her to have Bette call them when she was back in New York. "Getting in touch with her and Zebra is like trying to get an audience with the Pope," Justin said.

Mallory spotted Alec in the next room almost immediately. How could she miss him, standing next to Billy Barton, who wore one of his trademark, flamboyant, three-piece suits. Tonight's fashion statement was a hunter green suit with matching green, polka-dotted tie. If he hadn't been so hand-some, with thick, dark brown hair and piercing blue eyes, she doubted he would get away with his outfits—no matter how much money he had in the bank or how many magazines he owned. She could see the enormous, gold, Yacht-Master Rolex watch on his wrist from six feet away.

"Hey, Mallory. Nice to see you. You look fetching, as always." He kissed her on both cheeks. "You're just in time for the good news."

"Oh, what's that?" she said. Alec put his arm around her, but she shrugged it off. She was still pissed off about last night, and no matter how late it was getting or how spirited the party, she wasn't ready to kiss and make up.

"I was just telling Alec I'm flying him to LA next week for a major interview."

"Oh, yeah?" She glanced at Alec, but he was looking at Billy expectantly.

"Kendall James: our March cover story. She's in the new Kathryn Bigelow movie coming out that month. Major score."

Mallory looked at Alec. A year ago, he had been lucky to get an interview with Bette Noir, a New York burlesque performer. Now he was flying to LA to interview the hottest starlet in Hollywood? She hated to admit it, but she felt jealous.

"Are you serious?" Alec said, clearly elated.

"Serious as cancer, my man. So here's your excuse to have a Kendall James movie marathon this weekend. Just to save you some trouble prioritizing which ones to watch first: she's topless in the Ryan Ellison one."

Mallory rolled her eyes. "I'm leaving," she said.

"I'm leaving, too," Alec said. "Billy, great score. I won't let you down—*Gruff* readers will see a whole new Kendall James when I'm done with the article."

"I kind of like the old, topless Kendall James," Billy said. Alec laughed.

Mallory walked to the door.

4

Violet was a visual person. She had seen a lot of beauty in her twenty-five years—not the least of which greeted her in the mirror every morning—and she was difficult to impress. And still, Ryan's three-story, 3,200-square-foot penthouse suite at the Hotel on Rivington made her gasp.

Floor to ceiling glass walls. A panoramic view of the city. The room was glass, dark wood, and steel. It was elegant, masculine, and very, very, hot.

Ryan opened the bar.

"What do you want to drink?"

"Champagne," she said, without hesitation. She only drank champagne. In fact, she only drank carbonated beverages, period. Sometimes she even brushed her teeth with seltzer water. Another girl at the Blue Angel, Poppy, shared her affinity for bubbles. Poppy had gorgeous long legs, and Violet had hit on her one night, but apparently she was in a committed relationship with her hideous dyke girlfriend.

He pulled out a bottle of Krug.

"Cool," he said. "I didn't even know that was in there."

He poured her a glass.

"Ready for the tour?" he said. Violet did want a tour—was dying to see the place. But she didn't want to become any more impressed. She was losing too much power as it was. She gulped her Krug. It tasted amazing, and she wondered if it was very expensive.

"Why don't you just make yourself comfortable and point me to the bathroom?" she said.

"The big one is upstairs, but come here for a sec. Check this out."

Reluctantly, Violet let him steer her to the back of the loft-like first floor to the home theater, complete with a DVD library of what seemed to be hundreds of films.

"Holy shit," she said. She loved movies. She used to collect DVDs but had realized it was a huge waste of money—so much more practical to collect sex toys. But this . . . It was the most luxurious thing about the suite. More movies than she could sift through.

"Very cool," she said, pulling out a selection from the "classics" row. "They have *The Blue Angel*."

"Who's in that?" Ryan said, pulling it away from her, no doubt wondering if it was something his agent should have gotten him a part in.

"Marlene Dietrich," she sniffed. "It's the favorite film of the old lady who owns the Blue Angel. Her inspiration."

"This is really old," he said.

"I know. But it's amazing. Really." The film was German and from the 1930s, about a guy who falls in love with a beautiful cabaret performer named Lola Lola. He was a very rigid and in-control guy, but Lola Lola awakens this mad passion that ultimately destroys him. That was the thing about passion—it felt amazing but would kill you in the end.

She thought about her own Lola Lola, and that was the last thing she wanted.

"Where's the bathroom?" she said.

He looked up from the DVD, as if suddenly remembering that he had a woman in his suite who had promised him an alternative to the Slit. He tossed the film onto a chair.

"You are insanely hot," he said, moving closer to her with a smile. He slipped his hand under her top, running his thumb over her nipple. She didn't feel especially turned on.

I'm hooking up with Ryan Ellison, she told herself, trying to get some mental heat going.

They locked eyes, then he kissed her mouth. He kissed like a college boy, overeager and a little sloppy. She pushed his face down to her breasts, and he kissed them over her shirt, cupping them hard and pushing against her so she felt his stiff cock against her waist.

"The bathroom," she repeated.

"What?"

"Where is the bathroom? The master one."

Time to get down to business. She already had an idea about what her "performance" would be. It was something she had been planning for next week at the Angel, and she couldn't do it twice in the same week. But tonight was clearly a better use of the particular creative expression she had in mind. Besides, it was probably something that would make Agnes completely furious.

"Upstairs."

She took his hand and led him up the steel and glass stairwell in the center of the floor. Turning to her left, she saw the Empire State Building glowing green and purple, the rest of the city splayed beneath it like a tableau created solely for her personal viewing pleasure. She was tempted to stop right there, to fuck Ryan Ellison in front of all of Manhattan. But if there was one thing she knew, it was that it always, always paid to delay gratification.

But Ryan Ellison was clearly not with that program. His

arm circled her waist, and he started unbuttoning her jeans. He stroked her over her panties, and she felt herself get wet. Thank God. If the hottest actor in Hollywood couldn't get her going, she was in trouble.

Violet looked at the green glow of the building in the distance and wanted nothing more than to lean over the railing and let him put his movie star cock inside of her.

"Stop," she said, pulling his hand away. He drew back, a questioning look on his face. She pulled off her boots and jeans, throwing her pants over the side of the stairs to the floor below. He looked at her standing in her tank top, thong, and combat boots. She knew what a great visual she was in that room, on those stairs, against that view. She knew what an amazing sight they would be together, fucking, hot on hot. It was a shame no one else would get to see it. For the first time, she understood the appeal of doing porn.

He knelt down and licked her pussy over her underwear.

"Follow me," she said, leading him by the hand up to the mezzanine and planting him on a couch.

Violet walked through the spacious bedroom, all neutral colors with cherry wood floors and a sleigh bed with pristine white linens. She couldn't wait to dirty them.

Next to the bed was an iPod in an iDock. She turned it on and scrolled through Kings of Leon, the Black Eyed Peas, and Duffy, wondering if she was getting a glimpse into Ryan's musical taste or the whole thing was courtesy of a Rivington staffer. She clicked on Duffy.

She grabbed the ice bucket from the bar, then indulged herself in a peek into the walk-in closet. Ryan's jeans and shirt were in a pile on the floor. Good—he didn't mind a bit of a mess.

On to the bathroom.

"Holy shit." The bathroom was an entirely other level of spectacle—all Italian mosaic Bisazza tile, with glass shower and walls, and, best of all, a two-person Japanese-style soaking tub. She was tempted to jump in for a soak, but decided against it. Ryan would probably come looking for her and join her, and that wasn't the direction she had planned for the evening.

She looked through the Ren of London bath products, making a mental note to pocket a Moroccan Rose Otto Bath Oil before leaving. Then: down to business.

She picked through the basket of bath products and pulled out the High Glide Cooling Shave Cream and a washcloth. In the shower, she retrieved Ryan's Gillette. Then she filled the ice bucket halfway with water.

She took off her tank top and and returned to the iPod to select her performance music. Nothing, nothing, nothing.... bingo: the song "Phone Call" by the Faint. She hoped the music was Ryan's: guys who liked the Faint usually fucked well.

Maybe she'd finally break her losing streak and come.

She cranked the music loud enough to reach Ryan, grabbed the shaving cream, razor, and ice bucket, and made her way to the couch.

Mr. Movie Star was messing around with his BlackBerry, but promptly dropped it when Violet appeared with her bare breasts and her props.

Violet set the bucket of water, razor, washcloth, and shaving cream down on a beveled glass end table across from the couch.

Ryan was smart enough to keep his mouth shut.

Violet swayed her hips, circled around slowly, dancing as if she was the only one in the room. She felt Ryan's eyes on her but ignored him. When she was ready, she eased her thong off and kicked it aside. She ran her hand over her light pubic hair, just an inch-wide "landing strip," as if wondering how it got there. She glanced at Ryan, and she would have sworn he was already breathing heavily. She loved when the guys in the audience looked at her like that, like they could come just from the sight of her. It made her want to start fingering herself, not for his benefit, but because that blatant adoration was the best aphrodisiac, and she felt it most intensely at the beginning of a performance. Once she got too far into the zone, she tuned out and was almost numb. But to stop now would ruin the rhythm of the performance, so no, she wouldn't let herself come. She was sure Bette Noir hadn't lost her discipline when she scored that skanky musician. Now it was her chance to shine, and she wasn't going to lose her game.

Violet turned her back to Ryan and retrieved the shaving cream with an exaggerated bend so he could get a full view of her ass.

"Jesus fucking Christ, you're perfect," he said.

That was it—she couldn't resist. She had Ryan Ellison as a captive audience staring at her ass. When would she get an opportunity like this again? She hadn't had a good orgasm in weeks. What would Bette do? Ah, fuck it.

Her back still to him, she set the shaving cream aside, propped one leg up on the table, and eased her index finger inside herself. She had barely gotten three strokes in when he came up behind her and put his own hand on top of hers.

"What are you doing? No, no, no," she said, turning around and guiding him back to the couch. God, you'd expect more from an A-list movie star. But in the end he was just a guy, like every other guy. But it was her own fault—she was putting her pussy before professionalism. "Just watch."

He opened his mouth to protest but thought better of it and smiled at her. The last time she had seen that particular version of his smile it had been directed at Reese Witherspoon.

Yes, she would come tonight.

She retrieved the shaving cream and the razor, turned back to face Ryan, and lathered up her pussy. After one sharp stroke, she languidly reached over and dipped the lathery blade in the bucket of water. The key to this act was really taking her time, almost making the razor against flesh a dance in itself.

But she wouldn't have that kind of time tonight, because Ryan was already off the couch again.

"What did I tell you?" she scolded, but she couldn't help but smile. He took the razor from her hand and knelt down. She was about to say no, but decided to simply go with it.

Ryan pressed his left hand against her, making sure her skin was taut enough for him to slide the razor without nicking her. His movements were slow, cautious, but deliberate and confident. She closed her eyes, trying to allow herself to give up control, if only for a few minutes. It was impossible.

"Sit," she said, taking the razor from him. He leaned back on his heels, and she resumed her methodical stroking of the razor against her pussy. He watched her with rapt attention. When she was bare, she reached back, dipped the washcloth into the water, and then handed it to him. He took it and, on his knees, reverently wiped the last specs of shaving cream away.

She sat down, setting her bare ass on the cool glass table. He pushed her legs apart and dipped his face to her pussy, licking her in strokes almost identical to those of the razor just moments earlier. She looked down at his shiny dark hair and let herself run her fingers through it. He was beautiful, no doubt. And she couldn't wait to see his cock.

He pressed his tongue against her clit, and she groaned, arching back against the wall. She put one heel up on the table, opening herself to him more fully. If he stuck his finger in me now, I would come, she thought—but of course he would not know that about her. That was the trouble with sleeping with random men—they rarely knew the right buttons to push. With women, you had a better chance of them intuiting what to do right off the bat.

She thought of her Lola Lola, imagined her tongue inside of

her. But no, not tonight. Ryan Ellison was lapping at her pussy, and she was not going to waste it.

She cupped her hand under his jaw, tilting his face up. He stood, and she ran her hand over his erection straining against his jeans. She liked what she felt. Ryan undid his fly and pulled his pants over his hips. She slipped her hand inside the flap of his plain white boxers, her fingers circling around his thick cock. He pulled the boxers down and smiled at her. She knelt, closed her eyes, and ran her tongue slowly along his cock from the base to the tip, then took the whole thing in her mouth. He was big, but then she remembered she might have read that about him somewhere. Nice to discover you *could* believe some things you read in the tabloids.

She took him out of her mouth.

"What's wrong?" he said.

"Let's go back downstairs."

"You sure do like to move around a lot," he said, but he helped her stand. He kissed her mouth, better this time, then her neck, his hands on her breasts then sliding down to squeeze her ass and pull her pelvis against his. The feel of him hard against her stomach made her pussy throb, and she knew she had to get him in place to fuck her properly.

"The stairs," she said huskily, and she didn't have to ask twice.

They stopped halfway down, and Violet again turned to look out at the winking lights and the glow of the Empire State Building. In her state of arousal, it seemed for the first time to be such an obvious phallus, a brightly lit cock beckoning in the center of the city.

But the best part of the view was the reflection of Ryan Ellison.

Ryan pressed up against her, his cock rubbing against her ass. He slid his hands around to play with her nipples, and he licked the small of her back, which gave her a chill up her spine.

"Fuck me," she said, leaning slightly over the railing, watching herself in the window. She locked eyes with her reflection, anticipating what Ryan would do, how he would enter her and what that cock would feel like inside.

She was surprised when he took a minute to eat her pussy from behind before grasping her hips and pushing deep inside, long hard thrusts that made her gasp. But she relaxed into his rhythm and watched their beautiful reflection. Between his thickness buried deep inside her and the sight of herself with a movie star, she knew her dry spell was going to be broken. She was almost giddy with anticipation of her orgasm, when his movements slowed.

"Don't stop," she breathed.

"I want to fuck you in the ass," he said.

Of course you do, you latent homo perv, she thought. *All you guys do.*

"Hmm, is that so?" she said.

"Yeah—that tattoo of yours is very ... suggestive."

It had been a while since she'd agreed to take the submissive position of accepting anal. She loved getting fucked in the ass, but so few guys were any good at it. But if she didn't give her ass up to Ryan Ellison ... who was she saving it for?

But now the chance of an orgasm was over. She never came from anal. It was only pain—but the best kind of pain. Besides, this night had never been about her getting off. It was a dance— a show from one performer to another.

"Okay," she said.

"Cool." He pulled out slowly. "Be right back."

While he went to the bathroom—hopefully to find some lube—she fingered herself, admiring her reflection. Thank God she was beautiful. At least that was one thing she could count on. Everything else was such a hassle.

Ryan padded back down the stairs, resuming his position behind her. He used both hands to spread her ass and stuck one finger inside of her. She gripped the railing, resting her head on the back of her hand as he slowly eased his cock into her ass.

She felt the familiar sting of pain and near-pleasure, the intense sensation that confused every synapse in her body. Ryan made a noise, his hands grasping her hips tightly.

Violet wished she could come. She closed her eyes and thought of a girl she had met after a show a few weeks ago. She hadn't been that pretty, but she had the softest, pinkest pussy Violet had ever seen. She ate her out for an hour and lost count of how many times the girl came. But Violet left unsatisfied.

Violet reached down and touched herself, thinking of that pink pussy. Surprisingly, she felt tension building in her cunt, and she kept rubbing as Ryan moved his cock in and out of her with cautious strokes, his breathing heavy. And then she felt it, that blinding shudder. The girl in her mind changed with a click, and Violet moaned as she imagined her Lola Lola.

She thought of Mallory.

Alec knocked on the door.

"Are you coming to bed soon?"

Mallory looked at herself in the mirror, her mascara slightly smudged under her eyes. She opened the bathroom cabinet, searching for another container of Almay eyemakeup remover pads with oil. The waterproof mascara Poppy had lent her backstage must have been some crazy designer brand because she couldn't get it to budge off her lashes. She'd already gone through half a dozen pads with no progress. She decided she'd have to break one of her cardinal rules and go to sleep with makeup on.

She knew she'd look like a wreck in the morning, but she gave up and tossed the cotton pad into the garbage.

Alec knocked again. "Are you alive in there? I'll never figure out what you do in there all that time. Come on, Mal, open the door."

She opened the door. "It's open. Happy now?"

He looked adorable in his powder blue, long-sleeved T-shirt and navy blue boxers. He had great legs, an even better ass, and she loved nothing more than the feeling of his arms around her. It took all of her strength not to fold herself against him.

"No. Why are you so pissy?" Alec said. "I know Billy's a jerk sometimes, but he signs my paycheck. And trust me, he's not a bad guy. Just a lot of talk."

"Can I finish taking off my makeup now?"

She closed the door. Guys were so dense. Did he really think she was this upset about Billy? Did he think the argument last night had just evaporated—that there was an expiration date on the issue of his inviting Violet Offender on their date?

She pulled her long dark hair into a ponytail and surveyed herself in the mirror. It felt good to be in a simple white cotton T-shirt after a night in costume, but she thought better of it. Maybe she was getting too domesticated—maybe that was why Alec was so intrigued by that crazy bitch, Violet Offender. It was difficult to imagine that woman in anything but corsets and leather. She probably slept in a spiked bra, handcuffed to her headboard.

Mallory pulled off her T-shirt and wrapped a towel around herself. She crept out of the bathroom to her closet, where she pulled out a red camisole and matching underwear. She had zero interest in having sex with Alec, but that didn't mean he shouldn't want to get a little something. She couldn't wait to say no.

He was in bed reading *Vanity Fair*. As soon as he noticed her in the room, he put the magazine down, watching her closely for any sign of warmth or forgiveness.

She gave him nothing.

The covers were tightly tucked on her side of the bed. She pulled them away just enough to slip her slim body between the sheets. She turned out her bedside light, her back to him.

He moved under the covers, too, but didn't make an attempt to touch her. She appreciated that. After a moment, he turned out his bedside light, too.

The thought of going to sleep without talking suddenly made her want to cry.

As much as she wanted to just shut him out, she couldn't. Going to bed angry—or ending an argument with one of them storming out—had caused a lot of problems in the past. She hoped she had at least learned something after all of these years with Alec.

"I'm really upset about last night," she said. There. Simple and direct—healthy communication 101.

"I know," he said. "And I'm really sorry. Violet asked what I was doing after the show, I told her we were going to get a late dinner at the Stone Rose, and I just asked her if she wanted to go to be polite. The last thing I wanted was to upset you. I know you think I was trying to orchestrate something, but I swear I wasn't."

"You're telling me you have no sexual interest in her?" Mallory said, sitting up and turning on her light.

"I don't," he said, sitting up, too. His hair was tousled, his gray-blue eyes sleepy. She wanted to reach out and stroke his face, press her lips against his neck, and breathe him in.

"Be honest."

"Okay, 'sexual interest' in her is an overstatement. But I guess I find her intriguing."

Mallory took a sharp breath. Even though she had known it without his saying it, the words stung.

"What am I supposed to do with that information?" she said, crossing her arms in front of her chest. He looked at her arms—she knew he hated when she got into defensive body posture. Sure enough, he reached over and pulled gently on her arm. She kicked him under the covers.

"Ow!" he said.

"You know, I see lots of 'intriguing' guys—and women, for that matter. But I don't ever put those thoughts or feelings before our relationship. And that's what you did last night."

"I wasn't putting it before our relationship! God, Mallory. I can't win with you. I'm being honest—yes, I find her attractive. Who wouldn't? If anything, I was diffusing any potential sexual tension by inviting her out with my girlfriend. Everyone knows we are together—there was no subtext. I would have invited Poppy or Scarlett in the same situation. Unless..."

"Unless what?" She finally let herself look him in the eyes.

"Unless you're projecting all this onto me because *you're* attracted to her."

"Don't be ridiculous," she said. And yet she knew he wasn't being ridiculous. Last year, he had been interested in Bette Noir. And yet Mallory was the one who ended up fooling around with her—surprising even herself with the expansiveness of her own sexuality. But that wasn't the case this time—far from it. Mallory not only didn't trust Violet, she didn't like her, regardless of how hot she was.

"Am I being ridiculous?" he said.

"Yes!"

"Okay, then can't you admit that maybe you are, too?"

"No," she said. But she knew the tone of her voice was giving away the fact that she'd forgiven him. Sure enough, under the covers, his hand traced the lace of her underwear along the outer curve of her ass. She was glad she'd changed out of that T-shirt.

"Even though you were mad at me, your pussy so was so wet backstage," he whispered in her ear. "It took a lot of self-control not to fuck you right then and there."

Mallory smiled, arching her back against him. She felt him hard against her, and she moved her hand behind her to stroke him over his boxers.

"What makes you think I'm not mad anymore?"

"Okay—maybe you're mad at *me*. But I think you've forgiven my penis."

"I should be most angry with your penis. That's obviously what you think with half the time."

"Only the half that I'm in bed with you." He scooped her in his arms and turned her around so she was lying on top of him. It was a clumsy maneuver, and she laughed.

"This isn't comfortable."

"So get comfortable," he said, stroking her hair. She threw the covers aside, then inched down lower until her breasts were between his legs, her arms were resting on his thighs, and she was able to run her tongue along his cock over his underwear. "Yeah, that's definitely better," he said. She could tell by the catch in his voice how turned on he was. Maybe she was a pushover, but fucking was so much better than fighting.

She eased his boxers down, gliding her lips against his bare cock as she undressed him.

She loved Alec's body, everything about it—from his legs to his cock to the hollow between his collarbone that she liked to kiss. But maybe her favorite part—the part that she had first noticed—was his hands. They had been study partners in a prelaw class senior year, and she had immediately noticed how beautiful his hands were—large but elegant, with beautiful, tapered fingers like those of a sculptor or a piano player. And when he got excited about something he gestured with them broadly. She would just watch his hands, shamefully imagining how they would feel on her breasts or between her legs. And then one day he wanted to show her something in a document on the library computer, and she was scrolling for it with the mouse but kept missing the paragraph. He placed his hand on top of hers to guide her, and that was it.

She had confided in Julie over coffee the next morning.

"I am in major lust with my study partner."

"Do you want to break up with Jeremy?" Julie asked about Mallory's boyfriend of six months.

"No! Of course not. I love Jeremy."

Three weeks later she was in bed with Alec Martin. And that was the end of Jeremy.

Now those hands wound in her hair as she pulled down his boxers and took the tip of his cock into her mouth. She tongued his foreskin, lifting it slightly then licking his shaft downward until she reached his balls. Cupping them, she flicked her tongue at them gently, until he gave her the satisfaction of moaning.

"Turn around.... Let me eat your pussy while you do that," he said. She smiled. She loved that he could be that direct with her, that he could talk so dirty. When they first got together it had shocked her. Now she wondered how she could ever be satisfied without it.

Mallory eagerly complied, switching her position so that her legs were on either side of his face, her pussy bent toward his mouth. Now that she had access to his cock from a different angle, she focused on the tip, running her tongue around the rim before taking his entire length into her mouth. She sucked firmly, moving her lips back and forth, her tongue circling the tip every time her oral strokes reached the head of his penis. She trailed her mouth with one hand firmly on his wet shaft, working it up and down in tandem with her mouth. She tasted the first bud of semen. And between her legs, his tongue lapped at her cunt while his finger massaged her clit.

When she got excited, it became more difficult for her to concentrate on working his cock with her mouth. She tried to focus, but when he started circling the rim of her asshole with his thumb, she knew it was over. He gently pressed his thumb into her ass, his mouth sucking on her clit like a pomegranate seed. A low moan escaped from her.

He held her by the hips, his tongue moving from her clit to the center of her pussy, then pressing deep inside her, fucking her, while his thumb worked in and out of her ass. She didn't want to come like this—apart from him, while he played her like an instrument. She pulled away.

"What's wrong?"

"I want you inside of me," she said. He sat up, pressing her down to the bed. Instead of letting her mount him, he moved his full weight on top of her. She slipped her arms around him, kissing his neck, running her lips along the rough stubble on his chin. He brushed her swollen outer lips with his cock, and she felt a familiar surge of anticipation knowing he was going to enter her. But he kept his cock outside, rubbing against her until she was in a frenzy. She grabbed his ass, pulling him to her as hard as she could.

"Alec..."

"What?" he said, kissing her temple.

"I want you," she said quietly, wondering if she would get away with only saying that much. Sometimes he made her beg for it; as much as she loved sex, she hated articulating what she wanted. And really, when it came to pleasing her, he never needed her to say a word—he knew her body almost better than she did.

"I want you, too," he said. And then, so quickly it was almost startling, he thrust his hard cock inside of her. She gasped, adjusting her hips so he didn't get quite so deep. His mouth moved down to her breasts, biting her nipple. She didn't know why she liked it rough sometimes, but with Alec she had learned the interplay between pleasure and pain.

He slid in and out slowly, and she had to fight the urge to tell him to stop moving, to just stay inside of her. She felt like she could come just from feeling him fill up her pussy. Then, his movements quickened and shortened to hard thrusts, and she knew he was close to coming. He pressed his finger inside her ass, and her pussy convulsed in waves.

"Oh, my God," she said, clutching his back. His thrusts grew harder, animalistic in their intensity, and then he cried out. Her pussy clenched against his cock over and over, the waves of pleasure overtaking her.

When he pulled out, her pussy still throbbed slightly, as if reluctant to let go of the orgasm. Breathless, they lay side by side, and he pulled her closer so she could rest her head in the crook of his arm. She looked at his profile, his flushed cheeks and strong nose, and marveled at his beauty. There was an adage that before sex, men aren't thinking clearly, and after sex, women aren't thinking clearly. She wondered if that was true, because in that moment, all she could think was that she was madly in love.

5

The line inside City Bakery stretched from the register almost back to the farthest reaches of the buffet. Mallory, Julie, and Allison quickly broke off strategically: Julie would snag a table upstairs, Mallory would get the baked goods, and Allison would buy the "real food" they felt compelled to eat along with the shop's signature pretzel-croissants and zucchini chocolate cake.

"This place reminds me of the dorm," Julie said. Their coordinated efforts landed them a prime spot on the upper level, with three trays heaped with food, coffee, and hot chocolate.

"If Penn had served food like this it might actually have been worth the fortune in tuition," Allison said.

"Don't knock the old alma mater," said Mallory.

"Says the only Ivy League–educated burlesque star on the planet."

"For your information, not only am I not the only Ivy League burlesque star on the planet, but I'm not even the only Ivy burlesquer in New York."

Allison shook her head. "Then they really are charging too much for tuition."

Mallory threw a straw at her. Julie laughed, covering her full mouth with her hand. And that's when they saw it.

"Um, excuuuse me—what is that giant object weighing down your ring finger?" Allison said.

"I'm blinded!" Mallory jumped up and hugged her oldest friend.

Why had she not noticed it as soon as she walked in? Julie was glowing. *I'm too wrapped up in all this crap with Alec, that's why.*

"Jonathan proposed last night. I was dying to tell you guys, but I knew if I just waited twelve hours I could tell you in person." She looked at her ring as if seeing it for the first time.

"Where did it happen?"

"Oh, my God, it was so romantic. We went to the Shake Shack in Madison Square Park, waited on line for like forty-five minutes, then took our stuff to a bench near the Fifth Avenue side. And we were just sitting there eating, and there were pigeons kind of milling around waiting for scraps of food. And so Jonathan got down on one knee, and I swear I thought he was feeding the pigeons or doing something like that, and the next thing you know he was holding out this gorgeous ring and asking me to marry him! And it was just like in a movie—after I said yes and was hugging him, the people on the bench across from us started clapping."

"Julie, I'm so happy for you." Mallory said. And she was. But she couldn't help but think that while Julie's boyfriend was proposing marriage, she had been trying to figure out if her boyfriend was still trying to get other women into bed with them. And sure, she and Alec had had many laughs about how "vanilla" Jonathan was. But Julie didn't seem to be complaining.

A child shrieked at the table next to them.

"Ugh, there are too many babies here." Allison made a face.

"Allison!" Julie said.

"What?"

"I knew it: you guys are totally going to ditch me when I move to Westchester."

"You just got engaged last night, and already you're moving to Westchester?" Mallory said.

"For the record, we won't ditch you when you move to the 'burbs—at least, not until you pop out your rugrats," Allison said. "Right, Mallie?"

Mallory played with her mug of hot chocolate. "I like kids," she said.

"Well, I'm going to take a pass on that particular life experience."

"Oh, really? And how does Andrew feel about that?" Mallory said. Allison had met her boyfriend, Andrew Goldmark, at one of the PR events she had coordinated a year ago. He worked on Mayor Bloomberg's staff, was five years older than her, and together they made a typical Manhattan power couple.

"We're completely on the same page. Marriage, yes. Kids—no. And we both want a traditional wedding: a hundred guests, white dress, the whole deal."

"I love weddings," Mallory said. "Every time I pass Vera Wang on Madison I get a pang."

"Really?" Allison and Julie said in unison.

"Yeah. Why do you seem so shocked?"

Allison and Julie looked at each other, then down at their food.

"What?" Mallory said.

"Well, we just worry about you," Julie said. "You want the same things we do out of life—a career, a good relationship. But you're going about it in a...strange way."

"What do you mean?" Mallory said.

"I think what Julie's trying to say is, where the hell is this burlesque thing really going? I mean, we get that it's cool and fun and it's great that you took a leap and did it for a year. But really, Mallory—what's the future?"

Mallory fought the urge to say something nasty and defensive. The truth was, sometimes she wondered the same thing.

"You say that you want marriage and kids, but you've been dating Alec for years and you guys still act like you're in college," Allison said.

"What's that supposed to mean?"

"Don't get defensive, Mal. It's just that you run around in that crazy burlesque world and then you wonder why Alec is always looking at other women. It's not the best environment for a healthy, monogamous relationship."

"I told you, we are monogamous now."

"When was the last time he suggested bringing another girl home?"

"Months."

"Well, I don't think the verdict on Alec is in yet."

"Who asked you to be judge and jury?" Mallory snapped.

"Okay, let's stop. Mallory, we're just concerned about you."

"Thanks, but I'm fine."

She thought about Alec's stunt with Violet the other night. And she didn't feel fine at all. And as long as Allison and Julie were already down on her relationship...

"But this thing did happen the other night that sort of bothered me," she said.

Allison and Julie leaned close across the table, as if Mallory were about to reveal the secret of the universe.

"As you so critically mentioned, you know Alec and I have had the occasional three-way...."

"Yes, and we think you're insane," Allison said.

"Can you cut the editorializing and let me tell you this story?"

"Yeah, I want to hear the story," Julie said, twisting her three-carat princess-cut diamond.

"But we agreed it was more trouble than it was worth and that we were done with all that—it was going to be just us. Monogamy. Traditional relationship."

"Except for the time you saw that e-mail to him from the chick from Village Tavern," Allison said.

"Seriously, shut up and let her talk."

"Okay. Aside from that. And anyway, *she* was e-mailing *him*. He can't control that. So two nights ago I had a show, and we decided we were going to go out to dinner afterward. We've both been working like crazy, and we knew we needed a date. He asked me where I wanted to go; I said the Stone Rose, and it was all good. We get to the restaurant, we're waiting at the bar for our table because of course it's a scene and the table isn't ready, and as we're waiting that chick, Violet, from the Blue Angel shows up."

"The one with the crazy tattoos who works as a dominatrix?"

"Yep. That's the one. At first I thought, what a coincidence. So she walks over to us, and Alec is all, 'Hey there, Violet.' And she says, 'Cool place—I've never been in here before.' And I realize that he invited her!"

"No way," said Allison.

"Yes!"

"Did you walk out?"

"No. I thought about it. But then I was like, I'm not leaving the two of them alone."

"I'm sure if you had left he would have followed you," said Julie.

"I know. But still…"

"So what did you do?"

"The hostess seated us, and we had drinks and dinner and it was friendly enough, but Alec knew I was pissed, and I didn't talk to him when we got home. I didn't take his calls at work yesterday. But then after the show last night he told me she asked what we were doing after the show that other night, that he told her we were getting dinner and invited her just to be polite."

"Such bullshit!" Allison said.

"Maybe not," Julie said. "What if he just said it casually, thinking she'd never actually accept, and then she did? Why would Alec do something so blatant and piss off Mallory like that?"

"But this is what I'm talking about," Allison said. "You guys live in this world where the natural boundaries don't exist. You take off your clothes on stage, you've hooked up with other women in the past, and then you wonder why the lines are blurred."

"So you're saying it's my fault?" Mallory said.

"Not completely. But the combination of Alec's personality and the fact that you haven't been great at drawing the line yourself...It's hard to say if he even did anything wrong the other night."

"I can't believe you're defending him," Julie said.

"I'm not. I'm just saying it's not Alec; it's not Mallory—it's the dynamic between them that creates this constant tension."

"So what's the solution?" Mallory said.

"Get out of that burlesque culture. As long as you're in it, your relationship will suffer."

Mallory shook her head. "You're wrong," she said. But a small part of her had already begun to wonder.

6

Violet stood outside the building on Mercer street in SoHo. At not quite 10 a.m., she had already been running around the city for four hours. She awoke at the Hotel on Rivington and let Ryan Ellison eat her pussy one more time before she hurriedly got dressed and fought her way through the paparazzi staked outside the hotel to get a cab to Brooklyn. She needed to find a place to store her dom equipment in Manhattan—it was such a hassle to drag it back and forth, especially when the sessions were last-minute. But that was the price she paid for going freelance; when she had worked exclusively at the notorious midtown dungeon the Cellar, she had the convenience of storing all of her costumes and equipment in her locker. But for the convenience, she had to give more than half the price of her sessions to the house. As a private operator, she could charge whatever she wanted and walk away with every cent. It was worth the occasional last-minute subway ride carrying a suitcase full of whips and nipple clamps.

If only she could figure out how to make such a lucrative move with her burlesque career.

She pulled the keys out of her trench coat pocket. Yes, she had keys to this client's well-appointed loft. His particular, elaborate fantasy included the feigned element of surprise.

She opened the heavy exterior door and took the small elevator to the top floor. It was warm for late October, and she was sweating in her thigh-high, black patent leather boots and constrictive corset. She set her suitcase down and took a moment to powder her pale complexion. It was vitally important, as the saying went, to never let the customers see her sweat. She was superhuman. She was master of the universe.

She was Mistress Violet.

With a quick time check—10 a.m. on the dot—she inserted her key in the door to the penthouse apartment. Slowly, she pushed the door open. Sure enough, as always, the man sat the middle of the room on an antique wooden chair, dressed in a vintage red ball gown pulled up to reveal his small cock, which he was methodically stroking.

Violet strode into the room, her sharp-heeled boots making a menacing clatter against the marble floor.

"Billy! Are you doing that naughty, naughty thing again?" she said, feigning shock.

"Yes, mistress," the man said, with equally feigned sheepishness.

"This is very, very distressing to me, Billy," she said, moving closer, shedding her trench coat to reveal her leather and satin-clad body. The client's hand continued to work his cock while his eyes swept her from head to toe.

Violet reached forward and slapped him hard across the face.

"Did I give you permission to look at me?" she screamed.

"No, mistress. I'm sorry, mistress," he said, immediately reverting his gaze downward.

"You are being a very bad girl," she said. "I'm going to have to punish you, you realize, don't you?"

The man nodded, cowering slightly. Violet pulled a whip out of her small suitcase.

"Remove your dress," she said. The man complied, unzipping the back seam with practiced hands and stepping out delicately. He folded the dress and placed it carefully on the chair. "Now turn around and show me your ass," Violet commanded. When he followed her orders, she waited a few beats, letting him savor the anticipation of the first tear into his flesh. Then, raising her arm and with expert precision, she flogged him across his ass cheeks. She noticed the familiar shudder run through him, and she didn't know—never knew—if it was pleasure or pain. And her arm rose again.

After a few minutes, when red welts formed in a crisscross pattern on both sides of his buttocks, she dropped the whip and sighed.

"That was for looking at me without permission," she said, walking around him in a slow circle. The man kept perfectly still, dared not look at her. "Now we still have to deal with your playing with your dirty parts, don't we?"

"Yes, mistress," he said.

"Bend over the chair, you little whore," Violet said. The man slowly moved into the dictated position, bracing his torso with his forearms on the chair, his legs nearly straight, his ass high in the air.

Violet struggled not to yawn. The tedium of following the same script week after week, coupled with her lack of sleep last night at the hotel, was making this session unusually difficult for her. She used to love sessions like this—simple S&M, a little verbal abuse. Classic and very satisfying. Midway through the session she'd get a high that would last for hours. Now she needed a little bump just to get started most days, and that was getting expensive. It was a vicious cycle, spending money on coke just to get through the dom sessions to make money. Now, the high that she had to get through her nose with her domination work she could only get naturally on the Blue Angel stage. But that gig didn't pay shit. It was a problem—one she wasn't quite sure how to fix.

"I'm going to have to teach you a lesson," she said, kneeling by the suitcase. She pulled out a wide black dildo, and squeezed a liberal amount of lube on it. "Teach you not to play with that pussy of yours. Do you hear me?"

"Yes, mistress."

She advanced toward him slowly, then reached out her foot and skimmed his waiting asshole with the heel of her boot.

"Do you think you are worthy of having my beautiful boot in your dirty, ugly pussy?" she said.

"No, mistress."

"No is right. I'm going to fuck you with my dirty cock— and you're barely worthy of that." And with that, she plunged the dildo deep into his anus. He liked a rough entry and then for her to work it slowly in and out while he jerked off.

While she waited for him to come, she looked around the apartment, marveling at the art, the photographs on the walls, the brilliantly composed furniture and color scheme. She thought about how many celebrities had been to parties in this very apartment, perhaps sat in the chair that their host was now leaning on while being fucked in the ass while drooling over a ball gown, his cock in his hand.

It was hard to recall the times when this had been fun for her. She knew she had once felt that way, but the memory was so intangible, it was like a dream hours after waking. Now all she felt was resentment. It was difficult to always be the one giving satisfaction, never receiving it. She thought maybe she had been on her way to some gratification the other night when Alec invited her to join Mallory and him for dinner. But then Mallory showed up with that sour look on her face. God, she'd love to shove this black rubber cock up her ass and loosen her up a little. But who was she kidding? If she got her hands on

Mallory Dale, she'd forget all about her frustration and start eating that pussy like a kid in a candy store.

"Mommy!" her client called out, as he always did when he came.

Violet looked at her watch. Maybe she could call Alec and see if she could lure him out for coffee.

Her client slumped over the chair, spent.

"Thank you," he said, breathless.

"My pleasure, Mr. Barton," she said.

Time to clean up.

She went to the bathroom, washed her hands, and repacked her bags. She didn't feel the high she used to get from these encounters; she felt drained. It was so exhausting to always give and never receive any satisfaction.

By the time she returned to the living room, her client was transformed from a sniveling sex slave to a media mogul. The entire countenance of his face was different, and he wore slacks, a jacket, and a green, blue, and pink-striped shirt she recognized from the window at Thomas Pink on Madison.

Wordlessly, he slipped her three hundred-dollar bills.

"See you next week," she said.

"One more thing," he said. "One of my writers got comped for this show. It's sold out and supposed to be phenomenal." He handed her tickets to a Jack Terricloth show at Joe's Pub.

"Thanks. I love your connections," she said, pocketing the tickets. "You know, you should own a club. Ever think about it?"

"Not really," he said. "Huge time suck, and few are profitable. I'll stick to media domination."

She couldn't help but smirk at the word "domination." As a magazine editor he should have a better sense of irony. And for some reason, an image of Mallory flashed through her mind. "Suit yourself. But do you have one more ticket for this thing?"

"No. My editor needs the other one to cover the show for the magazine."

"That's a shame," she said, holding out her hand. "You know, my schedule is really looking tight next week. I hope I can fit you in."

He handed over the ticket.

Outside, she dialed her phone.

Mallory grasped the barre with both hands, her right leg extended on top of the smooth horizontal pole, arching her foot. She brought her right arm up over her head, bent slightly at the elbow, her face turning slowly toward it as she arched her back and slid her leg forward on the bar, extending her body into a long stretch.

In the reflection of the floor to ceiling mirror, she could see the ballet dancer behind her, Nadia. They split the cost to rent practice space at Ballet Academy once or twice a week. Nadia was hoping to land a spot with a major dance company so she could make a name for herself. Mallory doubted Nadia had any idea about the type of performing Mallory did—or that the name she was making for herself was "Moxie." Although when Nadia saw Mallory working on her new routine to the Marilyn Manson song, "Heart-Shaped Glasses," she would start to realize her practice space partner wasn't training for *The Nutcracker*. Usually Mallory saved her choreography for practice at the Blue Angel, but lately she felt the need to get away from the other girls.

A knock at the studio door broke her concentration. She turned to see Alec waving outside the glass window. He waved her over.

"What are you doing here?" she said breathlessly, opening the door. Cool air rushed to meet her, making her realize how sweaty she had gotten. There was no workout like ballet—not Pilates, not yoga, not spinning—nothing.

"I want to take you to lunch. I know we have plans to meet later, but I couldn't wait."

"I still have a half hour left."

"Mind if I watch?"

"No, of course not. I'd kiss you but I'm gross."

"You're gorgeous."

She shook her head and returned to the studio. Nadia was packing her bag.

"I'm sorry. Is it bothering you that he's watching? I can have him wait for me outside," Mallory said.

"Why would I mind? I'm all about the audience. I just have to run—practice downtown."

Mallory was amazed at the discipline and rigor of Nadia's life. It was an endless chain of practice, rest, practice. She felt guilty complaining about how little time she had between her paralegal job and shows at the Angel. It was a cakewalk compared to what real dancers went through.

Now that she had the room to herself, she slipped the Marilyn Manson CD into the ancient, wall-mounted stereo. She was glad she'd saved her old CDs and even bought new ones every once in a while just because of the practice space.

She cued up the song, "Heart-Shaped Glasses." It was her favorite song of the album, a dark, decadent Lolita tribute. The video featured a young Evan Rachel Wood, and it was rumored at the time that she had broken up Marilyn Manson's marriage to the most famous burlesque star of the modern day—Dita Von Teese.

Mallory's idea for the "Heart-Shaped Glasses" routine was to play with the audience's notions of desire or what is desirable. Unlike most acts in which the performer starts dressed and slowly removes items of clothing, she would start the routine naked—in just a G-string and pasties. Her character would wake up in bed, stretching and teasing the audience with brief glimpses of her ass, her legs, her breasts. She would have to figure out the best way to get a prop bed on the stage—maybe just a folded comforter and a cardboard "headboard" and pillows would do the trick. She would cover the comforter with heart pillows and stuffed animals, and these objects would partially obscure her nudity while she stretched in an exaggerated awakening. Then she would need a vanity table, and she would sit in front of that in just her G-string and pasties, and put her hair in pigtails.

By that point, the audience might wonder what grown woman slept with stuffed animals and wore pigtails. And when she shimmied her breasts and pulled on her plain, starched white blouse and short, plaid schoolgirl skirt, the audience would begin to realize that they should not be desiring her. Mallory liked to find ways to provoke her audience, not just turn them on.

Excited with her idea, she grabbed her bag and met Alec outside the studio, throwing her arms around him.

"Um...you taste like salt," he said.

"I have a great idea for an act to a Marilyn Manson song."

"You and Marilyn Manson! I think his music is synonymous with sex for you because the first time you saw Bette perform, it was to one of his songs."

"You might be right. Whatever the reason, I'm pure inspiration, baby."

"What show are you planning this for? The Halloween show?"

"No—the theme for Halloween this year is 'Scary Tales,' so this wouldn't work."

"Fairy tales?"

"No—*scary* tales. We're going to do dark takes on classic stories. I want to do something with Snow White and Rose Red. In fact—now that I'm thinking of it—we might need you to dress in a bear costume." She kissed him on his cheek. "I'm going to get changed. Meet you outside."

"A bear costume? That's not what I had in mind when I got into burlesque. I was hoping one of these days you would ask me to take my clothes off, not wear a furry suit. Although I am open to a merkin...."

"Very funny. You'll just have to leave that to us. Now let me get out of these sweaty clothes."

The dressing room was filled with high school girls just getting out of pointe class. Their bubbly chatter reminded her of what it was like to be that age—life stretching ahead of you like an endless road, while the only things that mattered were right in front of you: grades, friends, and boys. She looked at them, all long limbed and fresh faced, and she envied them the simplicity of their choices. Of course, the idea of carefree youth was a retrospective illusion. She knew she had been filled with angst and doubts at that age. But she at least had the illusion that things would make more sense when she was a grown-up. No one had told her that things just became more complicated and less clear. But then again, even if someone had warned her, she wouldn't have believed them.

She dressed in her street clothes, thinking about how ambitious she had been in high school: honor student, captain of the field hockey team senior year, editor-in-chief of the yearbook. Accepted at Penn, Cornell, and Columbia. With the certainty that she would be a lawyer, just like her father, married by age twenty-eight, with two kids just like her parents had, living in Main Line Philadelphia in a stone house with a creek in the backyard. Now look at her: she was a paralegal moonlighting as a burlesque dancer living with a boyfriend who might or might not have his eye on another woman. She imagined trying to explain that to her fourteen-year-old self.

Most of the time, she felt triumphant about her exciting deviation from "the Plan." But when she thought about her former self, she wondered if she had chosen the right fork in the road.

One of the girls looked at her black, four-inch lace-up Dolce boots—a gift from Bette.

"I love your shoes," she said, wide-eyed.

"Thanks," said Mallory. "I like your jeans."

They were simple Levi's, perfectly worn, with a hole in one

knee and a heart drawn around the hole in blue ballpoint ink. The girl blushed and went back to her friends.

Outside, Alec paced in front of the building talking on his phone. When he saw her he hung up and asked her if she wanted to go to Eli's Restaurant or Gracie Mews Diner for lunch. She shrugged.

"What's wrong?" he said.

"Nothing. Either place is fine."

"You seemed so happy when you got out of practice, and now it's like you're deflated." The last licks of sweat on her body chilled in the October air. Alec took her hand, and she immediately felt calm. She never got tired of how it felt when his big hand enclosed hers, their fingers laced together in that practiced way. "Maybe this will cheer you up." He handed her a plastic shopping bag with the Ballet Academy East logo on it.

"What's this?" she said, looking inside.

"I saw it while you were getting changed, and I thought you could use it."

She pulled out a black duffel bag embroidered with the pink letters BAE. The straps were pink, and the date of the current ballet season was stitched across the top.

"I love it!" she said. "That was so sweet of you."

"Your old bag is kind of banged up and getting more wear and tear from all the shows at the Blue Angel."

"This is true," she said, smiling and unzipping the new bag. "I want to put all my stuff in it right now."

His phone rang. She watched him hold the phone and couldn't help but smile. Ever since he had used the phone to videotape himself fingering her one night, then played it for her while he fingered her again, she saw every iPhone as an erotic object.

She turned back to her new bag, but something about the tone of Alec's voice speaking with the caller distracted her. Mallory could usually tell within thirty seconds who Alec was talking to, but not this time. His voice was oddly constrained, and he just said, "Uh-huh...Don't worry about it....Not a big deal." He glanced at Mallory but then away. "I think we have plans but thanks anyway."

He was clearly in a hurry to get rid of the call and didn't look at Mallory as he put it away.

"Who was that?" she asked.

"Violet," he said.

Mallory resisted the urge to say, "What the hell is she doing calling you?" Instead, she remembered Allison's prediction that their relationship was doomed to fail as long as they were in the burlesque world; Mallory was determined for that not to be the case. She was going to stop being paranoid and trust her boyfriend. If Violet was getting out of line, she'd deal with her directly.

"Oh? What did she have to say?"

"She, um, apologized for upsetting you the other night."

"I wasn't upset."

"Mal, you didn't speak to me for almost twenty-four hours."

"Yeah, but she doesn't know that."

"You gave me dirty looks all throughout dinner. I think she got the hint."

"So that's it? She just called to apologize?"

"Yeah. And I guess as a peace offering, she invited us to the Jack Terricloth show at Joe's Pub tomorrow night. I told her thanks but no thanks," he said, finally looking at her and smiling. He took her hand again.

"Really? I'd kind of like to see that show."

He stopped abruptly.

"You want to go to the show—the three of us?"

"Yeah," she said. "Why not?"

Alec shook his head. "I'll never understand you."

"That's right," Mallory said, squeezing his hand. "You won't."

7

Another Saturday night, another *Law & Order* marathon.

It was getting to the point that if she didn't have a show at the Blue Angel, Poppy and her girlfriend, Patricia, didn't go out. Anywhere.

"I work hard all week, and you have shows a few nights a week, so let's just enjoy some quiet time together," Patricia said. It was true that Patricia had just made partner at the prestigious law firm Reed, Warner, and her work hours were insane. Poppy didn't have a day job, and Patricia's career afforded them a great lifestyle. Poppy understood that and appreciated it. The problem was, their "quiet time" together more and more involved lying around in bed watching television. As for sex—well, there was only the occasional rote session.

Poppy pulled the floral comforter up around her waist. Patricia passed her the bowl of popcorn without taking her eyes off of the television screen. Poppy took the bowl, put it on her nightstand, and discreetly checked her BlackBerry. No messages. Of course not. Everyone else was on their way out to having a good time.

Maybe this was what relationships always looked like eight months in. She wouldn't know—she'd never had a serious relationship before. And who better to have one with? Patricia was her best friend; she'd saved Poppy from the loneliness she felt after moving to New York and feeling, for the first time, like just one of the crowd. She'd saved her from the pain of her unrequited crush on Bette Noir. And yes, her interest in Bette had started out as careerism, but the hurt she felt when Bette turned her attention to Mallory Dale had been far deeper than any sense of professional setback. But then Patricia took her in, showed her love—made her feel like she was a part of something special. Maybe that was more important than sex.

"Pass me the remote," Patricia said.

Poppy dutifully complied, glancing over at her partner. It might help if Patricia did more with herself physically. She knew it wasn't fair to make comparisons, but it was difficult when Poppy spent so much time in the sexually-charged atmosphere of the Blue Angel, with women who, while not all beautiful, certainly did the absolute most with themselves. But Patricia had literally never seen the inside of a gym, and for her a garter was a type of snake, not an undergarment.

"I kind of want to go out tonight," Poppy blurted. Patricia looked at her in surprise.

"Really?" She flipped on NY1 News. "It's cold tonight—look at that. Forty-two degrees. I say we stay here where it's cozy."

"Um, okay. I'm going to go on the computer and see if I can find a movie for us to see tomorrow."

"Sounds good," Patricia said, happily flipping back to *Law & Order*.

Poppy pulled a cardigan over her sheer camisole from La Petite Coquette. Patricia was right about one thing—it was cold.

She turned on the light and the computer monitor in the office and locked the door. Removing her underwear, she sat in the desk chair and logged onto the Web site Fleshbot. She flipped through a few links to videos of women using dildos on each other, giving blow jobs, and even a strange fetish video of two women passing a small ball back and forth using only their assholes. None of this was doing anything for Poppy. She knew the only woman on the site who would help her get off was the porn star Stoya. With her alabaster skin, black hair, and tight body with perfect, small, pert breasts, she bore an uncanny resemblance to Bette Noir.

She found a link to a video of Stoya having double penetration—one guy's cock in her ass, the other in her pussy at the same time. Stoya's face was flushed with pleasure, and the guy on top had his hand wound in her hair, then he pressed a hand against her neck. Poppy clicked off—a little too much penis. She wanted to see Stoya alone or with another woman. She settled on some stills of Stoya with a woman identified in the tags as "Jizz Lee." She clicked through the two dozen photos of the pair allegedly frolicking in bed the morning after the AVN Awards. Some with Stoya underneath Jizz, her breasts being sucked, a wicked smile on her lush lips. Others, Stoya on top, her hand between the other woman's legs. Stoya and Jizz kissing, both smiling, either crazy about each other or putting on a good enough show for the cameras.

Now that's what a couple should be doing in bed!

Poppy slipped her hand between her legs, her middle finger skimming her clit, then moving down to reach inside. She was amazed at her own wetness, and she considered stopping right there and going back into the bedroom to fuck Patricia. But then she thought of the last time they'd had sex, and how she barely had been able to come, and so she continued pressing her finger more deeply, looking at Stoya's porcelain body entwined with that of the butch lesbian with the buzz cut. She closed her eyes, and Stoya turned into Bette, and it was Poppy's body she was pressed against, her own breast being suckled by the dark-haired beauty. She imagined the feeling of her nipple between Bette's teeth, half memory, half fantasy. She imagined Bette's fingers expertly playing between her legs, her thumb on her clit, her middle finger inside of her—the way it had been that night a year ago. She could smell Bette, that vanilla and citrus perfume she had worn the first—and only—time they made love.

Poppy arched back against the hard desk chair, her hand working quickly in and out. Her breath quickened, and she felt the swelling in her pussy that told her the rush of pleasure was moments away.

"Poppy? Why is the door locked?" Patricia called out, knocking.

"Sorry—just a sec," Poppy said, opening her eyes, looking at Stoya, trying not to lose the pleasure that was achingly close.

"See if that Colin Firth movie is playing at the Angelika," Patricia said from the other side of the door.

Poppy kept one hand in her pussy, the other clicking furiously through the images on her screen. But it was a lost cause—her fledgling orgasm dissipated like a quickly deflating balloon.

"Can you just give me a minute?" Poppy snapped, surprised at her own anger.

Silence from the other side of the door.

Again, she wondered: Is this what it meant to be in a relationship? And if so, how much longer could she last?

The "pub" in "Joe's Pub" was a misnomer. It was a lounge with a small stage that was made for intimate, high-quality shows. Tickets could be hard to come by, but Billy Barton's seats were arguably the best in the house. Mallory, Alec, and Violet weren't sitting front and center, but were instead in a booth that was wide and intimate, in the shadows but slightly elevated for a perfect view of the stage.

A waitress took their drink order.

"Anyone else drinking champagne? Let's get a bottle," Violet said. Alec looked at Mallory. So far, he had been deferring to her all night like she was his mother—about what time they left to meet Violet, what order they sat in (Mallory slid in first, followed by Violet, with Alec on the end), and now, what to drink.

"Champagne is fine with me," Mallory said. She hated to admit it, but Violet was stunningly gorgeous, with her widely set green eyes, porcelain skin, and rosebud mouth. But the delicacy of her natural beauty was heightened by her extreme style, the white blondness of her boyishly short hair, the stud in her tongue, and her multitude of tattoos: she had a full sleeve on her right upper arm, an ace of spades on her shoulder blade, and a bouquet of—what else—violets above her left breast. And she certainly dressed to draw attention to herself, in torn black jeans, a black bustier top, and a leather jacket.

The musicians were already on the stage. Jack Terricloth and his bass player, Sandra, were seated on stools, facing each other. Mallory had read in some magazine that they were a couple and that they met when Sandra joined Jack's band The World / Inferno Friendship Society. She knew the group had a cult following, but she'd never been to a show before.

Sandra and Jack began some banter. She was arresting, with big, blue eyes, dark lipstick the color of a bruise, and long dreds.

"She's hot," Violet said to Mallory, nodding toward Sandra.

"Um, yeah," Mallory said. And with that, Violet put her hand under Mallory's short black dress, on her upper thigh. Mallory was startled and stared straight ahead, wondering if Violet's other hand was on Alec's leg and assuming it must be. She moved Violet's hand off and shot Alec a look. He was focused on the stage, and nothing in his expression indicated that anything was going on under the table.

The duo on stage launched into their first song, and the champagne arrived. Mallory took a long swig and then settled back against the booth, trying to relax. Violet's hand returned to her leg, her fingers now stroking her thigh up and down, until she reached the edge of Mallory's panties. Mallory glanced over at Alec, and he winked at her. Mallory noticed that Violet's left hand held her champagne glass, so there was no way she was touching Alec. She just wondered if Alec knew what was going on under the table on her side.

Violet's fingers traveled to her inner thigh, then lightly brushed her pussy over her underwear. Mallory jumped up.

"Excuse me—going to use the restroom," she said.

"Are you okay?" Alec said.

"Yeah. Sure. Be right back."

But she wasn't okay. She hated to admit it, but Violet's touch was turning her on.

The bathroom was a single stall and was so dimly lit she could barely see her reflection in the mirror. It was difficult to tell if she looked pale and needed blush or if it was just the lighting. She was tempted to apply more but it was too risky— might look garish in better light. And then she wondered why she cared so much what she looked like. Why she cared if Violet found her attractive or not. Maybe it was because lately, she felt like the plain Jane in burlesque. She couldn't keep up with the peacocking among the girls, and she was the one without tattoos, without dramatically colored hair or haircut, without nude photos of herself on Fleshbot. For her day job, or by street standards, she was remarkably attractive and maybe even edgy. But in the burlesque world, she was plain and demure. Even her tagline, the Burlesque Ballerina, suggested rarification or reserve, not raw sexuality. On the one hand, this was distinctive and as much a trademark as Violet's trademark combat boots and body ink. But sometimes she felt like a part of her was still holding back, one foot in the real world in case she did not "make it" in burlesque—although by most standards she had already arrived with her steady gig at the Blue Angel, mentions in *New York* magazine and the *Village Voice*, and a thousand "friends" on Facebook and almost as many Twitter followers. But she wondered if she had the drive to become as big as Bette Noir or as buzzed about as Violet. And if Allison was right—that her life in burlesque would be the death of her relationship with Alec . . . well, that wasn't a trade she was willing to make.

She dabbed a little Tarte Flush on her cheeks and headed back to the table, where Violet and Alec were locked in conversation like guided missiles. She pushed back the swell of annoyance in her gut and took her seat.

"Let's get out of here," Violet said, casually putting her hand on Mallory's knee like she was a possessive girlfriend. Mallory bristled.

"We just got here," she said.

"I got word of a pop-up at the Plaza. It's one of Mischa Galit's events. I say we blow out of here and check it out."

Mallory had heard about Mischa Galit. He was a twenty-three-year-old former DJ who had declared the New York velvet rope and bottle service club scene over, and, tapping into a network of tastemakers and beautiful people, had created an underground roving party scene of "pop-up" parties. They were in different locations every night, anywhere from a candlelit, abandoned building in China town to an art deco loft apartment in Soho to a suite at a five-star hotel. Mallory hated to admit it, but Violet had piqued her interest.

"That could be cool," Alec said.

"Fine. Let's go," Mallory said.

Violet smiled. "Done. There's just one thing: you need a hat to get in."

"What kind of hat?"

Violet shrugged. "It doesn't matter."

"So we have to go back to our apartments, find hats, and meet out again?" Mallory said.

"No, of course not. We can stop by Village Costume. It's just a few blocks away. And then we head uptown," Violet said.

"Is it open this late?"

"It's always open late on weekends. You'd be surprised how many people need a last-minute costume on a Saturday night."

"I find that hard to believe," said Mallory.

"My roommate at NYU used to work there. She told me that costumes increase your chance of getting laid by sixty percent."

"That's ridiculous," said Mallory.

"Really?" said Violet. "You think Halloween is so popular for the free candy?"

8

Mallory had not been to the Plaza Hotel since she was six years old and her mother took her to show her where "Eloise" lived. Now, twenty years later, she was wearing a fedora and following her heavily tattooed, bleached blond, pirate hat-wearing nemesis into the side of the building and the entrance to the now private residences. People had been outraged in 2002 when the famous hotel was purchased for over seven hundred million dollars and a plan was announced to convert it to a private apartment building. Mallory agreed with the outrage, but in the end some of the rooms were declared interior landmarks, and many were kept as hotel rooms. The new owners restored and maintained the regal elegance that had made the Plaza Hotel one of the most famous hotels in the world for over a century.

A white-gloved door attendant showed them to the elevator and pushed the button for the top floor. When the gilded door slid closed, Violet said, "One more thing—you have to have a tattoo."

Mallory and Alec looked at each other.

"Mallory doesn't have a tattoo, Violet. You should have said something earlier," Alec said. Obviously, Violet was in the clear, and Alec had a shark on his left arm. But Mallory had not yet succumbed to the needle, to the amazement of her fellow burlesquers.

"I wasn't finished," Violet snapped. "If you don't have a tattoo, someone there will give you a temporary one."

"Like the kind children wet and press on?" he said.

"Why don't you just wait and see?" she said.

Mallory and Alec exchanged another look. With a smile, he rolled his eyes as if to say, *This night was your idea.*

The door opened to a majestic space that, with its high ceilings, crystal chandeliers, and antique furniture, perfectly matched the elegance of the building that housed it.

The richly appointed backdrop was incongruous with the Rihanna-Eminem song playing over the sound system and the hipster crowd showing lots of skin and yes, ink-covered skin at that.

A super skinny, tall, blond Ann Coulter look-alike greeted them at the door. She wore a towering purple hat festooned with feathers and semiprecious stones. It was the most remarkable headpiece Mallory had ever seen. Mallory thought she looked familiar—like she had seen her picture in Page Six or maybe the *New York* magazine "Intelligencer" pages.

"Come on in! I'm Penelope. Do you mind if I take a photo of your tattoos? It's for an art project."

"Sure," Violet said.

"I *loooove* this," the woman said, twirling her finger in the air around the purple flowers on Violet's chest. She aimed her digital camera for the shot, then proceeded to take photos of Violet's back and arm while Mallory and Alec stood off to the side.

"This is weird," Mallory said to him.

"Would you rather be home watching TV?"

"I feel like I'm on TV. Maybe this is all a setup for someone's reality show."

Penelope turned to them.

"I know you," she said to Mallory.

"No, I don't think we've met."

"I've seen you in my club. I *never* forget a face from my club," she said dramatically.

"What's your club?"

"The Slit. I'm Penelope Lowe."

Now Mallory knew why she looked familiar. Penelope Lowe was a notorious party-girl heiress who owned the club the Slit. Most true burlesque performers bristled at Penelope's calling her shows burlesque—they were more highly sexualized performance art.

"Oh, sure. Great place. I saw your Christmas show last year. My friend Bette Noir brought me."

"I love Bette! How *is* she? No one sees her anymore now that she's a celebrity."

"She's great. She does a lot of shows in LA because that's Zebra's home base." Zebra was the eccentric, flashy, pop music superstar who had turned Bette from a burlesque performer to a tabloid staple and fashion icon.

"You should do a show with us sometime."

"Thanks, but I'm exclusive to the Blue Angel."

"Don't be ridiculous! Agnes has to get with the times and relax a little. You girls are the only ones who don't rotate throughout the clubs here, and it's only going to hurt your careers. I mean, who does the exclusivity help? Only the old lady."

"Well, she gave me my start, and I'm happy there," Mallory said. She looked at Violet, who had not gotten her start at the Blue Angel but who was benefiting from the consistency and quality of the shows there. She hoped she wasn't going to use this as an opening to pad her schedule. Or maybe Mallory should hope she would—and in the process, get herself fired from the Blue Angel. That would end the little problem of having her in Alec's face all the time. But she felt conflicted because she was protective of the Blue Angel; she wanted Agnes to remain on top.

But Violet had already mixed into the crowd, and Mallory didn't know if she'd even heard Penelope's invitation.

"Fair enough," Penelope smiled. "So show me your ink—burlesque dancers always have the best work."

"I don't have any tattoos."

"Unbelievable! Virgin flesh. Phenom. You're first of the night. Go down that hallway and turn right. When you're finished, find me. I'll take a photo. Oh—and if you want a better hat, Brenda Waites Bolling is debuting her fall collection in the library."

With that, she turned her attention to the shark on Alec's arm.

Mallory made her way through the crowds to the hallway, stopping only to take a mimosa from a roving cocktail waitress. She wore an elaborate hat that looked like a peacock sitting on her head.

At the end of the hallway, she walked through an archway to find a small, well-lit room with a woman seated at an easel surrounded by paint. She had artwork propped up all over the room, elaborate colored-pencil sketches of nudes, flowers, ornate crucifixes, and old movie stars.

She had waist-length brown hair, a wide nose, and smiling brown eyes. Her arms and legs appeared to be covered in splattered paint, but on closer look, Mallory realized the swathes of vivid color were tattoos.

"Is that... Are those...?" Mallory had never seen anything like it.

"Tattoos? Yes. Come on in." She gestured at the stool in front of her.

"I don't want a tattoo," Mallory said. The woman laughed.

"I'm not a tattoo artist. I'm a painter."

Mallory stared at her leg. It looked like a Jackson Pollock.

"It really looks like paint."

"That's the idea," she said. "I got them from Amanda Wachob."

Mallory sat on the wooden stool.

"So what's the deal with this? Penelope told me I had to come to this room if I didn't have a tattoo."

"I'm going to paint one on," the woman said. "I'm Celeste."

"Mallory," she said. "So how does it work?"

"You can describe an image to me, or pick one from my drawings or paintings."

"How long will it last?"

"The paint?"

Mallory nodded.

"You can completely remove it later tonight with baby oil. Or if you want to keep it a while, just tape Saran Wrap over it while you shower. If you don't protect it while you shower, it will start to crack and wear off in a few days."

Mallory stood and looked through the paintings and sketches. She didn't see anything that she could live with on her body, even just temporarily. She couldn't imagine how people could commit to a permanent design.

"I don't know...." she said.

"Well, tell me about yourself. What do you do?"

"I'm a burlesque dancer." It had taken Mallory a while to be able to say that. In the beginning she had felt like a poser, and after three years of law school and half a year working at a Park Avenue law firm, saying she worked in law was almost as deeply ingrained in her as her name.

"Cool," Celeste said. "Where do you perform?"

"The Blue Angel," said Mallory.

"I love that club! I haven't been there in a while, but it was the first place I ever saw a burlesque show."

"It's one of the oldest in the city. It featured burlesque when it was nowhere else to be found. Now burlesque is everywhere. Or, at least, everyone calls their shows burlesque," she said, thinking of Penelope and the Slit.

"I'll have to come by and check out your act. Well, let's think of an image for your painting. How about a blue angel?"

"Sure," Mallory said, liking the idea.

"I can do like a sexy, Varga girl with wings or more of a straight-up angel. What do you think?"

Mallory thought for a minute. It was a tough decision. This was why she could never get a tattoo.

"You decide," she said.

"I say go for the hot chick," Violet said. Mallory turned, having not even realized she had entered the room. Celeste looked her up and down.

"I can see you don't need my work."

"No, I don't," Violet said. But they were looking at each other in a way that told Mallory they might like to work each other over—in bed. "Mind if I watch?" Violet said to Mallory.

"No," she said.

Violet took a seat on an Edwardian couch. Celeste arranged paint on a palette—half a dozen different shades of blue, black, white, and purple.

"So we've decided on a fallen angel Varga girl?" said Celeste.

"Sure. Sounds good."

"On your bicep?"

"Okay."

Mallory looked around the room while Celeste took the fine-tipped brush to her arm. The paint was cool for the first second it touched her skin, then she didn't feel much at all.

Violet moved closer, sitting on the floor near Celeste, ostensibly to watch her artwork. But Mallory could feel her eyes on her body, roaming from her legs, to her breasts, and back down again. It was unnerving, but she didn't know what to say or do about it. She felt oddly controlled by the two women, Celeste using her skin as a canvas, and Violet viewing her like an object. She felt her mind slipping into a fantasy of Violet's walking over to her and slipping her hand under her dress again, this time her fingers moving under the elastic of her underwear, brushing over her clit before dipping inside of her.

"That's cool," Violet said. "Can I try?"

"What? Painting something?" Celeste said.

"Yeah. On her."

"Sure. But not on this design—you'll wreck it," Celeste said. She smiled flirtatiously at Violet.

"You want to paint something on me?" Mallory said.

"You're the one in the chair," said Violet.

"I think one painted tattoo is enough," Mallory said.

"Don't worry—I'll put mine where no one will see it."

Mallory felt something twitch between her legs.

She couldn't look at Violet. Instead, she focused on the beautiful image appearing stroke by stroke on her arm. It was a long, lean brunette, wearing a blue corset and black hot pants. Her legs were drawn in black stockings, and the brush danced around the lower end of her bicep to create small stilettos. The woman was looking to the side, her hands behind her back, on which Celeste created a large blue ostrich feather that looked like wings.

After ten minutes, Celeste put her brush aside and appraised her work.

"Are you finished?" Mallory said.

"Yes," Celeste said, giving her a hand mirror. Mallory held it to her arm. The burlesque angel looked even more fantastic when she could see it straighton.

"I love it," Mallory said. "It almost makes me want a real one!"

It was true. She had sat in that stool intending to wash the paint off as soon as she got home. Now she was hoping it really would last a week if she took care of it. She wondered if Alec would like it. Maybe that was why he was so hot for Violet—all the images adorning her flesh.

"My turn," said Violet.

"Are you an artist?" asked Celeste.

"Yeah," she said dryly. "I'm a real Renaissance woman."

"I can't think of another image I want painted on," Mallory said.

"I know what I'm doing on you."

"Don't I have a say in what's going on my body?" Mallory laughed nervously.

"No," Violet said.

Celeste relinquished her stool, giving Violet access to the paint and brushes. Mallory glanced at the entrance to the room, wondering if Alec would be looking for her.

"Pull up your skirt," Violet said. "Actually, you'd better take it off. I don't want to get paint on it."

"You can paint on my other arm. I'm not taking off my skirt."

"I thought you said you were a burlesque dancer," Celeste said. "Don't be shy around us."

Thanks a lot, Mallory thought.

"I've seen her backstage getting dressed a dozen times, so I don't know what she's so uptight about," Violet said. Both women looked at her expectantly.

"How long does the paint take to dry? I don't want to spend the whole night sitting in this room in my underwear."

"I'm sure we can find a way to entertain you until it dries," Violet said. "Now take your skirt off."

Something about the sharpness in her voice and the stone cold serious look in her bewitching eyes made Mallory want to do as she said. She imagined Violet must make her S&M clientele very happy.

"Fine," Mallory said. She was about to instruct Violet to

make sure it was something small—that she didn't want paint all over her. But she decided not to say anything. Protesting or trying to direct her would no doubt just provoke her into doing the opposite. If Mallory was going to take off her skirt, she might as well just enjoy the ride.

Mallory stood, unzipped her skirt, and stepped out of it. She folded it and placed it on the shiny hardwood floor. She stood in front of Violet in her blouse, black lace underwear, and suede Tory Burch boots.

"Sit back down," Violet said.

Mallory returned to the stool.

"Spread your legs."

"What?"

"I'm going to paint something right there." She poked Mallory's inner thigh with the wood end of the brush.

Mallory moved her legs apart, and Violet slid her stool closer. She selected a fine-tipped brush and, after dipping it into purple paint, began working on the highest, innermost section of Mallory's thigh, inches from her pussy.

Celeste walked to the door and closed it.

"What if Penelope sends someone in for painting?" Mallory said.

"They can wait. Besides, I'm surprised I got even one partier who doesn't already have a tattoo. I don't think they'll be beating down the door."

She returned to stand behind Violet, who was intent on her handiwork between Mallory's legs. Celeste leaned down, and at first Mallory thought she was getting a closer look at the image on her legs, but then she realized Celeste was reaching around to cup Violet's breasts. Violet ignored the woman's touch and kept painting. Celeste pulled down Violet's bustier, baring her ample and—Mallory hated to admit—perfect breasts. She couldn't help but watch Celeste's fingers graze Violet's hard nipples, and she felt a quiver between her legs.

"Almost done," Violet said calmly, as if a hot woman wasn't feeling her up. Mallory looked at the image on her leg. Violet had painted wide open purple flower petals that looked like an engorged vulva.

"What is that?" Mallory said.

"It's a violet, obviously," she said.

Violet leaned back to admire her handiwork.

Mallory looked at Celeste, who winked at her.

"Want me to blow on it so it dries faster?" Violet said, and before Mallory could reply, she leaned in and pulled aside her panties, blowing gently on her pussy.

Mallory's heart started to pound. She knew she should get up, that she should put a stop to whatever it was that was going on with Violet, but when Violet held Mallory's underwear aside with one hand, and with the other brushed her thumb against her clit, Mallory just looked at her. They locked eyes, and Violet pressed a finger deep inside her. Mallory had to bite her lip not to moan.

And that's when the door opened. Alec.

Violet let Mallory's underwear snap back into place, but her own toplessness was a dead giveaway that more than body painting was happening in the room.

"Took you long enough," Violet said. "Maybe I should have drawn you a map."

He appraised the scene in front of him and looked at Mallory questioningly. She stayed silent, and he took a few steps toward them.

"Sorry to interrupt." He looked at Mallory reproachfully. "Just pretend I'm not here," he said.

"Well, that's impossible. So if you're going to stay, at least make yourself useful. See if that door locks," Violet commanded. Alec examined the old-fashioned knob and turned something until a sharp click echoed in the high-ceiled room.

Violet sat back on her heels, and Mallory closed her legs, careful not to press her thighs together and smudge the flower.

"Why don't you sit on the couch and watch. If you're a good boy, maybe we'll invite you to join in."

Mallory could tell Alec was about to say something—maybe tell her to fuck off. But Celeste was now kneeling beside Violet and tonguing her breast, and Alec kept his mouth shut and took a seat on the couch.

Violet turned back to Mallory and tugged off her underwear. Mallory didn't want to look at Alec—she was uncomfortable with her desire for Violet and uncomfortable knowing how much Alec probably wanted Violet, too.

The issue of whether or not to look at Alec was solved when Violet blindfolded her with her panties. Mallory reached up to adjust the fabric so it wasn't so tight, and Violet pushed her hand away.

"Spread your legs," she said. Mallory complied, but still Violet pressed her knees apart further. She felt warm wetness as Violet licked the outside of her pussy as she slid her finger back inside slowly. Mallory's mind couldn't process the pleasure because she was too busy imagining Alec watching and also wondering what Celeste was doing.

Violet's tongue stopped, and all Mallory felt was the slow pulse of her fingers—one inside, one massaging her clit. If she had been more relaxed, she would have come, but it was impossible. She reached up and pulled down the makeshift blindfold. Violet was watching her intently.

"Don't make me tie you up," she said, her voice throaty with desire.

But Mallory was looking at Alec—more specifically, at where Alec had been sitting two minutes ago. He was gone.

Mallory felt her stomach tilt.

"I have to go," she said, scrambling to pull on her clothes.

"Forget about him. Let me fuck you," Violet said.

"I think you just did," said Mallory.

* * *

Mallory was shaking when she walked out of the Plaza and ignored the white-gloved doorman's offer to hail her a cab. It was a painfully perfect October night—the kind of evening that would usually send her and Alec to the East River to sit on a bench, hold hands, and look at the moon. Alec always said that even when they were old and not running around the city doing exciting things or having crazy sex, they would always have that—long walks, holding hands, and the moon.

But now she wasn't so sure.

"Damn it, Alec. Pick up your phone." It went straight to voice mail for the third time.

She sobbed out loud, almost stumbling on the cobble-stoned walkway alongside Central Park. A couple turned to look at her.

Mallory sat on a bench and told herself to pull it together. Okay, he had to pick up his phone eventually. Or not.

She pulled herself up from the bench and hailed a cab. He didn't have to pick up his phone, but he had to show up at the apartment eventually.

During the cab ride, she continued to call and text him but got no response. At Eighty-third Street, she handed the cab driver a twenty, didn't pause for change, and, once inside her building, took the stairs to the eighth floor instead of waiting for the elevator.

Out of breath, she pushed the door open and found Alec sitting on the couch, tapping on his iPhone.

"I've been calling you!" she said, closing the door behind her. Her heart was pounding.

"I know," he said calmly and without looking at her.

"Why did you run off like that?" she said, taking off her coat, tossing it on a chair, and sitting next to him. He didn't move his eyes from his phone, and a quick glance at it told her he was reading his LA flight itinerary. Her stomach tightened.

"Is that a rhetorical question?" he said.

Okay, so he wasn't going to make this easy for her.

"Alec," she said, putting her hand on his arm. He shook it off. She forced herself to stay calm, and she took a deep breath. "Remember when Bette took us to the Slit last year, and you told me you wanted to have a three-way with her, and that I should just see where the night took us? And it didn't happen that night, but that was a major turning point in our relationship where you were asking me to be open to adventure. And then we decided the openness was making our relationship too complicated, and we agreed to keep things just between us. But I thought the other night, when you invited Violet to dinner, that it was a sign you were getting restless again. I was trying to be a good sport—to not be threatened by your interest in Violet and not to go back to the way things were when I first moved to New York. When you were the adventurous one and I was intimidated by everything."

"This always happens: You suspect that I'm interested in someone else; I admit that I fantasize about a three-way or something—just being honest with you because most guys would never admit that to their girlfriends but trust me they all think it—and then while I'm all talk, you are the one who goes out and actually hooks up with people! It happened with Bette, and it happened again tonight. How do you explain that? How do you expect me to feel about it?"

Mallory didn't know what to say. He had a point. Was this all her fault? Or was Allison right—the burlesque world, with its focus on the body as art, as a means of expression, where public nudity was no big deal, was skewing their perception of normal. Once Mallory accepted that anything was possible, was anything *impossible*? And was she using Alec's curiosity or mild attractions and flirtations with other women as an excuse to explore her own fantasies? She really didn't know.

"I'm sorry," she said, combing back his hair with her fingers. She wanted to lean in and kiss his temple, but she was afraid he would push her away. And she was afraid that the feel of her lips against his skin, or the smell of him, would be her undoing. "I love you. I wish I could take it back. You know I don't want anyone else—any more than you do."

"How can I know that?" he said. And she could tell by the look in his eyes that he was in pain—that he wasn't just arguing with her as a power play or out of ego. He truly doubted her.

"Alec, please don't say that. I love you. I've never loved anyone but you. I think this is all just growing pains. We've been together a long time."

"Maybe too long," he said.

She gasped. "What does that mean?"

"It seems like this trip to LA is good timing. We need to be apart. Let's not talk until I get back in a week. I need to think, and if you're honest with yourself, you probably do, too."

"You don't want to talk the entire time you're away?"

He shook his head.

The last thing she needed or wanted was a week of not speaking with him—especially knowing he would be running around LA with Kendall James. This was a disaster. She had tried to make things better and look at what she'd done!

"I don't need to think!" she said. "I know how I feel about you. I know I want this relationship." She reached for his hand, but he stood and walked into the bedroom. She followed him and watched him pull the blanket and a pillow off of their bed.

"I'm going to sleep on the couch tonight," he said.

"Please don't," she said, knowing it was useless to try to change his mind. Alec was very stubborn, and she could tell by the coldness in the way he looked at her that this was beyond anything she could say in the moment. Now she was more than upset: she was scared.

And there was absolutely nothing she could do about it.

9

_____

"Hey there," Gavin said, walking into her office with his overcoat thrown over his arm.

Mallory had spent the past two hours burying herself in the mountain of paperwork piled on her desk at the office. It was the only thing to keep her from checking the time, from obsessing, *Alec is boarding the plane now. Alec is halfway to LA now. Alec will land in two hours....* The thought of going home that night was dreadful. She had packed her ballet clothes so she could go straight from the office to BAE and avoid the empty apartment for as long as possible.

"Do you have court this morning?" Mallory said.

Gavin was dressed in a navy blue, pin-striped suit. He looked good in suits, and she thought for the umpteenth time how handsome he was—in a preppy, magazine-ad sort of way. She wondered what his relationship was like with his girlfriend. She was sure that Connecticut-born, horse-loving Susan Moreland had never infuriated him by letting another woman finger her.

"Yes, unfortunately. I could use the morning to go through

paperwork, but that is not going to happen. Everything under control here?" he said.

"Yes, fine," she said brightly, surprised to find her mood had surged at the sight of him. "I'm going through the Marchand depositions."

"Great. I have Fiona going through some of those, too. I need that by the end of the day tomorrow. "

"No problem," she said. "Good luck with Klein."

"Thanks. And thanks for all your help on that one. You never know with Judge Hager, but I think we're going to get good results." He glanced over her shoulder to something behind her. "You're a ballet dancer?" he said.

"What?" she said, turning around to see what he was looking at. She spotted her BAE bag on top of a filing cabinet. "Oh. No, I'm not a ballet dancer. I just do it for exercise. I hate the gym."

"That's so great!" he said, with a boyish enthusiasm she had never seen him exhibit. "Cynthia Hobbs is on the board of the New York City Ballet, you know."

Cynthia Hobbs was one of the plaintiffs in one of Gavin's most successful recent litigations. Thanks to his strategy in the courtroom, she had been awarded millions in alimony.

"No, I didn't know that." It was strange to talk to Gavin about personal stuff—if ballet could be considered personal. Which it was, compared to their usual discussions that were all work, work, work.

Mallory was aware of her desire to prolong the conversation, but she didn't want to hold him up by forcing him to make polite conversation with her.

"Great. Well, see you later," she said. Was it her imagination, or did he linger in her doorway an extra beat?

She turned back to the depositions on her desk. She wished she hadn't told Julie and Allison about her plans with Violet and Alec, because they'd each called twice to find out how it went, and she couldn't bring herself to tell them. It was much easier to be the good friend who confided everything when it was the boyfriend who was screwing up, not herself. She couldn't imagine what Allison and Julie would say if she told them about last night. Actually, she could; they would tell her that she finally had Alec behaving somewhat decently, and she had gone ahead and behaved more irresponsibly than he ever had. And they would be right. They would tell her she deserved for him to want some time apart.

With a sigh, Mallory picked up the file marked *Klein v. Klein*. Gavin was going to trial for one of his clients, Marcy Gold Klein. The Kleins' case was a perfect example of money not buying happiness; Marcy was a successful producer of fashion shows and her soon-to-be ex-husband was a major Wall Street rainmaker. They had the town house, the Hamptons house, the parties with Rachel Zoe on the West Coast and Donald Trump on the East. And they had beautiful twin girls. Yet theirs was one of the nastiest divorces Mallory had seen or read about in her seven months at the firm. And that was saying a lot; it amazed her that people who at one time had pledged their lives to loving each other and making each other happy could go to such lengths to destroy each other sometimes as little as a few years later. When she expressed her reaction to Gavin, he said that he had ceased to be surprised or particularly affected by anything, but conceded that the burnout rate for matrimonial attorneys was especially high.

"Does this ever affect the way you think about the future with Susan?" she asked one day across the conference room table. She had no idea what gave her the idea that it was okay to ask such a personal, audacious question, except that she truly was just wondering. Susan Moreland was a pretty blonde, a competitive horseback rider, and someone Gavin had known since his days at Horace Mann, though they hadn't started dating until a year ago.

Gavin did not seem put off by the question, and in fact answered it in the careful, thoughtful way he answered her questions about choices he was making in his casework.

"It would be easy to become cynical, doing this job. But I am trying to remain an optimist. A romantic, even." He smiled as though he were half joking, but she didn't think he was.

Now, after a decidedly unromantic night, she couldn't help but think about that conversation.

Her cell rang, and her heart soared. She allowed herself to hope that it was Alec, saying he was willing to talk some more. That he wasn't leaving for LA with things like this. But it wasn't.

"Bette?" she said.

"Hey, gorgeous. Where am I catching you?'

"I'm at work—the law firm I told you about."

"Ugh. I thought I'd rescued you from the clutches of corporate America."

"Yeah, well, living *la vida loca* doesn't exactly pay the rent."

"It does for me."

"That is why you are my idol," she said, only half joking. "How is life in the fast lane?"

"Um...okay."

"Just okay?"

"I'll tell you when I see you."

"Does that mean you're in town?"

"I will be tomorrow."

"Perfect timing! We're doing the Halloween show tomorrow night. Want to come by for old time's sake?"

"Aren't I still banished from the kingdom?"

When Bette had unceremoniously quit the Blue Angel after falling into a relationship with the beautiful, androgynous pop star, Zebra, Agnes banned her from the club and quickly hired Mallory to fill the vacant slot in the show, thus launching her career as a burlesque performer.

"Nah. Agnes has your Dolce ad in the dressing room. She'll

never admit it, but she's proud of you. Besides, I think she has bigger things than your defection to worry about now."

"Like what?"

"I'll tell you when I see you."

"Sounds like we have a lot to talk about."

"You have no idea," she said, and thinking about last night, her happiness at hearing her old friend's voice burst like a bubble.

Poppy walked up and down the aisles of M&J Trimming, her go-to place for buying ribbon, buttons, feathers, and appliqués. Just setting foot in the door made her happy—it was the candy shop of costume creation.

She tried not to get distracted by the bins of Swarovski flat-back rhinestones in gorgeous shades of blue and green, colors with names like mint alabaster, peridot, olivine, and Capri blue. They were expensive, and she really had come to the store just for the tassels she needed for the Halloween show costume. Every time she walked into the store she saw ten things she wanted to buy just to have or because they inspired another costume. But one of the first things she'd learned about shopping for material was to go with a list and never deviate. Otherwise she would spend too much money on things that sparkled that she didn't really need. In that sense, it was like being in her relationship with Patricia. She needed to just focus and stop worrying about shiny distractions, sexy women who would never care about her the way that Patricia loved her.

The other night, she'd felt so bad about locking Patricia out of the office so she could look at porn, she immediately went back into the bedroom and made it up to her. Patricia had surprised her by easily agreeing to turn off the television, and their lovemaking was filled with an intensity that Poppy had not felt since the first few times they had been together. It was as if Patricia had sensed that Poppy was restless, and she, too, wanted to set things right.

A quick turn down an aisle brought Poppy out of the danger zone into the display of tassels. She honed in on the gold ones she needed and put them in her shopping cart. That's when she heard the commotion at the front door.

"You can't come in here with that camera," yelled one of the store employees.

Poppy picked out one more pack of tassels—black in case she changed her mind about the gold—and made her way to the front of the store. She was only mildly curious about the yelling at the front of the store, but when she noticed, out the window, the crowd on Sixth Avenue, she felt a surge of interest.

"What's going on?" she asked a bored-looking young woman at the checkout register.

"I'm not sure," the girl said with a shrug. "I think someone famous is here. There's paparazzi outside."

Poppy placed her items on the counter. Having lived in New York a while, she had become indifferent to rubbing elbows with celebrities. While the girl scanned her tassels and put them in a plastic bag, Poppy gave the store a once-over, wondering if she had forgotten anything.

And that's when she saw her.

Poppy would have known that shiny black bob anywhere. She instinctively started following the woman, like an animal turning after its prey.

"Hey, you forgot your credit card," the girl at the counter said to her. Poppy ignored her—she had to make sure, had to know for certain if it was really who she thought.

From behind, all Poppy could see was her gleaming dark hair and that she was wearing stiletto-heeled black ankle boots under a black leather trench coat. She didn't need to see more than that to know.

"Bette," Poppy said, feeling like a stalker as she closed the distance between them.

The woman turned around, and sure enough, there was that alabaster skin, the girlish smattering of freckles across the bridge of her nose. Her deep blue eyes were hidden under over-sized, round-framed black sunglasses.

"Jesus, don't sneak up on me like that!" Bette said.

"Sorry! I just...I'm so surprised to see you here," Poppy said, her heart racing.

"I just got back into town. Getting my M&J fix. There's a place like this—better than this, even—in Paris. But aside from that one store I've really missed what I find here. Here, walk with me. I want to get what I need before the paparazzi talk their way in here and I have to bolt."

Poppy looked around as they walked. Despite the throng of photographers outside, none of the other customers seemed to notice the tabloid darling in their midst.

"Is it always like that—with the photographers, I mean?"

"Lately. LA is the worst. I thought maybe it would be different here but no such luck."

Bette's phone rang, and she scrambled for it in her purse as if it were a lifeline.

"Hey," she said into her phone, shielding it with her cupped hand as if the casual observer could actually see who was on the other end. She stopped in the middle of the aisle. "Because you told me not to!" she hissed at the phone. And then she turned her back to Poppy and walked off.

Poppy stood watching her for a moment, then headed back to the checkout register to retrieve her tassels and American Express card. The thought of going home to Patricia gave her a sinking feeling.

She had found something that sparkled that she didn't really need, but that she wanted. Badly.

10

Violet peeked out from behind the stage curtain at the crowd. The Blue Angel was packed. There was a hyped-up energy in the room, and she felt good about the show.

Her only disappointment was finding that Mallory wasn't on the schedule.

"Mallory isn't here tonight?" she asked Agnes, hoping she had somehow misread the lineup.

"No. So Poppy ends the show and you open it."

Violet hated going first. The crowd was always excited for the first performer and easily impressed—too easily. Plus, they never remembered the first performer when they walked out the door after an hour-long show. How was she going to make a name for herself when she was practically the warm-up act?

And fucking Ryan Ellison hadn't increased her exposure; the paparazzi hadn't caught her leaving the club with him or leaving his hotel. And he hadn't tried to contact her or returned to the club. It was her fault—she had held back in fucking him. If she had unleashed Mistress Violet on his skinny ass, he would have been back for more. Any woman can give a man pleasure. But few can inflict pain.

By the time she took the stage she was in a foul mood. She was glad her act was loud and aggressive; the Rob Zombie song "More Human Than Human" cranked over the sound sytem, and she took the stage in her dreadlocked wig, leather jacket covering her black corset, her legs clad in thigh-high, six-inch-heeled biker boots.

Some might have construed her performance as a bit artless, but the way she threw off her clothes, gave the audience the finger, and flashed her pussy at them like a dare was every bit as choreographed as the more subtly teasing dances of her peers.

One person in particular seemed to be enjoying her audacious display; she caught Poppy watching her from the side of the stage, an expression of jaw-dropping awe on her obnoxiously conventional pretty face. For the first time, Violet realized, *Hmm. I could hit that.* But she had no interest. There was only one Blue Angel pussy she wanted, and she'd had a taste last night. She had every intention of going back for more.

Backstage, Agnes pulled her aside by the elbow.

"I told you we do burlesque here—not stripping."

"That was burlesque."

"Not by Blue Angel standards."

"Get with the times, Agnes. No one wants to see fat chicks dancing to 'Diamonds Are a Girl's Best Friend,' waving around a bunch of feathers. That's why people come here as a warm-up before going to their real entertainment for the night at the Slit."

"Then perhaps that is where you belong. One more show like that, and you're out. And keep your mouth shut, while you're at it."

"I'm the best performer you've got here, and you know it," Violet said.

"I've seen dozens of you come and go. And every one of you thinks you're something special. The truth is you're all re-placeable. So do what you wish."

Violet picked up her bag and searched for her cell phone. She didn't need the old lady and her passé club. She would leave—and she'd take Mallory with her.

Poppy was staring at her from across the dressing room.

And that stupid bitch will probably follow me out the door, too.

She pulled her cell phone out of her bag and dialed Mallory.

Mallory leaned in toward the bathroom mirror, examining her arm. That morning, she'd thought about washing off the painted lady, but she couldn't bear to part with it, despite the fact that it was a symbol of relationship disaster.

But Alec was gone, on the other side of the country, without so much as a text to say he had landed safely. So she set to work with a bottle of baby oil and a pile of cotton balls.

She watched the blue paint turn liquid, the angel's face melting.

Her cell phone rang in her handbag on the floor. Could it be?

She fished it out, trying not to smear baby oil on it.

"Hello?"

"Hey," said Violet. "What are you up to?"

Mallory cringed at the sound of her gravelly voice, a dozen erotic and excruciating images flooding her mind. She closed her eyes as if that could make them disappear.

"I'm getting ready for bed," Mallory said, immediately re-gretting her choice of words lest they be perceived as an invita-tion.

"It's early," Violet said.

"Not for me. Good night."

She hung up her phone. What did Violet want from her?

Maybe she wanted a do-over for Saturday night so she could get a chance to fuck Alec, too.

Mallory turned back to the painted tattoo, mashing the oily cotton against the image until it disappeared.

Her phone rang again. She could not believe Violet had the audacity to keep pushing her!

"What?" she snapped.

"Mallory?"

"Gavin?"

"Yes—I hope I'm not disturbing you."

She took a moment to compose herself.

"No, not at all. Are you still at the office?"

"I'm on my way to a dinner party at Cynthia Hobbs's. She's hosting a benefit for the ballet, and I paid for two seats but Susan just informed me she can't make it. It's a shame to waste a seat, and this is an event you might enjoy. The principals of this season's *Swan Lake* will be there. And Cynthia would be happy to have you. She raved about the work you did on the case."

Mallory's mind clicked into fast action. She loved the idea of getting out of the apartment, of being saved from having to brood about where Alec was and whether or not he would call. She wouldn't have to think of Violet, or of the performance she had to do tomorrow night that she was already dreading because of her state of mind. But she was in leggings and a T-shirt, and he was already on his way out!

"It's kind of short notice. I'm not exactly party-ready," Mallory said.

"Just throw on a black dress. The median age there will be sixty. You'll be the most glamorous one there in the simplest thing you own. Trust me."

Mallory laughed. She was already opening her closet.

"How long do I have to get ready?"

"Can you work fast?"

"Yes."

"I'll be there in fifteen minutes."

Mallory was giddy with anticipation.

Violet turned off her phone in a cold fury. It hadn't crossed her mind that Mallory would refuse to see her tonight. All during her performance, she had imagined Mallory in the audience, waiting to get her pussy licked when Violet was finished. The thought that she wouldn't be able to satisfy herself tonight was almost too much to take. She tossed her phone to the floor, where it clattered and slid to the nearest vanity table. Everyone in the dressing room looked at her for a second and then returned to changing and texting and getting ready for the next phase of their nights. All except Poppy, who could barely seem to take her eyes off of her.

Violet pulled on her jeans and combat boots, threw her bag over her shoulder, and strode to the door. As she passed Poppy, she said, "Come with me."

She didn't have to ask twice.

In the cab, on the way to her apartment, Violet pulled a T-shirt from her bag and used it to blindfold Poppy. This wasn't just some cheesy rip-off move from a bad gangster movie; she really was a private person and had no intention of allowing Poppy to know where she lived or see what her apartment looked like. And the fact that Poppy complied with the blindfolding made her confident that the woman would let her do whatever she wanted to her.

Ideally, she would have been able to take her to the Cellar or another one of the dominatrix clubs where she worked and occasionally rented space. But Friday nights were too expensive for her to rent space just to give Poppy a freebie, no matter how much she would love to have access to the equipment. She'd just have to improvise tonight. Besides, she was sure Poppy would be back for more, and Violet felt turned on for the first time that night, anticipating how delicious it would be to wage a campaign of sexual control over Poppy LaRue.

But for tonight, she would start slowly—relatively.

The cab pulled up in front of her building, and she helped Poppy navigate the wide cement stairs to the front door of the four-story brownstone. Her legs were long and lean in her short leather skirt, and Violet couldn't wait to get her hands on them.

To her credit, Poppy had been silent for the ride and even as she made her way into Violet's apartment, leaning into her so she didn't stumble.

She led Poppy into her bedroom and helped her off with her coat. Then, with Poppy still blindfolded, Violet tied each of her arms to the wrought iron headboard.

Poppy's chest was heaving up and down with her heavy breathing. Violet didn't know if it was from the exertion of climbing four flights of stairs in stilettos, or nerves, or excitement.

"I like that you're quiet," Violet said, as she looked through her closet for appropriate attire. "Conversation can be so tedious."

She stripped off the clothes she only wore after a show, the same old jeans and a shirt she'd had so long she didn't care if they got covered in glitter or if they were lost or stolen backstage. She turned to make sure Poppy was still in place on the bed, not trying to take off the shirt covering her eyes or loosen her wrist restraints. She didn't want her getting too comfortable.

Violet changed into a crotchless leather catsuit and thigh-high patent leather boots. She rifled through her drawer of masks and decided on a Victorian studded favorite of hers that she'd bought at a fetish shop on West Twenty-second Street.

A quick perusal of a duffel bag full of supplies from her last dom session with a client yielded a good leather blindfold to re-place the makeshift one she currently had wrapped around Poppy's eyes. And switching the blindfolds would give her the opportunity to let Poppy have a glimpse of her in her Mistress Violet ensemble—she wanted her to have an accurate mental image while she was being defiled.

She strode over to the bed and untied Poppy's arms.

"Sit up," she said. Poppy obeyed her immediately. Violet bent closer to her, untying the clumsy knot holding the shirt against her head.

She stepped back so Poppy could get a good look at her. The expression on her face was the perfect blend of awe and trepi-dation. She knew Poppy wanted to tell her she was beautiful—that for once she was looking at someone more outstanding than herself. But—and rightfully so—she was hesitant to speak.

Violet tied the leather blindfold around Poppy's head and instructed her to lie back down. She fastened restraints around her wrists, bondage ropes that were the best quality she had, the least likely to leave marks.

"I need to get something from the other room. Don't move an inch while I'm gone."

Silence.

"Do you hear me?"

"Yeah," Poppy said.

"Good girl. And while we're at it, don't speak unless I tell you to."

Violet wasn't sure what the girl's deal was, but she knew enough about human behavior to know she was desperate for a good fuck.

She made a quick trip to the kitchen to get a pair of scissors, then returned to find Poppy still in place on the bed. In a way, she was disappointed. It would have been nice to return to find her untied, naked, masturbating—and eager to tell Violet she could shut the fuck up and watch. But people rarely surprised her.

Annoyance flared in her; why did she always have to do all the work?

On the floor beside the bed, she laid out the basic equipment she needed: a pair of scissors, a paddle, a-cat-o'-nine-tails, and ankle restraints. She added a ball gag to the collection, just in case her sexual servant suddenly became chatty.

Poppy was wearing a tight black T-shirt that Violet hoped for Poppy's sake was made by Old Navy and not Vince or James Perse, since it was about to meet an untimely end.

She stood at the side of her bed, looking down at Poppy.

"Stay very still," she commanded, pulling the bottom of Poppy's shirt taut and lining up the mouth of the scissors. Then she began to cut. Violet made sure that Poppy felt the cool press of the metal against her belly as she worked her way up.

"What are you doing?" Poppy said, trying to sit up.

Violet pushed her back down.

"What did I tell you about speaking unless spoken to? I'm going to have to punish you for that. And, not that it's any of your business, but I happen to be removing your shirt. Your hands are tied—since I obviously can't trust you—so I have no choice but to cut it off."

Once the T-shirt was split down the middle, she parted it like a curtain and looked at Poppy's breasts. She had to admit—the girl had a damn good body. Violet recalled now, although she hadn't thought about it before, seeing Poppy's ugly girl-friend at the shows a few times. Violet was a tough critic, and she had to admit Poppy was technically the most beautiful girl at the club. So what was with the subpar pussy she kept at home?

Poppy squirmed under her gaze. Violet didn't know if it was because she felt self-conscious or because she wanted her to do something.

Violet unzipped Poppy's jeans and tugged them off roughly, tossing them on the floor. Then she took the scissors to her underwear, and she could see Poppy holding her breath when she grazed her lips with the cool metal. Her pussy seemed moist and inviting—was she wet already?

Violet still wasn't sure what she wanted to do with her, but decided she'd like to get a look at her ass.

She untied her wrists again.

"Turn over on your stomach," she said. Poppy hesitated. "Now!" Violet yelled.

Poppy turned over slowly.

"I shouldn't have to ask you twice. Now get up on all fours."

Poppy hesitated for only a second before getting onto her hands and knees. Violet picked up the paddle, and with a heavy arm, smacked it hard against Poppy's left ass cheek.

"Ow!" Poppy said.

"Don't ever make me ask you twice to do something." She smacked her again. Poppy's body remained rigid and still. Violet circled the bed and then landed one more blow against Poppy's right ass cheek. "Lie flat on your stomach," she said.

Poppy flattened herself against the bed, and Violet pulled each of her arms out so she could re-tie them to the bed posts. She swept her hand along the floor until she found the ankle restraints, and secured Poppy to the bottom of the bed, her legs spread wide apart.

Violet looked at the alabaster skin of her ass, marred with two angry red splotches like states on a map.

She knew Poppy was tense with anticipation for what would happen next, so Violet did nothing. Finally, she said softly, "I'm going into the other room. You had better not move a muscle. Do you hear me?"

Poppy nodded her head.

"Say, 'Yes, Mistress Violet.' "

"Yes, Mistress Violet," she said, her voice low and quiet.

Violet stood from her perch on the edge of the bed and

moved to the doorway of her bedroom. For ten minutes, she silently watched Poppy. Sure enough, she did not make any discernable movement the entire time. Violet was almost disappointed—she had been looking forward to punishing her.

She strode back into the room, making sure her boots announced her presence loudly against the hardwood floor.

"Did you move?" Violet asked.

Poppy shook her head.

"I can't hear you."

"No," Poppy said.

"No, what?"

"No, Mistress Violet."

"Good girl. Just for that, I'm going to stick my finger in your pussy. Would you like that?"

"Yes, Mistress Violet."

Violet sat on the edge of the bed, angled so she had a perfect view of Poppy's cunt. She licked her thumb and index finger and then pressed her thumb into Poppy's pussy, easing it in and out slowly. Poppy moaned, and Violet pressed her index finger deep into her asshole. Poppy's anus clenched slightly in resistance, but she soon gave into it. Violet held her finger inside her ass while working her thumb inside her pussy, occasionally slipping it outside and up against her clit. Poppy was breathing hard and occasionally murmuring something. Violet couldn't discern what she was saying, and she didn't really want to. She decided she wanted to see her breasts.

Poppy raised her head questioningly, but knew better than to say anything. Violet quickly untied her restraints.

"Get on your back," she commanded. Poppy complied, although her body moved clumsily, as if she weren't accustomed to having the use of her limbs. Violet re-tied her arms and restrained her ankles. She used this time to strip off all of her clothes. Completely nude, she climbed onto the bed.

"Don't move your head—keep that blindfold exactly where

it is," Violet said. Poppy was still. Violet straddled her face, her pussy poised inches above Poppy's mouth.

"Stick out your tongue," Violet said. Poppy complied, and Violet lowered herself onto Poppy's mouth. "Lick my cunt," Violet said. Poppy complied, eagerly running her tongue along Violet's pussy lips and pressing it inside of her when Violet grabbed her head and forced her mouth deeper.

Violet didn't feel close to coming. And then, like the night with the Asian and Irish girls, and the night with Ryan, she felt her mind drifting to Mallory. Suddenly, it was Mallory's glossy dark hair fanning out on the bed beneath her, Mallory's delicate features pressed against her cunt. It was Mallory's mouth sucking on her clit, and Mallory's hands that cupped her ass, bringing her closer, pressing her tongue deeper, until Violet was able to feel some release.

Violet withdrew from Poppy's mouth and began fingering herself. She remained poised above Poppy's face, so Poppy could sense her and no doubt smell her but had no idea what she was doing or would do to her next. Silently, Violet worked her own clit until it was hard as a bead. She slid down slightly so she was at the level of Poppy's navel, and while she brought herself closer to orgasm, she looked at Poppy's breasts. She imagined how she would touch them in a few minutes, imagined twisting the woman's nipples until she begged her to stop. And then she came, silently, but with a violent shudder that shook the bed.

Without missing a beat, she moved down between Poppy's legs. She saw the girl was more wet than before and wondered how much she had liked eating her pussy.

"Did you like the way my pussy tastes?" Violet asked, pressing a finger back inside of Poppy.

"Yes, Mistress Violet," Poppy said softly.

Violet observed her carefully: Poppy's cheeks were flushed,

her chest was rising and falling in shallow breaths, and her breasts were full, her nipples erect and rosy.

She moved up so she could reach Poppy's breasts with her mouth. While her tongue teased Poppy's nipples, occasionally punctuated with a sharp bite of her teeth, Violet switched the rhythm between Poppy's legs so that she had her thumb on her clit, one finger moving in and out of her. Within seconds, Poppy cried out, an orgasm shuddering through her, her thighs gripping Violet's wrist like a vice.

When Poppy was finally still, Violet untied her arms and feet.

"You may take off your blindfold."

Poppy slowly, with fumbling hands, pulled off her blindfold. Her blue eyes focused on Violet in a mix of lust, awe, and yes, fear. She sat up, her cheeks flushed, her eyes bright, and pretty smile on her face. She looked like someone who'd been properly fucked for the first time in a while.

"I suggest you don't mention this to anyone," Violet said, pulling on a black robe from her closet.

"I won't," said Poppy.

"After all, you're the one with a girlfriend."

"She can't find out about this!" Poppy said.

"I would imagine not. But that doesn't change the fact that you're my bitch now, and when I call you for a good fuck, you'd better be available to me. Understood?"

"Um, yes. I mean, I think so."

"Yes, *what?*"

"Yes, Mistress Violet."

Mallory was grateful to Allison for giving her as a birthday gift one year the Nina Garcia style handbook, *The One Hundred: A Guide to the Pieces Every Stylish Woman Must Own.* Mallory actually followed it, and as a result she had a closet full of staples that, mercifully, included the classic little black dress, evening clutch, and overcoat at the ready. Getting dressed for the fundraising dinner was completed with the precision of a military operation.

Gavin picked her up in a silver Mercedes.

"You're driving?" she said.

"Yes. I hate cabs."

"But then you can't drink," she said, trying to cover what she suddenly felt was a gauche remark.

"I rarely drink during the week. Especially not at work functions, which I consider this. Especially now that you are coming with me."

Mallory felt a sting at his remark, yet knew that was ridiculous. What did she think—that this was a date? Of course it was a work event. Yet somehow, sitting next to him in her best black cocktail dress, it felt like the furthest thing from work. What was going on with her?

Cynthia Hobbs lived in an enormous, art-filled three-bedroom apartment between Central Park West and Columbus. The living room overlooked the glowing dome of the American Museum of Natural History's planetarium.

Cynthia kissed Gavin on both cheeks when they arrived and introduced him to everyone as "the man who saved my life!"

The living room was filled with eight round tables set with crystal and heavy silver. The seating was assigned and was strictly boy, girl, boy, girl. Mallory was couched between Gavin and a Wall Street dude who looked at her like she was being served for dinner.

Twenty minutes into the evening, Mallory was buzzing on a big glass of earthy red wine and the thrill of just having met Anna Sandrine, the dark-haired, doe-eyed principal dancer in *Swan Lake,* who was seated at what was obviously the "A-list" table, next to Cynthia Hobbs.

"If you 'saved her life,' why aren't you at her table?" Mallory whispered to Gavin with a smile.

"Seating is strictly by checkbook," Gavin said. "And there were only three zeros on the one I wrote."

That sounded like a lot of zeros to her.

But Mallory was happy right where she was—despite the errant hand on her leg courtesy of Mr. Wall Street. She pushed it away, and he laughed like it was a joke they shared.

Every few moments, Gavin checked in on her with a glance and a smile, making sure she was holding her own. She was.

"Every lawyer I know is miserable," the Wall Street guy was saying.

"Yes," she said, because it was easier to agree than to debate him. Mallory looked across the room at Anna Sandrine and thought that she couldn't wait to tell Alec. But then she remembered she wouldn't talk to Alec for a week. That was the deal, and she knew he would stick to it. She would have to do the same. At least she could tell Nadia the next time she was at the practice space.

"But, to be fair, a lot of people in my business aren't happy. It takes a lot of money to be happy doing what I do," he said. "I'm one of the lucky ones. Do you like your job?"

"I love it," she said automatically, thinking of the Blue Angel. Then she realized he meant her paralegal job.

"Well, good for you," he said, clearly surprised by her affirmative response.

She took another sip of her wine, wondering what the guests in that rarified room would think about her burlesque career. She doubted it would meet with the approval of these self-proclaimed patrons of the arts. And then she felt a sudden surge of loneliness.

The waitstaff began serving Tartufo for dessert. She clumsily tapped on the hard chocolate shell with her spoon, realizing it was time to stop drinking. Her fine motor skills were officially shot.

"Excuse me," she said, and asked the server to point her in the direction of the bathroom.

The bathroom walls were covered in a salmon-colored fabric threaded with gold. Behind the toilet—a piece so sleek and modern she could barely find the flusher—hung a black-and-white photograph of Cynthia taken by Herb Ritts.

Mallory touched up her eyeliner and lipstick, thinking how in twenty-four hours she would be taking off her clothes on the Blue Angel stage. Only in New York could she find herself traversing the lines of low and high culture so quickly. Would she be able to successfully swing back and forth indefinitely? She doubted it. With a sinking feeling, she knew she was going to have to choose. It was just a matter of when.

Outside, in the hallway, Gavin was waiting for her.

"Oh! You surprised me."

"Are you having a good time?" he said.

"Yeah. It's interesting. "

"That isn't too convincing," he smiled. "I'm ready to go when you are."

"Really?"

"Sure. Nights like these tend to have diminishing returns. It's all downhill after dessert."

"That's one of my basic life philosophies," she said, and he laughed. "Okay, well, you're the one driving."

"Let's say our good-byes."

In front of the building, a valet produced Gavin's car. Gavin held her door open for her before getting behind the wheel.

"The man to your left at dinner—Jackson Deer? He asked for my card before we left. He's divorcing his wife of ten years, and I think he's worth about half a billion dollars," Gavin said.

"Sounds expensive."

"Yes. It could be a good case for the firm." Gavin turned

onto Columbus to get them back around to the cross street through Central Park at Eighty-first Street. "He specifically asked if you could be in the room for the consultation."

"That's weird," Mallory said.

"Not really. You're smart; you're attractive. Whether or not you realize it, you're a huge asset to the firm, Mallory. And you're doing a very good job. I know you didn't have the most positive experience at Reed, Warner, but I hope you're feeling on more solid footing now. And I hope you're thinking long-term with us."

She was taken aback. Gavin had no idea that she had lost all interest in a legal career—that the firm was just a way to pay the bills while she established her real career, the career that had become central to her identity and to her relationship.

"I think I drank too much wine to talk shop," she said, and it was true. Her thinking was slow and fuzzy, and she was smiling for no reason.

"Fair enough," he said, returning her smile. She let her head drop back against the leather seat, wishing it was the summer so Gavin could put the convertible top down. But even in the dark, in the closed car, with the late October chill, she felt lighthearted, warm, and more carefree than she could remember in a long time. And she realized that while Alec made her feel sexy, Gavin made her feel like a lady.

And she liked it.

11

The following night, almost exactly twenty-four hours later, Mallory stood outside of the Blue Angel, trying, without success, to psyche herself up for the show.

She couldn't remember the last time she'd felt so lackluster on the night of a performance. She hated to admit it, but it probably had something to do with the fact that she had almost never done a performance without Alec at the club. He was her primary audience of one, the person who inspired most of what she explored and expressed in her act, and the person she trusted to give her feedback on her performances.

But tonight he would not be there.

And she was confused by how much she had enjoyed Gavin's company last night. When she didn't see him at work all day because he was in court, she was disappointed. It made her think that her misstep the night at the Plaza—and maybe all of her arguments with Alec over the past year or so—had happened for a reason. It wasn't her fault, and it wasn't his fault. This was what happened when people tried to stretch a college romance into the real world.

She spotted Poppy strolling down the street, her mile-long legs impossible to miss.

"Hey," Mallory said.

"Why are you standing out here?"

"Just, you know, psyching myself up for the show."

"Oh." Poppy put her hand on the door and then hesitated, turning back to Mallory. "Can I ask you something?"

"Sure."

"You and Alec have been in a long-term thing, right?"

"Well, yeah. Although now probably isn't the best time to be asking me about that."

"What do you mean?"

"Nothing. Ignore me. Go on."

"Okay, well, in all the time you guys have been together, did the sex ever get kind of boring? Like, routine?"

"No," Mallory said, without hesitation.

"Never?"

"No. Why? What's going on? Are you and Patricia having problems?" She really didn't want to hear about her the sex life of her former boss, Patricia Loomis, but Poppy was clearly in distress.

"Yes. I mean—no. We're not fighting if that's what you mean. But I don't feel attracted to her anymore. The sex is always the same. It was good in the beginning but now it's ..."

"Too predictable?"

"Yes, that. But also...sometimes I'm attracted to other people."

Mallory sighed. "I think it's normal. I mean, I see people I'm attracted to. But when you're in a good relationship, you make the conscious decision not to act on that feeling. But those feelings never stop just because you're in a committed relationship." Poppy was visibly pained. "Is it someone in particular?"

"Yes. And no. There's someone, and I'm going to try not to see her anymore—I know she's bad news. But more than that, I still keep thinking about Bette."

"Oh, Poppy. You have to let that go. Bette is in a whole other world right now. And she's in love with Zebra."

"I know, I know. It's ridiculous. I just had to ... say it aloud. Maybe that will help me let it go."

"Yeah, just think of her as someone you would see in a magazine or in a movie. Not accessible. Not an option."

"I know. You're right."

"But if you're not satisfied with Patricia, maybe you should end it. Don't string her along."

"I care about Patricia. Sometimes I'm even happy with her. I'm just confused."

"Well, stay away from other women until you figure it out. You're not going to see things more clearly by messing around."

"Okay. I'm going to just keep reminding myself of that." She held Mallory's arm. "Don't mention this to anyone."

"Of course not."

"Thanks, Mallory."

"Sure," Mallory said, checking her BlackBerry for the time. "I'm going to head in now, too." She couldn't procrastinate outside any longer. People would show up for tickets soon, and she didn't want audience members to see her in her street clothes before the show. But she was dreading seeing Violet for the first time since the night at the Plaza. She was relieved to have Poppy with her.

The club was decked out in keeping with the Halloween theme, tables covered with fake cobwebs, orange glitter, and as centerpieces, silver jack-o'-lanterns glowing with votive candles. Blocks of dry ice were set at the edge of the stage to create the illusion of fog, to eerie effect. Even the small, cramped backstage area was decorated with plastic skulls and pumpkins.

Despite the festive atmosphere, Mallory was tense. She noticed that for some reason, Poppy looked uptight, too.

The dressing room was full. All the girls were there: Cat-o'-Nine-Tails, Scarlett Letter, Kitty Klitty, and, of course, Violet, who looked particular fetching, her green eyes almost glittering against her bright stage makeup.

"What character are you supposed to be?" Kitty asked her.

"Why don't you watch me and find out," Violet said, and Mallory could feel her eyes following her as she staked her claim on a vanity in the farthest corner of the room.

Suddenly, a scream erupted. Mallory jumped, and then realized the MC for the night, Rude Ralph, had lurched into the room wearing an executioner's costume and thrown a fake, decapitated head onto Kitty Klitty's lap.

"Get out!" Scarlett tossed shoes at him.

He laughed and ducked, the shoes hitting the wall.

"Hey, Violet, I need you to check the props you have out here and make sure we're setting it up right. That thing is heavy."

"I'll be there in a minute."

Ralph bounced a rubber eyeball at Poppy.

"Eww!"

After a rousing chorus of "get the fuck out," he left.

"Ugh. So annoying. Why isn't Alec here tonight, Moxie?"

"He's in LA interviewing Kendall James."

"She's hot," said Violet.

Mallory focused on her makeup and costume, ignoring the bait. She was dressing as a super-sexy Snow White, in a blue corset with red bustier and custom cap sleeves with blue ruching that were reminiscent of Snow White's traditional dress. Her ass was squeezed into yellow hot pants, under which a few inches of bare leg showed before her thigh-high white stockings began. Her favorite part of the costume was the mid-calf length white patent leather platform boots. On her head she wore a black, bobbed wig with a headband, and on her right arm she had a press-on tattoo of one of the Seven Dwarfs.

Agnes, looking weary and a bit aggravated, opened the door.

"The lineup is Violet, Poppy, Kitty, Cat, and Moxie with Scarlett."

Mallory was doing an act together with Scarlett Letter. They were performing to the Hole song "I Think That I Would Die," off of one of Mallory's all-time favorite albums, *Live Through This*. In the song, Courtney Love sang with melancholy and passion about loss, and the character Rose Red was central to the chorus. To accompany the tune, Mallory and Scarlett had choreographed a dark interpretation of the Snow White and Rose Red fairy tale. As she had told Alec weeks ago, they needed a bear on stage with them. Since Alec was gone, they had enlisted Scarlett's boyfriend, Eric, who told them the last time he had been on a stage was his fifth grade Christmas pageant.

"We have two stage kittens tonight because of all the costumes and extra glitter and who knows what," Agnes said. "But be careful on the stage because they might miss this or that. I don't need any problems tonight. That's all. Moxie, I want to speak to you outside."

Surprised, Mallory put down her eyelash glue and followed Agnes outside, where they stood directly behind the stage curtain.

"I see you have a special guest on the list tonight."

"Yes! Bette is here. Is that okay?"

Agnes smiled. "Yes. Tell her to come by and say hi after the show."

Mallory felt good thinking about Bette in the audience tonight. She hadn't forgotten that she would be there, but in all of her stress about Alec and trepidation about seeing Violet, she'd pushed the one bright spot of the night to the back of her mind. But she knew that once she was out there on stage, she'd feel the rush of knowing her mentor was there cheering her on. She could almost forget about Alec in LA, almost forget Violet's eyes following her every move.

Her BlackBerry beeped with a text:

Sneak out and watch the first act w/us? Table in front. I'm with Martha and Justin.

Mallory typed back:

Is there a seat? Agnes will kill me.

To which Bette responded:

Blame it on me! We have a seat. Get your hot ass out here.

Mallory smiled and threw on a robe.

Out in the audience, she spotted Bette immediately. Even among the dark and glittering decorations, she was the most dramatic sight in the room, with her luminous pale skin, trademark black bob, and pillowy, heart-shaped lips always painted a deep, matte red. She was wearing a floor-length, red suede trench coat that must have cost a fortune. Mallory wondered if she was getting free clothes from designers now that she was being photographed everywhere with Zebra.

"Hey, beautiful," Bette said, jumping up when she saw her. She pulled Mallory into a hug, and Mallory felt all the eyes in the room on them. She remembered the first time she was at the club—she had spotted Bette before the show and had been immediately fascinated.

"I'm so glad you're here," Mallory said. Justin Baxter and Martha Pike were at the table. "Hi! It's great to see you guys."

"Hi, doll," Justin said, hugging her warmly.

The lights dimmed, and the audience settled down, a frisson of anticipation in the air. "So what's the deal with this Violet chick?" Bette whispered.

"You'll see for yourself. She's opening."

The curtain rose, and in the center of the stage was a floor-to-ceiling pole. Mallory and Bette looked at each other. This was a first.

The staccato, military-style opening to the Marilyn Manson song "The Beautiful People" began, instantly changing the vibe of the room from anticipation to nervous excitement. Violet appeared, wearing a Belle mask from *Beauty and The Beast,* a black leather jacket cinched tightly at the waist, black fishnet stockings, and combat boots. Her platinum, cropped hair was covered with a long, dreadlocked wig.

She marched in place, her body rigid and almost robotic in

motion. As the song picked up momentum, she unzipped the leather coat, baring her breasts, her nipples covered in skull and crossbone pasties. The crowd cheered and clapped wildly, and Mallory saw that Bette was watching the performance with rapt attention.

The chorus of the song began, and Violet jumped onto the pole, clambering up it like a dark spider. At the midway point, she released both hands, and, supporting herself with only her legs, leaned back so she was virtually lying on her back in midair. And then, to the collective disbelief of the audience, she started rotating around the pole in a complete 360 degrees.

"Oh...my...God," Bette said.

"I thought I'd seen everything," said Justin Baxter.

Mallory could only imagine what Agnes was thinking. She hated anything that smacked of stripper culture. To her, there was a world of difference between burlesque and the modern day strip club, and to blur the lines was the worst kind of affront to the discipline she'd built her life around.

Violet continued to wind her body around the pole, finally leaping down to tear off her fishnets, leaving her in only a thong and combat boots and the Belle mask.

"Walt Disney must be rolling over in his grave," said Bette.

"Agnes is probably digging one for Violet," said Mallory. Bette laughed.

At the end of the act, the audience whistled, cheered, and stomped their feet in a frenzy Mallory had rarely—if ever—heard before.

She was torn between wishing Alec were there so she could talk about it with him, and feeling competitive and relieved he hadn't seen it. She hated how exhilarated she felt from watching the performance. She had to admit it was the most interesting thing she'd seen onstage in a long time.

It would be a hard act to follow.

* * *

Mallory posed in the darkness, facing Scarlett and hearing the whispers and rustling of the audience. The curtain pulled back to reveal a makeshift forest—Agnes and Kitty's handiwork of small fake Christmas trees and cardboard roses painted glow-in-the-dark white and red.

The foreboding opening strings of "I Think That I Would Die" filled the stage, and Mallory felt a tremor of delicious anticipation. No matter what else was going on in her life, the rustling and murmurs of a live audience waiting in the dark, giddy with expectation, would never fail to make her feel alive and powerful.

Mallory and Scarlett moved into their choreography, skipping around the flowers in a circle. Scarlett's costume was a mirror image of Mallory's, except her bustier and boots were red, her hot pants were black, and she wore a long, cherry-colored wig. They both carried wicker baskets full of flowers, and Mallory carried a baby doll wrapped in a blanket. Eric lurked off to the side of the stage in his bear costume, waiting for his cue. When Courtney Love's mournful lyrics began, he moved into the open so the audience could see him, and he inched closer to Mallory and Scarlett, the unsuspecting Snow White and Rose Red. Then he snatched the doll from Mallory's arms—and removed her corset in the process—and retreated back into the shadows of side stage.

Mallory felt the hot stage lights on her bare skin and heard the roar of the audience at the sight of her breasts, covered only with small pasties over her nipples. She felt the audience's energy, and the heaviness of her mood finally lifted. She wished that she were not sharing the stage with Scarlett, because she had the urge to peel away the rest of her costume, to reveal her body to the audience as quickly as possible so she could feed on their excitement and adoration. This, performing, was the closest she had ever gotten to taking drugs, and she needed a dose that night more than ever.

Scarlett was busy following the script of their carefully paced disrobing and removed her bustier to offer it to the freshly bared Snow White, who demurred. As the chorus began with the rousing "Rose white, rose red...," Snow White and Rose Red danced around the stage, "searching" for the bear, all the while shedding clothes. When they were down to their G-strings and boots, jumping up and down frantically, the tassels on their pasties twirling in unison, the audience roared their approval.

While Mallory had liked the idea of the act when they planned and choreographed it, as she went through motions, it felt forced and unsatisfying. She didn't fall into the groove she had felt the night of the Marie Antoinette performance, and although the audience didn't seem to know the difference, she did.

Eric reappeared on stage, and Rose Red and Snow White removed their shiny boots and, to rousing applause, hammered the "bear" with their shoes until he relinquished the baby and retreated, in defeat, back into the depths of the forest. Snow White and Rose Red bent over to retrieve their baskets, giving the audience a good long look at their asses, bare except for their floss-thin G-strings. The shouting and clapping reached a fever pitch, and Mallory and Scarlett, nude and barefoot, their respective white and red tassels twirling in triumph, skipped back amongst the flowers.

Mallory didn't experience her usual post-performance high. In fact, she felt like she had bombed.

"Don't be ridiculous!" Kitty Klitty said, when she confided this to her, near tears as she took off her fake eyelashes. "You're always the best one."

"Well, thanks, Kitty. But I don't think that's true, and it's certainly not true tonight."

"At least you're not getting fired," she said.

"What does that mean?"

"While you were onstage, Agnes came in and told Violet to pack her stuff and get out."

Mallory looked around the room. She had noticed Violet wasn't there, but it wasn't unusual for the girls to filter out to the club after their set.

"She fired her?"

Kitty nodded, and then asked, "Is Bette really in the audience?"

"Yeah."

"Are you guys coming out with us? We're going to Elixir."

"I don't know, Kitty. I think Bette wants to keep a low profile. Everything's different for her now that she's with Zebra. She can't go anywhere without the paparazzi stalking her, and I think she wants a quiet night for a change."

Kitty looked crestfallen, but Mallory was too distracted to try to promise to get Bette to meet up with her one night before she left town again. Instead, she went looking for Agnes and found her in her office.

"Agnes? I'm going to meet Bette outside. I'm sure she'd love to see you."

Agnes turned to her, a bitter expression on her face.

"They liked it. I've never heard them applaud like that."

"Who? Liked what?" Mallory said, although she was fairly certain she knew what Agnes was referring to.

"Violet's stripper dance."

"Oh, well, they don't know, Agnes. I mean, it's all just entertainment to them. You can't expect the audience to be offended that someone doesn't do classic burlesque."

"Offended? They don't even want burlesque. I think now they want to see strippers but to feel better about themselves to call it burlesque. The closer to stripping, the happier they are." She shook her head. "My day is past."

"Don't say that, Agnes. We have a full house every night. If people wanted stripping they could go anywhere else. Or they could go to the Slit to see something raunchier. But they don't. They come here."

"For how much longer?" She waved Mallory away. "Go meet your friend. I will come say hello."

"Okay. We'll wait for you outside."

But waiting outside proved impossible; when she met Bette at the front of the club as planned, Bette told her they couldn't leave.

"The sidewalk is literally jammed with photographers," she said.

"What do we do? Wait it out inside?"

"They won't leave until I leave."

"So what do we do?" Mallory repeated.

"We need a cab. Or a car."

"I have an idea." She texted Justin Baxter, asking if he could call a car for them. He said they were welcome to use his to get home—his driver was waiting for him and Martha around the corner and could take Mallory and Bette instead.

"I didn't think it would be like this here," Bette said. "LA, yes—but this was my last bastion of sanity."

"Well, not anymore."

Mallory saw Agnes making her way toward them.

"Welcome back, my bright star," said Agnes.

"Hey, great to see you," Bette said, letting the older woman hug her.

"The world is treating you well?" Agnes said.

"I can't complain," said Bette. "Except I do miss my old home base."

"You're welcome here any time. Just forewarn me next time so I can get security. These people are animals."

"Did you have a problem?"

"I had to lock the door! It's illegal but what can I do? They would have marched in here with their cameras....I would have to call police but then, who knows what problems. So next time, tell me first, okay?" She patted Bette's cheeks like she was a wayward grandchild.

Mallory's phone beeped.

"The car's outside. Let's go. Thanks, Agnes. I might take you up on a little guest appearance sooner than you think."

Bette took Mallory's hand, pulling her through the throng outside the door. It was a terrifying crush of bodies and cameras, creating a feeling so claustrophobic Mallory almost started hyperventilating. She realized the images of paparazzi ambushes on TV did not do justice to how terrifying the experience felt. Every instinct in her body turned to fight or flight, but she couldn't do either; she had to follow Bette's lead until the Town Car door was safety closed on them.

"What a nightmare! How do you live with that?"

"It's not always that bad, and Zebra has a tight security team. I didn't realize it would be like this even without her with me. Sorry about that."

"It's not your fault. But we're lucky Justin and Martha lent us the car."

"I guess I was deluding myself to think we could walk around and talk for a little bit."

"So where to?" Mallory said.

"The Standard," Bette told the driver.

"Just like old times," Mallory smiled.

"Oh yeah? Is that an invitation?" Bette said.

"Very funny. You're practically a married woman these days," Mallory said.

"No," Bette said. "I'm not."

"What do you mean? Did something happen with Zebra?"

"I'll tell you at the hotel." She pointed discreetly at the driver. "I've been in enough tabloids this year to become paranoid."

"Wow. Your secrets are worth money."

"Every inch of me is worth money," Bette said. "And I'm just getting started."

12

Violet didn't know what disgusted her more: getting fired after putting on the best performance of the night if not the history of the club, or the rabid throng of paparazzi waiting outside for Bette Noir. Who cared about her? So she was banging Zebra. Big deal—Violet had fucked the shit out of Ryan Ellison, and she didn't make it into one tabloid. Hadn't even gotten a mention on a stupid gossip blog.

Her phone rang. When she saw the incoming number, she felt a surge of hope that the night could turn around yet. At the very least she could take out her aggression.

"Mistress Violet," she said.

"It's Billy. I know this is last minute, but are you free?"

"No. I'm quite expensive."

"You know what I mean. Are you available?"

"Now?"

"Yes," he said.

"Where?"

"My apartment. But the thing is I have a...friend with me. Can you handle that?"

"I can handle anything. But since I'm doing you a favor tonight, I have a little favor I want to ask you."

"Name it."

"Not now. Another time."

"So we'll see you within the hour?"

"I don't have my equipment with me."

"We have everything you need."

Yes, you do, Violet thought. *You just don't know it yet.*

Mallory curled up on the couch in Bette's suite at the Standard.

"So what happened?" she said.

Bette poured herself vodka.

"It's my fault," she said. She looked younger and more vulnerable than Mallory had ever seen her, her face clear of makeup, her pale skin stark against her black hair. "I fucked it up."

"I doubt that," Mallory said. And she wasn't just saying it to make Bette feel better; Bette had always displayed a cool, rational mind when it came to relationships and sex.

"No. I did. I need a cigarette," she announced, pulling a pack out of her Chloé bag.

"Since when do you smoke?"

"Since the Paris leg of Zebra's tour."

"You're going to wreck your perfect skin."

"I'll quit in a year."

"Why a year?"

"That's the time I'm allotting myself to get over Zebra."

"That's too much time. You know the formula: it takes half the time you were with someone for you to get over the breakup. You were together less than a year, so in five months or so you should be in good shape." Mallory smiled warmly at her and patted her arm. "Besides, things probably aren't really over. Maybe you guys just hit a rough patch and it will work out."

Bette shook her head, leaning back into the folds of the thick, white couch cushions.

"I blew it. I tried to make it into something it wasn't. A bush league mistake." She tapped her cigarette into a wide shallow glass. "It started out great—the sex was phenomenal; we talked all the time about art and music and dance. She was fascinated by burlesque, and you know I performed at some of her shows. We were like this creative, singular organism. We fucked and performed and dressed up and partied. But I got so wrapped up in her and wanting to be around her as much as possible that I stopped working at building myself. I didn't practice; I stopped thinking of acts; I stopped paying attention to new music because everything was about Zebra. And before I knew it, she was the only artist in the room, and I was just another hanger-on, like the stylists and backup dancers and makeup artists and designers. She totally lost interest in me. And the more I sensed her losing interest in me, the harder I clung to her. It was a vicious cycle. I can't even blame her for losing interest in me. I wasn't even interesting to myself."

"That doesn't sound like you."

"It wasn't me! I'm telling you, love is a dangerous drug. Worse than coke. The highs are high, but you can't maintain it. You keep trying to, and it just makes things crash that much faster."

"I think ideally love is supposed to mellow into something sustainable."

"Yeah? How's that working out for you?"

"Not so well, actually." Mallory told Bette about her suspicion that Alec was attracted to Violet, and the ill-fated night out for the three of them.

"That chick is bad news. Alec should know better. And you

should have known better than to hang out with her. So where do things stand with you and Alec?"

"He left for LA the night after the Plaza, and I haven't heard from him since. I don't know if he's hurt, angry, trying to figure things out—or maybe he's not thinking about me at all. Maybe he's partying with Kendall James and has decided our relationship isn't worth the trouble."

"I doubt it. That guy loves you."

"I messed things up."

"Yeah, maybe. But he's fucked things up in the past and you forgave him. Now it's his turn."

"Maybe. Or all this messing up and forgiveness—or not—is a sign that the relationship just fundamentally doesn't work. We met when we were twenty-one-years-old. How often do those types of relationships really go the distance? And I'm not talking about people who stay in miserable marriages. I mean really work—like, people stay happy together."

"I don't know. But I think it's too soon for you to give up. Unless you want to."

"Why would I want to?"

Bette shrugged. "Do you have your eye on someone else?"

"No!" Mallory said defensively.

"There's no other guy?"

"No! Except sometimes I fantasize about my boss."

"The lawyer?"

"Yes. It's not just that he's gorgeous—which he is. Or that he's extremely smart and good at what he does..."

"Uh-oh," Bette said.

"No, it's not those things. It's more that when I'm with him, I don't have all the baggage of my relationship with Alec. It's like Gavin—that's his name—sees me through fresh eyes, and that lets me see myself that way, too. There's so much intensity with Alec, and as much as I love him I'm just exhausted from it. With Gavin, I can imagine how an adult relationship should be."

"Be careful, Mallory. You know what they say—the grass is always greener. You and Alec have something together. Don't let it go so easily."

"It's not my choice right now—to let it go or not. I don't know if Alec wants to be together anymore, either. And I'm just trying to see the possibility that it's not the worst thing in the world instead of curling up in a ball like I did the last time we broke up. I guess I have a lot to figure out."

"I'm sorry. For what it's worth, I think he really loves you."

"Maybe. But that doesn't mean we'll make each other happy in the long run. And I don't know what to do about it except take a step back."

"That makes two of us. But I'm going to try to forget about Zebra—which, considering she is on the cover of every magazine, playing over the sound system of every store I walk into, and permeating every corner of pop culture, will mean I basically have to move to another continent. Or planet."

"I think you need to focus on yourself. Do a show at the Blue Angel. Agnes would love it. And you need to remember that you're a star in your own right."

"If there's one thing that being with Zebra confirmed, it's that I want real success. I want that level not just of fame, but of influence. I just have to figure out how to get to the next level."

"I know you're hurting now, but being with her did help you get exposure. And in the beginning, that's what you told me you wanted, remember?"

"Yes. I remember. And you were disappointed that I wasn't looking for my soul mate. Ironic, isn't it?"

"Maybe you instinctively knew that she was just there to serve a purpose in your life. I was being a romantic sap. But I'm done with that."

"Now you're a cold, hard realist?"

"I'm trying to be."

Bette raised her glass in a toast.

A beautiful young man opened the door to Billy's apartment. Violet recognized him instantly from the Burberry billboard in Soho.

"Hey," the guy said.

Violet shrugged off her leather coat, revealing the steampunk princess costume she'd put back on after the show. The only thing she'd left out of the ensemble was the wig. The man—if he was even technically a man or still a boy—seemed unfazed by her dramatic attire. She wondered if he knew what was in store for him, or if Billy was orchestrating a little midnight surprise.

"Where's Billy?

"Um, in the bedroom."

"Why don't you be a good little whore and wait for us on the couch."

The boy looked like he'd been smacked. She did not, in actuality, think he was a prostitute. But he might as well get a sense of the tone of the evening. Things always went more smoothly when everyone knew the drill.

She walked into Billy's bedroom and found him doing a line of coke.

"Great. Party favors," she said, sitting next to him in front of the glass end table. She dipped her finger into the powder and rubbed some on her gums. "Maybe your boy toy in the other room would like to partake? We should all get in the partying mood, don't you think?"

"Don't worry about him," Billy said.

"I'm not worried. I just want him to be with the program. I'm not in the mood to have to do a lot of handholding. So what did you have in mind?"

Billy hesitated for a few beats. "I want you to do the usual to me—you know, scolding, humiliation. And then for punishment I want you to force me to...do stuff with him."

"Have you two fucked before?"

"I don't know why that's relevant," he said.

"I need to know the dynamic between you two so I can control the room. Answer the question or I'm out of here."

"Yes. We have."

"Super. Where is the equipment?"

He pointed to his nightstand. She stood and collected the large black dildo, the paddle, the butt plug, and the arm restraints.

"This will be a thousand dollars," she said. "Paid upfront."

She strode into the living room and got the men in position: Billy Barton on all fours, and Tyler, the Burberry model, was—at her command—inserting a butt plug into Billy's ass.

She enjoyed directing. She was like Sofia Coppola—except hot. Actually, she kind of liked Sofia Coppola's *jolie laide* sort of attractiveness.

"You know he wants your cock in his ass, not that substitute—don't you, Tyler?" she said.

The man-child, trying dutifully to play along, looked at her with utter shock every time she opened her mouth. He was a gorgeous specimen, with wide, muscled shoulders and the tapered, taut upper body of a swimmer. He was about six foot five inches, and had a nice big cock. When he first removed his jeans, she told him to stroke himself, and it took all of her willpower not to kneel down and take that cock into her mouth. She rarely craved cock, but when something looked perfect she had to have it. Maybe Billy's final humiliation of the evening would be to watch Tyler fuck her instead of him. But no, that would derail the most important part of her evening—something that would cost Billy Barton much more than one thousand dollars.

"Now say thank you," Violet said to Billy.

"Thank you, Mistress Violet."

"Not to me, you idiot. To Tyler!"

Billy started to thank Tyler and she interrupted. "You better show your appreciation by sucking his cock. Now! Tyler, get in front of him."

Tyler stood in front of Billy, who raised himself on his knees and eagerly placed one hand on Tyler's thick penis, guiding it to his mouth. He took it in as far as he could, grasping Tyler's ass with both of his hands, pulling him in a little deeper and holding him in place while his mouth worked him.

Tyler closed his eyes, moaning so quietly Violet almost didn't hear it. She circled around the two of them, pausing occasionally to smack Billy's ass with the paddle.

She could see that Tyler was getting so worked up he was close to coming, and she couldn't let that happen—not yet.

"Tyler, get over here and remove this butt plug. I don't think Billy is giving you good enough head, and he must be punished." Tyler looked at her pleadingly, as if to say, *Don't make us stop.* But she wasn't there to help some stupid model get off. "Don't make me use this on you," she said, brandishing the paddle. She knew from a little trial run earlier in the session that Tyler did not enjoy pain—not even a little.

He obeyed her, reluctantly pulling his cock away from Billy's hungry mouth, and circled around to where she was standing, tapping her boot with impatience, pointing at the offending butt plug, which needed immediate attention.

Tyler's cock was reddish purple, veiny with excitement and glistening with Billy's saliva. She was mesmerized by it, barely taking her eyes away as Tyler pulled the rubber plug from Billy's rectum.

She turned only to make sure her handbag was where she thought she had left it—on the floor under the antique coffee table. It was, just within arm's reach.

"Now put your cock in his ass—and don't take it out until I give you permission. Is that understood?"

Tyler did not answer, but he immediately put his hands on Billy's buttocks, his thumb rimming the opening, Billy's eager anus puckering at him like a tiny mouth. She watched in fascination as Tyler's cock burrowed inside of Billy, her eyes darting from the rhythmic pumping to the look of ecstatic concentration on the man's face. She didn't trust him to keep going for as long as she told him to—he probably didn't have that much control, and he probably didn't care about meeting with her approval. She watched them closely, circling around once to see that Billy's eyes were half-closed, glazed with impending ecstasy. Tyler was busy pumping away, and she doubted he would be paying much attention to her. He was not trained, as Billy was, to be acutely aware of her every move during these sessions.

She bent down behind Tyler, discreetly retrieving her handbag.

"Fuck me!" Billy cried.

Oh, I will. Violet smiled to herself while clutching her iPhone. She crept slowly from her perch behind the two men to a side position where she could get an angle on both Billy's face and the guy riding his ass, and snapped three shots. Just then, Billy's penis erupted with semen, and she clicked the camera one more time.

Tyler convulsed in spasms and moans, and she quickly slipped her phone back into her bag.

Her work here was done.

13

Monday morning, Mallory woke up with a start, wondering why her alarm clock had failed to go off. Even though she was late, she took the time to go through the morning ritual of turning on her BlackBerry and checking for a text or message from Alec.

She had seven new voice mail messages. Since midnight last night.

"What the hell..." She logged in and was met with Allison's excited voice.

"You're famous! Nice photo, by the way. Call me!"

What was she talking about?

The next message was from Julie. "Did you see Page Six? Call me!"

Mallory jumped out of bed, pulled on sweats—and sunglasses, because she knew she looked like death warmed over—and hurried to the Korean grocer on the corner. She slapped a quarter on the counter and didn't wait to leave the store before thumbing through the *Post* to the gossip page. There, on the lower left side of the page, was a photo of Bette exiting the Blue

Angel, surrounded by paparazzi, with Mallory at her side. The caption read, "Zebra's paramour Bette Noir exits hot spot Blue Angel with fellow burlesquer, Mallory 'Moxie' Dale."

"Oh…my…God." Mallory looked around the bodega, feeling as exposed as if she were standing there naked. This was a disaster. The one thing she'd worried about the most when she accepted the paralegal job with Gavin. When she was busted for performing at the Blue Angel by the last law firm that employed her, she was promptly fired. At the time, she hadn't been that upset. She hated the job and had been second-guessing her decision to become a lawyer. But she'd quickly realized that making no money while dancing at the Blue Angel was not a viable mode of existence in New York City. And so she had asked a headhunter to find her a legal job, and the first gig she interviewed for was Gavin's paralegal opening. She was surprised by how much she enjoyed working in the law without the pressure or commitment of making it her entire life's work.

But this would ruin everything.

She tucked the paper under her arm and walked back to her apartment. It was colder than she had anticipated—the first hint of winter. She pulled her sweatshirt closed and wished she'd worn a hat.

She dropped the paper on the kitchen counter and started the coffeemaker.

On the one hand, she knew working for Gavin didn't involve as rigid an environment as her previous job at the venerable law firm Reed, Warner, but she doubted he would be thrilled to learn his paralegal was a burlesque dancer. He represented some very wealthy, high profile New Yorkers in their divorces, and it was conceivable that having a paralegal known for taking off her clothes would impede his business.

She dialed Bette's cell, but of course she was still sleeping and didn't answer. The next call was back to her voice mail, where she erased two more calls from Julie, a call from Alec saying he couldn't wait to see her tonight, a message from Poppy telling her about Page Six, and a message from Gavin on his way to court saying he hoped she was okay since she was not at her desk and if she was sick not to worry, he had *Klein v. Klein* under control.

Her phone rang again. Gavin's cell phone number appeared on her screen.

"Gavin, hi. I'm so sorry—I overslept but I'll be in the office in forty-five minutes or less. Good luck in court today."

"Thanks. Um, Mallory?"

"Yes?"

"Do you read the *Post*?"

Her stomach dropped.

"Sometimes," she stalled.

"Well, I don't. But apparently Marcy Klein is a big reader of Page Six."

"Gavin, I can explain...."

"Let's not get into it now—I have to focus on what Judge Hager has in store for us. I don't want to upset you, but I do think this is something that merits further discussion."

"Okay," she said.

"Things should be wrapped for the day by eleven thirty or so. Meet me for lunch? I'll make a reservation at Park Avenue Autumn. Do you know where that is?"

"I'll figure it out," she said, looking at the photo of herself. She looked startled by the glare of the camera, like the proverbial deer in headlights. By her side, Bette looked cool and impervious, like a movie star. Yes, Bette was cut out for that life. She was not.

She had thought she could keep the two halves of her life separate, and if she had to choose one over the other it was a no-brainer: her future was as Moxie. But she didn't feel as sure-footed as she had the last time her worlds collided. And she was not looking forward to having to choose again.

Mallory waited by the hostess station at Park Avenue Autumn. She had read about the restaurant, which changed its décor and menu with every season. Although she had no idea what they did for summer, winter, and spring, she couldn't imagine it surpassing the simmering elegance of their take on autumn, with the dark wood and copper and perfectly attenuated lighting that was neither bright nor dim but some perfect meeting of the two that had the inexplicable effect of making Mallory feel beautiful.

"Sorry I'm late," Gavin said, looking unusually harried and slightly disheveled. He shrugged off his Burberry overcoat and handed it to an attendant.

"No problem. How did it go today?"

"Pretty well," he said, as they were shown to their table.

"This room is fantastic," she said. "I can't believe they change it every few months."

"I know. I thought they might get complacent and abandon that gimmick after the first year, but they haven't. I've been here a few times, and I have to say the best room is Spring. But this is a close second."

"I think that's true of New York in general. Spring is the best time of year, followed closely by fall."

"I know a lot of people who would debate you on that," he said.

She read the menu and appreciated the autumnal accents on all of the dishes. She decided on the roasted pumpkin soup with lobster croutons and then the shrimp Cobb for her main. Gavin ordered the fig carpaccio with goat cheese and the roasted chicken with pumpkin pie.

She realized all the food and décor talk was a way of stalling, avoiding the real reason they were having lunch at a fancy restaurant in the middle of the workday. The suspense was killing her, so she decided to bite the bullet.

"About that photo..."

"Are you really a burlesque dancer?"

"Yes," she said.

"What is that, exactly?"

"Well, it's a performance art, like any other kind of dancing. Costumes play a big role, and lots of the dancers put a feminist spin on it...."

"But there's an element of stripping, right?"

"Yes. But not fully. I mean, I take my costume off but I'm wearing...Look, I feel really uncomfortable talking to you about this."

"Mallory, I feel bad even having this conversation because typically, I'm not one to judge. And really, I don't care what you do in your spare time. But people make generalizations, and Marcy Klein depends on you a lot and this shakes her confidence, rightly or wrongly. When I'm running around at court or I'm in a deposition room with you, I can't worry that the opposing counsel or our clients may be taking you—and, as an extension, me—less seriously because of your, um, other job."

"I understand," she said, her stomach sinking.

"I'm not sure what to tell you, except to consider the fact that you might have to make a choice."

Violet pulled the covers off of her naked body and reached for her iPhone. She scrolled through the images of Billy Barton being ass-fucked by the Burberry model and it made her wet—not because the images were hot, but because they were going to get her what she wanted. Well, at least one thing she wanted.

She placed the phone down and rubbed her clit with her index finger, thinking of the way she'd fucked Poppy LaRue, but instead of Poppy tied up on her bed it was Mallory. What would it take to get Mallory in that position? Some help from Alec, that's what.

Emboldened by her success last night with Billy Barton, Violet felt she was on a hot streak and dialed Alec's cell.

"Hello?"

He sounded groggy.

"It's Violet. Can you hear me? Where are you? It's so loud."

"I'm getting on a plane. What do you want?"

"I'm ready for another outing. Think you can find something interesting for us to do tonight?"

"That's not going to happen."

"What's the problem? Too much partying in LA? Did Kendall James wear you out?"

"How did you know about Kendall James?"

"A little birdie told me. A hot little birdie." Silence on the other end. "So do you want to meet up tonight or what? Mallory might want some entertainment, party pooper."

"I'll pass," he said.

"Are you cranky because I didn't fuck you, too?"

"Jesus, Violet. It's a little early in the day for this. I don't think Mallory has any interest in your games."

"I think you'd be surprised what Mallory is interested in," said Violet. "You're being too hasty in answering for her. I bet she'd be up for a drink. Perhaps you should just stay home this time and let the girls have all the fun. Are you willing to take one for the team, Alec?"

"Mallory and I are the team, Violet. You aren't even on the bench."

"Is that so?"

"Yes," he said.

"We'll see. Oh—and Alec?"

"What?"

"I can't wait to taste your girlfriend's pussy again."

She hung up and began composing a text to Mallory.

* * *

Gavin peered at her over the dessert menu.

"I'm thinking the chocolate cube. What do you say?"

"Sounds great," she said, though she was too nervous to eat any more food. He hadn't pressed her further on the issue of her Page Six exposure, but now that dessert was on the way, she had a feeling her less-than-desirable night gig would be back on the table, so to speak. Sure enough, when the dark chocolate square appeared on a silver tray, he turned pensive.

"So, how serious are you about this burlesque career?" Gavin finally said.

"I'm not sure how to answer that," she said.

"Well, is this a passing hobby or something you plan on doing for a while?"

Mallory swallowed hard.

"To be honest, if you had asked me that a few months ago, I would have told you I was very serious about it. I love performing, but I'm starting to wonder what the endgame is. And I didn't think I had to know the absolute answer to that, but…"

"I only press you on this because I don't see how I can keep you on, knowing that you have such a high-profile, edgy nightlife."

"It's not usually high-profile—I don't even use my real name. This was a freak thing because of my friend Bette.…"

He put his hand on hers, and she felt something electric shoot through her. She looked at him in surprise. *Oh, my God, I'm actually attracted to him. Truly attracted to him.*

"Forgive me if I'm speaking out of line—and this is none of my business except for the part about how it affects the office—but I think you're brilliant, and it is a terrible waste if you don't at least consider taking the bar exam."

Mallory sighed.

"There was a time when I really thought that was what I wanted. Every choice I made in my life was centered on my goal to be a lawyer at a big firm. And then I got the job at Reed, Warner, and I hated it. Every day I dreaded waking up in the morning. I didn't know how I could be so miserable when I was getting what I'd worked so hard for. So I tried to pretend I wasn't miserable. And then I failed the bar. My boyfriend said he thought I failed on purpose on some level. I told him that was crazy, but maybe he's not entirely wrong."

"Reed, Warner is a tough gig. They burn out more lawyers than not. That culture isn't for everyone. But the fact that you even got a place there tells me you must be pretty damn good."

"Thanks," she said, feeling inexplicably bashful at the compliment.

"Will you at least consider giving law another shot? I think you'd be amazing at family law. My clients love you, and that is so important in this field where emotions run high and the most important things in people's lives are at stake—their homes, custody of their children. That's why I am particularly sensitive to the issue of your burlesque career. I don't want the clients to have less faith in you or to think differently about you in any way. It's not right that people should generalize because of something like that, but you know that's human nature."

"I know," she said. "And it bothers me to think that Marcy would have less faith in me because she perceives me as being flighty or less serious about my work here because I'm performing at night."

"Will you at least think about getting back into a legal career? And I don't mean as a paralegal. You're too good for that." And then...Was it possible? The way he was looking at her—the prolonged eye contact, the quick but unmistakable glance at her lips. It was more than the way a boss looked at his employee.

"I just don't know," she said, stalling. Was he attracted to her?

Her phone vibrated in her bag. She wondered if it was yet another person texting or calling about the Page Six photo. Hopefully, word had not yet spread to her mother, who was still clueless about Mallory's alter ego.

The text was maybe the one bit of news that had the ability to make her feel worse than getting busted by her mom:

Don't make any plans for tonight. I'll make it worth your while. —VIOLET.

Mallory's head filled with an image of Violet's head between her legs.

"I'm sorry," she said to Gavin. "What were you saying?"

"Will you consider getting back into law?" Gavin said. "Maybe let this burlesque thing run its course and get serious about your career again.

She looked at the text, then back at Gavin. "Yes," she said. "I'll think about it."

14

Mallory rolled down the cab window, not trusting what she was seeing through the glass. Was that a line down the block?

One street away from the Blue Angel, her phone rang.

"When are you getting here?" said Bette.

"I'm a block away," she said, looking at the street that housed the Blue Angel. The sidewalk was filled with people. "Am I seeing what I think I'm seeing? Is that a line to get in?"

"Yeah. I attribute it to the Page Six mention, combined with Poppy's tweeting about my guest appearance tonight. We're overwhelmed."

"I'll be right there." She told the cab to stop and hurried along the uneven sidewalk in her heels, hoisting her BAE bag onto her shoulder. Inside, her "Heart-Shaped Glasses" costume was folded, along with some documents from work that she needed to read over the weekend. Once again, she'd barely been able to leave work on time. She didn't mind; the avalanche of reading and research kept her from having too much time to think about her personal life. If it weren't for her excitement to finally perform her "Heart-Shaped Glasses" routine, she wondered if she would have been able to motivate herself to leave the office at all.

She made her way past the line, and the ticket collector inside the door with the guest list look frazzled.

"Can you believe this?" she said to Mallory.

"No!" she said. "Where's Agnes?"

She found Bette in the dressing room.

"Where is everyone?"

"Agnes is holding a staff meeting. You're late."

"Agnes doesn't hold 'staff' meetings."

"Well, she does now. She told me she felt she had to address the firing of Violet, and make it clear what she expected in terms of 'conduct' on stage and what the Blue Angel stands for in the 'context of New York burlesque.'"

"Interesting," Mallory said, though in truth, she didn't find it that interesting. She felt apathetic.

"Are you okay?" Bette said.

"Yeah. Great. I'm excited to see you on that stage tonight." Mallory began unpacking her makeup.

"It's going to feel good to be out there. Like breathing again."

Mallory said nothing, just looked at herself in the mirror. She made no move to begin doing her face, while Bette expertly applied false eyelashes one at a time to the outermost corner of her upper eyelid, then followed around her eye with the mascara wand.

"Why aren't you getting dressed?" she said, not moving her eyes from the focus on her own reflection. Mallory said nothing. "What's wrong?"

"My boss found out about the Page Six photo. He's not too happy about my nightlife."

"So? What's he going to do? Fire you?"

"I think he might."

"Isn't that what happened last time you were 'outed'?"

"Yes."

"And you just found another job. No big deal."

"So is that what I'm going to do? Just keep losing jobs while I do burlesque at night—which pays next to nothing—and living two lives?" Mallory knew she sounded melodramatic, but the anxiety in her voice was nothing compared to the knot of panic she felt in her gut.

"What are you talking about? You're not living two lives. You just have to pay the bills. We all do—until we hit it big. Or at least bigger than this."

"We're not all cut out to be famous, Bette. You're different. For me, I'm having serious doubts about where all this is going. Getting this far—performing at all—is a big deal for me. Maybe as far as I'm going to go. I don't see myself setting out to conquer the world."

Bette nodded. She put down her mascara wand and turned to Mallory. "It's good you can be honest with yourself about this. You're smart, Mallory. And you don't need me to tell you that if you aren't willing to do whatever it takes to become famous, there's no point in doing this except as a hobby. And then no, it's *not* worth losing a day job that pays decent money. But I thought you were in it for real. To make a name for yourself."

"I'm confused. I thought I was, too, but... I don't know." She put her head in her arms as the other girls started filing back into the dressing room. They were mostly dressed for the show, and Mallory felt even more tense for being late and behind.

"Hey, Moxie. You missed the meeting," Poppy said.

"Yeah. What makes you so special?" Scarlett Letter said. Mallory wasn't sure if she was being serious or not, but in her current frame of mind it sounded like a dig.

"I got here late," Mallory said. "That's what makes me special. And now I don't feel very well, so if you'll excuse me, I'll be on my way, and you can have the stage all to yourself tonight to get some attention for yourselves. Although, most of the audience is probably here for Bette, so what you guys do is irrelevant."

She threw her cosmetics case back in her bag. Bette followed her out of the dressing room.

"What's the matter with you?" Bette whispered.

"I need to get out of here," Mallory said. "Can you apologize to Agnes for me? Tell her I felt sick."

"Yes. But don't do anything rash, Mallory. This will pass."

"I'm sorry I won't see your act tonight. I know you'll be amazing."

Mallory made her way through the crowd starting to filter into the main room. Bette followed her and grabbed her arm.

"Where are you going?"

"Home."

"You better get your ass on that stage in twenty-five minutes."

"I'm not performing tonight."

Bette didn't say anything, but put her hand on Mallory's arm. The simple gesture brought her to tears.

The crowd of people buzzed around them, oblivious to their unfolding personal drama. They were excited to see the notorious Bette Noir, a hometown girl turned national celebrity. The people talked about her as if she wasn't standing right there, within earshot. *Did you hear Zebra is a hermaphrodite? That's why Bette left her—she just found out.... Did you hear Bette stole a movie role from Zebra? Now they're not speaking.... Did you hear Zebra fucked Angelina Jolie, and Bette's going after Brad for revenge....*

Bette hugged her. "Take care of yourself."

"Thanks," she said.

She pushed her way through the crowd.

* * *

Outside the Standard Hotel, Violet gave her name to the guy with the headset at the door.

"I don't see it on the list," he said, brushing her aside like a fly.

"I'm with Billy Barton."

When she'd called Billy from her apartment an hour ago, he had not sounded very happy to hear from her. Apparently, he was out with one of his celebrity friends and probably didn't like being reminded of his dirty little secret. But she had insisted that he meet her, and he had reluctantly agreed, warning her that he only had until ten, and then he had to "be somewhere." Don't worry, she'd assured him—she had to be somewhere later, too. And she did: Since Mallory never responded to her text, she made a little date with Poppy, during which she would either be celebrating the result of her meeting or taking out her frustration.

While the 'roid rager at the door made her wait, she silently fumed, thinking to herself that if Billy had failed to put her on the list he was going to seriously regret it. But the planning of her retribution was premature; sure enough, the Door Lord unhooked the red velvet rope, and to the envy and anger of everyone in the line behind her, she was granted entry to the mecca of New York City nightlife.

She made her way through the dark entranceway to the elevator, waiting alongside Josh Duhamel and an actress from *Gossip Girl*—she couldn't tell which one because with their bland, generic attractiveness they truly all looked the same to her. She could tell they were both looking at her and wondering who she was. With her cropped blond hair, inked-up arms, and killer bod, people scrutinized her wherever she went. But celebrities were especially attuned to up-and-comers who might push them from their perch at the top of the food chain.

The elevator deposited them at the top floor, and Violet sauntered into the room. She'd been inside once before, to the celebration party for *Gruff* magazine's "Hot" issue last spring. It was the night she'd discovered Mallory Dale. She'd never forget looking across the room and seeing her for the first time, wondering who she was, and learning—to her delight—that Mallory was a newbie burlesquer, like herself. But Mallory "Moxie" Dale was in the inner circle, with her journalist boyfriend and her new gig at the Blue Angel. Violet was still laboring in the shadows of the dom world, picking up burlesque gigs here or there at the Slipper Room or Public Assembly in Williamsburg. And then she told Billy, her dom client, that she needed a more high-profile gig. And he introduced her to Penelope Lowe at the Slit. And word got out to Agnes that there was a hot new girl in town, and Violet got the prestige gig—the Blue Angel. And that got her closer to Mallory—but not closer to her goal of more money and more recognition. And that's why she was taking matters into her own hands. Whoever said there wasn't a shortcut to success was an idiot. And probably not successful.

She found Billy at a table in the back talking to the hip-hop artist Nicki Minaj.

"Oh…Violet. Do you know Nicki?"

Violet shook her head, and the woman smiled sweetly at her, extending her hand.

"Okay, doll," Billy said to Nicki. "I have some business to discuss, but I will call your manager on Monday and talk to him about the cover. But you heard it from me first—we want Nicki Minaj on the cover of *Gruff* by the summer."

After a few more pleasantries, the woman strutted off, leaving Billy to shift uncomfortably in his seat across the table. Clearly, he was not a fan of the impromptu social encounter.

"I have to admit, I was surprised to hear from you like this," he said.

"Pleasantly, I hope," she replied. He didn't respond. "Well, you don't seem to be in the mood for small talk, so I'll get right to it. As you know, no one is more aware of your tastes and interests than I am," she said, and he squirmed noticeably. "And while I don't share your kinkier proclivities—although I'm happy to service them for the right price—we do have one passion in common."

"And what's that?" he said, visibly annoyed. She was fascinated how different he was at the club, in his element—Billy Barton, arbiter of cool. Oh, if these people only knew!

"Burlesque, of course."

He seemed to relax.

"Yes, we have that interest in common. So what?"

"So I have an idea I am hoping you will be excited about: I want to open my own burlesque club. Something like the Slit, but more exclusive."

"Okay. Sounds good. Go for it."

"I intend to. But I'm not here for your cheerleading. I need you to bankroll it. We'd be partners."

"Violet, I have no interest in owning a burlesque club. They aren't exactly cash cows. And besides, I'm putting everything I have into keeping *Gruff* afloat. Do you have any idea how difficult the magazine market is right now? The last thing I need is a vanity project on the side."

"All you need to do is write a few checks. I'll run the day-to-day, recruit the talent, the PR people. You can use your contacts in the press to make sure the club opens as the biggest thing to hit Manhattan since Studio 54. Or you can choose to be a silent partner and just let me worry about making it a success."

"I just told you, I don't have the interest—or the cash flow, frankly—to open a club right now. Even if I wanted to, which I do not."

"Well, I'm sorry to hear that, Billy. But unfortunately for you, I'm not willing to take no for an answer." Violet felt an adrenaline rush just saying the words. She knew there were two types of people: predators and prey. And, as a predator, she loved going in for the kill. Yes, she would have her club. And then she would have Mallory. Of course Mallory didn't want her yet—anyone worthwhile wanted to fuck their way *up* the food chain, not laterally. Violet was newer on the scene than Mallory; she had no clout. But when she owned the club, Mallory would want her. She'd heard the rumors about Mallory and Bette. Such a cliché: new girl at the club fucks the star. But she would forgive Mallory that pedestrian move. Bette was a hot piece of ass as well as being a star. As for herself, she knew it was too late for her to outshine Mallory on the stage. But she had found her shortcut to the top, and once she was there, Mallory would want her.

Billy smiled and shook his head.

"Well, the answer *is* no. Now if you'll excuse me, I have to get on with my night—I have real business to attend to."

"I just told you I'm not taking no for an answer."

"What are you going to do about it?"

She shrugged. "I will refuse to work with you anymore. I think you'd miss my services. I'm sure your ass would."

"Listen, you crazy bitch. You're not the only whore in town—far from it. I could replace you in a second. So don't forget it."

"Hmm. And how would you go about finding other 'whores' to take care of your pathetic, closet-homo needs? Put an ad in the paper?"

"I think you should leave now before I call security."

"I'm just saying, if you want to put an ad in the paper, I have the perfect photo for you."

She slid three prints across the table.

Billy looked at them for a count of three seconds, then crumpled them in his fist.

"Are you out of your mind?" he whispered.

"No. I've actually given this a lot of thought. Now, the burlesque scene is getting crowded. I'd say the last thing down-town needs is another club—and I'm only looking at Manhattan. None of this Brooklyn hipster shit. So the obvious move is to buy an existing club that's doing well and take it over. Maybe give it a little makeover, put our own stamp on it. Get rid of the dead weight; out with the old, in with the new and all that."

Billy glared at her.

"To get right down to it," she said. "I want the Blue Angel. So—are you in, or are you out? And I do mean...you will be *out*."

Mallory was just putting the key in the door to her apart-ment when her cell phone rang. She was certain it was Agnes, yelling at her to get her ass back to the Blue Angel. But a quick glance at the incoming number told her she was wrong.

"Gavin?" she said.

"Hey, Mallory. I'm sorry to call so late."

"It's not a problem," she said, surprised at how happy she was to hear his voice.

"I'm trying to find the folder with the summer 2010 deposi-tions for Klein, and it's not here. I just checked your desk, and I can't find it. Do you have any idea where it is?"

"It should be on my desk. Are you sure?..." Her heart started pounding. This was a disaster. She was so preoccupied with all the craziness in her life that she was misplacing impor-tant files at work. This was unacceptable.

"I don't see it."

"Let me check my bag." Was it possible she was so absent-minded she'd brought it home with the pile of reading she had to do? She opened her BAE bag, and sure enough, in the pile of papers wedged next to her costume, was one of the *Klein v. Klein* files. "Oh, my God, Gavin. I'm so sorry. It's in my bag,"

"You shouldn't take those out of the office," he said, but not too sternly.

"I know! It was a total accident. Do you need it now? I can jump in a cab and be there in fifteen minutes."

"Yes, do that. Just expense the cab. I'll be in my office."

"I'll be right there," she said.

Mallory put her phone and her bag down and walked straight to the bathroom to look at herself in the mirror. She was relieved she hadn't put on stage makeup that she would have to take time to remove before meeting Gavin.

She felt a flutter of excitement as she changed into a black pencil skirt and gray cardigan. This was ridiculous: Gavin was her boss. He wasn't interested in her. And even if he was, Alec was still her boyfriend, no matter how many problems they had at the moment. And yet she couldn't help thinking of Gavin's thick, sandy brown hair and teal-colored eyes, or the slight cleft in his chin and dimples when he smiled. Today at lunch he'd had an unusual degree of stubble on his square jaw, and she'd had the urge to rub her palm against it, to feel it brush her cheek. And the way he'd looked at her today—the hint that maybe he wanted her—it was the most exciting feeling she'd had in a long time. With Alec, she was always mentally taking the temperature of their relationship—did he still want her; did he love her but not lust for her; did he want his freedom? Did she?

She knew it was pointless to let herself feel attracted to Gavin. But even though his status as her boss would prohibit him from ever making a move on her, just the thought that maybe he would want to if he were able to made her feel the rush she thought she'd left behind at the Blue Angel.

15

Poppy was guilt-stricken. Her hands trembled as she laced up her boots backstage. The other girls were already changed out of their costumes, happily chatting on their way to the bar to get drinks and celebrate another great show. Poppy would not be joining them, although she'd told Patricia that she would be. That she might be late—don't wait up. That she loved her and would see her in the morning.

This thing with Violet was madness, and it had to stop.

What did she hope to gain by it? To make the routine of her relationship with Patricia more palatable? Or was she trying to accomplish something even more futile: to banish the specter of Bette?

Regardless of the root cause of this insane behavior, for the first time, Poppy gave credence to the notion of sex addiction; she had used to scoff when she read about the male celebrities who had to go to "sex rehab" for cheating on their wives. But now she knew. What was this thing with Violet if not some sort of sick addiction? Every time she let Violet fuck her, she vowed it would be the last time. And then a few days later, Poppy found herself craving it with an intensity that overrode everything else in her life. There was something about walking into that room, having no idea what would happen or how, but knowing that it would result in a rush of pleasure so intense and complete it would render her mind blank and her body like a single, vibrating nerve of ecstasy. She felt she could never get enough of watching Violet's perfect body swathed in leather, the coldness of her wide green eyes, and the cruelty of her fingers that wielded pain while doling out pleasure in the most excruciating increments. How could she go from that to Patricia's plain face and soft body, her eager-to-please lovemaking that was as predictable as her own menstrual cycle? Of course, there was the question of why: Why did Poppy enjoy being yelled at in bed, called a stupid whore, smacked, deprived of sensation, told she didn't deserve to be fucked? What was it about her psychological make-up that made this exciting and appealing to the point that she was beginning to have a difficult time reaching orgasm without it? That was a larger problem. For now, she had to deal with the immediate issue: her desire for Violet.

Tonight she would cut it off. Just one last time. She would do as Violet asked—meet her at the bondage club on Fifty-seventh Street. It was called the Cellar, and she had never been there before. She had only met Violet three times at her apartment, and each visit followed a similar pattern of blindfolding, scolding, spanking, and eventually being finger-fucked or penetrated with a dildo before being "allowed" to eat Violet's pussy. Each session left her more spent and emotionally raw than the last. And each one left her thinking about it and longing for it days later.

She wondered if the new setting would change the dynamic at all. The thought of what the strange space might hold was enough to get her wet.

The cab dropped her off at the corner of Fifty-seventh and Sixth. She walked west, looking for the address. She found the building, its small entrance framed by two older buildings on either side. It would be easy to miss, but she had a feeling no one who was looking for it would give up before finding it.

The street was empty, and the wind was colder than she had experienced since last winter. A part of her wanted to leave. Maybe she should stop this thing right now, cold turkey. In the doorway of the building, a camera turned its roving eye on her.

She turned to see if there were any cabs, but the few she spotted were either occupied or had their OFF DUTY lights on. Poppy was a strong believer in signs and took this to mean she should go into the Cellar. She pressed the button on the intercom and was buzzed inside.

The lobby, if you could call it that, was dark and spartan, the floor littered with unsolicited Chinese take-out menus. She stepped over them to the single elevator bank. Violet had instructed her to take the elevator to the fifth floor. Only in New York would a place called the Cellar be located on one of the top floors of a building.

The elevator was small and made her feel claustrophobic. It rattled to a stop on the fifth floor, and she tentatively stepped out.

The first thing she noticed was a gaudy chandelier hanging over an elegant, mahogany desk that looked like it belonged at someone's country estate. Seated at this desk was a young woman with thick auburn hair cascading from a loose bun, granny glasses, and ghostly skin. She wore a Victorian style black blouse, but the rest of her outfit was hidden under the desk.

"Can I help you?" the woman asked.

"I'm here to see Violet."

"Mistress Violet? Okay, your name?"

"Um, Poppy."

The woman pressed a button on the desk phone and announced her arrival.

"That will be two hundred dollars. We take cash and all major credit cards."

Poppy stared at the woman in disbelief. This was too much, even for Violet. She expected Poppy to *pay* for it?

"I think there must be some mistake," Poppy said.

"I'm certain there is not. That's the rate for a one-hour session with Miss Violet. Nonnegotiable."

She knew this was the time to leave—the line in the sand that she should not, could not cross. And yet somewhere behind the curtains and doors to the left of the reception desk, Violet was waiting for her.

She handed over her American Express card.

Mallory signed in at the security desk in the lobby of the massive Park Avenue building where Gavin Stone Associates rented office space on the twenty-first floor. She swiped her ID card at the turnstiles guarding the elevator banks and checked her reflection in the chrome framework while she waited. She knew she would be checking herself even more closely in the mirror inside the elevator.

What was wrong with her? She was just dropping off a file. It didn't make a difference what she looked like. And yet she felt a pulse of excitement in her that was so strong it scared her.

The twenty-first floor was dark and quiet. Only a few overhead lights were on. It was strange to pass the empty reception desk and make her way down the hall to Gavin's office without seeing another person or hearing a single phone ring. It was like being in a dream.

She found Gavin at his desk, his sleeves rolled up, tie askew, head bent in deep concentration over a document in front of him. He looked like a model in a Ralph Lauren ad staged to depict a hot young lawyer busy at work.

Mallory rapped lightly on the doorframe.

"Knock knock," she said.

He looked up and smiled.

"Hey. Thanks for bringing that over."

"Of course! I feel terrible that you were looking for it and it wasn't here."

"No harm, no foul," he said.

She reached into her bag, produced the file, and handed it to him. When he took it from her, his fingers brushed hers. She felt something shake through her.

"I just wanted to apologize for this afternoon," he said. "I realize that I maybe overstepped. It's not my place to tell you what to do with your life. I did have to tell you what would or wouldn't work for me as your employer, but I should have left it at that. But the thing is, I do feel strongly about your potential, and if I hadn't spoken up today at lunch I might have wondered for a long time if I should have."

"I'm glad you did," she said.

"Really?"

"Yes. This is a confusing time for me, and I appreciate your candor."

Silence.

"It's a confusing time for me, too," he said.

"Really? You never seem confused. You're the only person I know who always seems to know exactly what to do, to say. I think being around you has made it impossible for me to accept the craziness in my life."

"That's ironic," he says. "Because being around you makes it impossible for me to live with the boredom of mine."

She looked at him.

"What are you talking about?"

"I didn't know you were a burlesque dancer. But I had an idea you had some sort of other life—someplace you ran to a few nights a week that you never wanted to talk about. Sometimes you show up for work and there's shiny stuff on your face—like glitter or something. And I know you change into other clothes sometimes before leaving here. I thought maybe you were a major clubber or something—I didn't know. I always wanted to ask you but knew it wasn't appropriate. And then when I imagined where you were, I found myself wishing I were there with you. Part of it is because my life is getting so routine, but lately I think it's because I just want to be with you."

She looked at him, stunned.

"I realize," he continued, "that it's completely inappropriate for me to be telling you this. And that's why, regardless of what you decide to do with your legal career, it's probably best if we don't work together anymore."

"You're firing me?" she said quietly.

"I just don't think I can be your employer any longer. But I'll help you find another job, give you the best recommendation. In fact, I think opposing counsel in *Klein v. Klein* is looking for a paralegal."

"I don't want to work someplace else," she said, near tears. "This is the one stable thing in my life."

"But I'm telling you my feelings for you are less than professional. Don't you see that this is not a tenable situation?" His face looked as pained as she felt.

She sat down on the black Ethan Allen couch that faced his desk.

"Gavin, what do you want me to do?"

"I want you to quit so I can make love to you."

"Jesus! You don't mean that."

"I do. I can't stop thinking about you, Mallory." He stood up from his desk and starting pacing in front of the bookshelf stuffed with legal volumes. "It's making me crazy. And I realize that even just having this conversation is risky, and you could sue the hell out of me, so I am asking you to just put me out of my misery and quit."

"I'm not going to sue you," she said, quietly. "And I'm not going to quit."

She walked over to him, grabbing his hand to stop his manic movements. He looked at her with surprise, and when she wrapped her arms around him, he did not move to embrace her back, but stood completely still.

"What are you doing?" he said.

"I've been thinking about you, too," she said, breathing in the unfamiliar scent of him, resting her cheek on his shoulder. She pressed her body against his and could tell that he was hard.

"Are you going to quit?" he said, his voice husky.

"Probably."

"You'd better go back to the couch until you make up your mind."

She looked up at him, his chiseled good looks even better at that close vantage point. Alec was sexy and ruggedly handsome, but Gavin was technically, empirically, unequivocally beautiful. And for the first time in years, she felt free from the terrifying feeling that she would never be attracted to anyone but Alec and that if she didn't find a way to make the relationship work, she would never be happy. Standing there, holding Gavin Stone, she knew she could be happy with another man—even if just for one night. And she needed, for many reasons, to know what that would feel like.

"I quit," she whispered, kissing his neck. As if he were a statue in a fairy tale brought to life by her touch, he grabbed her face and pressed his mouth against hers. For a few seconds, she wondered how this would play out. But then her body took over, and she couldn't think of anything at all.

Gavin pulled her closer, his hands moving to her ass. They stood against his desk, kissing like teenagers, so hard and fast it almost hurt.

Gavin pulled away, holding her hands and looking into her eyes.

"What's wrong?" she said.

"Come over here," he said, leading her by the hand to the couch. She sat next to him, trying to discreetly assess the bulge in his pants. "As much as I want you right now—and believe me, I can't remember ever wanting anyone more—I'm afraid this is a bad idea."

"Do you actually think I would sue you? I mean, Gavin, that's crazy. If you don't want to do this, that's fine, but please don't blame it on our work relationship."

"I feel like I'm taking advantage of you." He raked his hand through his thick hair. He had the strong wrists of a lacrosse player. She imagined he'd gone to boarding school. He probably had had a roommate named Biff.

"You're not," she said feebly. "I don't know how to prove something like that, but you simply aren't."

"I think I'd feel better if we both slept on this for a few days and then saw where we're at."

"Okay," she agreed, because what else could she say?

And then they locked eyes, and she leaned in and kissed him, and he pulled her to him with a roughness that seemed to negate his objections. She straddled him, pressing her crotch against his erection. His hands wound through her hair, and their mouths clashed together, teeth against teeth. She wanted to put her hands in his pants, to guide his cock into herself. But she had too much pride to be that aggressive, though maybe it was, in fact, the dynamic he needed to go through with fucking her. Or maybe he wasn't sure he really wanted her. She didn't know, and so she head-tripped herself out of doing anything, letting him kiss her until her mouth felt raw.

She climbed off of him, and he squeezed her hand. She grabbed her hastily discarded coat and her bag, and he walked her wordlessly to the elevator banks.

"Monday, okay? I'll see you Monday," he said.

"See you Monday."

* * *

Violet was waiting for Poppy behind the door. But it was a Violet that Poppy barely recognized, dressed in a pink rubber nurse's costume, with red latex gloves up to her elbows, and a rubber old-fashioned nurse's hat affixed to her head.

"Hello, Ms. LaRue," Violet said, with odd formality. "Did you pay the receptionist? I don't take insurance."

"What? Um, yeah." Poppy tried to ignore the nervous squirming in her gut, the nudge that there was still time to leave.

"Then, right this way."

Violet led her down a narrow hallway lined with closed doors. Poppy didn't hear any noise and wondered if the rooms were soundproofed. Finally, at the end of the hall, Violet opened a door with a set of keys and held it for Poppy.

Poppy stepped inside. She didn't know what she had expected, but certainly not this place that looked like a gynecology examination room, complete with a table and foot stirrups, an anatomy chart of the female reproductive system, and a tray full of latex gloves, lube, and some very official-looking instruments.

"I ... I think I should leave," Poppy stammered.

"Don't be silly." Violet handed her a pink paper gown. "Put this on, open in the front."

Poppy couldn't believe the scenario she was in and was both freaked out and oddly turned on. Violet's cheeks were flushed, her green eyes bright, her lips lacquered to an impossible sheen.

Poppy undressed, her hands shaking too much for her to fold her clothes, so she ended up tossing them on a chair. She kept her back to Violet while she nervously stepped out of her panties and pulled on the paper gown.

She slowly turned to face Violet, who was busy arranging items on the supply tray.

"Get on the table," Violet said, without looking at her, her voice emotionless.

Poppy climbed onto the examination table, the tissue paper covering crumpling underneath her. It was surreal. She half expected to find a stack of magazines next to her.

"Ms. La Rue, please slide down and put your feet in the stirrups."

Poppy complied, placing her bare feet against the cold metal, her legs spread apart.

Violet stood and moved next to the table. She peered down at Poppy and began feeling her breasts with her gloved hands. Her touch was rough and clinical, and yet Poppy felt a surge of excitement pulse between her legs. Violet's touch had little to do with an actual breast exam, but the detachment and brevity of her contact made it clear that's what she was supposed to be doing.

She moved away and took a seat at the end of the table.

"Come down closer," she said. Poppy slid her ass down more, feeling very self-conscious that her pussy was splayed open in front of Violet's face in that bright room.

Violet busied herself slathering lube onto her gloved finger, then inserted it inside of Poppy, as clinically as she had felt her breasts, then removed her hand. She straightened up in her chair.

"Have you experienced any sexual dysfunction lately?" Violet said.

"What?"

"Any trouble having an orgasm?"

"Uh, no."

"I thought you said you were having problems. That's why you made the appointment," she said.

"Oh, um, yeah. I'm having problems," Poppy said, playing along.

Violet slowly removed her rubber gloves. Poppy shifted her feet against the cold metal.

"You can't even come when you masturbate?" Violet said.

"No?" Poppy said, wanting to get the answer right.

"Hmm. This sounds serious," Violet said, rubbing Poppy's clit roughly with her thumb. She massaged, rubbing gently and then more firmly, pressing until it was almost painfully swollen. Poppy squirmed on the table. She was afraid she was going to moan, but didn't want to make any sound. She felt that if she did anything wrong she would ruin the script, and the thought of this somehow terrified her.

"You don't feel anything?" Violet said.

"No," Poppy whispered.

Violet shuffled through the items on the tray next to the exam table, and Poppy nervously shifted her ass against the paper underneath her. Her palms were wet with anxiety, her pussy throbbing with the need for release.

"Turn around and get on all fours," Violet said.

"What?"

"I'm going to cure you. Get on all fours—face the opposite direction from me."

Poppy had no interest in putting her ass in Violet's face.

"I don't know. I . . . I think I feel better all ready."

"If you're not going to let me treat you then you can leave."

"Leave now?"

"Yes. Do you want to come or not?"

"I want to come."

"Then get on all fours. Doctor's orders," she said with a wicked smile. She moved to the side of the table, adjusting it to make it flatter. "Oh, and take off your gown."

Poppy slowly pulled off the paper gown, dropping it to the floor. Despite all of the times she had taken her clothes off in front of a room full of strangers, she had never felt as self-conscious as she did getting into the position Violet demanded. But she dutifully turned around and got on her hands and knees, her ass in front of Violet.

She felt Violet's hand, once again in a latex glove, gently tracing the curve of her ass. Her finger moved down, brushing her labia so lightly it was as if Poppy were imagining it. She longed to feel that finger press deep inside her, to trigger the release she needed so badly it was like her entire body was becoming a coil of tension.

And then, nothing. She held the position for a few minutes, resisting the impulse to ask Violet what was going on. And then she felt Violet's gloved hands spread her ass cheeks and then push something slippery and hard into her anus.

"What are you doing?" Poppy said, turning around and feeling for the object. Violet slapped her hand away.

"I'm treating you. It's just a butt plug. Relax. Now get on your back again with your legs spread."

"This feels weird...."

"Keep it in there. Get on your back."

Poppy turned around, taking deep breaths, trying not to think about the sensation of heat and pressure in her asshole. She spread her legs and lay back on the table. Looking up at the ceiling, she wondered what was wrong with her—why she was in this situation. Surely, this was not healthy behavior.

And then she felt Violet's bare fingers skimming her pussy lips, then the flick of her tongue against her clit and her fingers pressed inside of her. The combination of the pressure in her ass and the touch on her G-spot made her come so violently, the wave of pleasure was almost like pain. She cried out, calling Violet's name, saying nonsensical things, shamelessly pressing her pussy closer to Violet, begging for more.

When the last tremor of orgasm subsided, Violet stopped touching her.

"You're cured," she said. "You can get dressed now."

Poppy was too spent to move. She was dizzy with the aftermath of intense physical sensation and the confusion of the encounter. She was vaguely aware of the foreign object still lodged in her rectum. As she raised her pelvis to do something about it, Violet pulled her hand away.

"Leave that in until you get home," she said.

"It's uncomfortable," Poppy said, realizing she sounded like a child.

"I don't care. It's part of your treatment. Doctor's orders. I'm going to sit here and watch you get dressed to make sure you don't disobey me."

Poppy stood from the table, her legs shaky. She pulled on her panties, conscious of her anus working to hold the butt plug in place. When she was completely dressed, Violet walked her wordlessly to the door of the room, and sent her down the dark hallway alone.

Mallory's lips still felt slightly bruised from Gavin's kiss, and this distracted her enough as she opened her apartment door that she didn't notice the lights were on in the bedroom, when she had most certainly left them turned off.

She flopped down on the couch, leaning back and smiling. Kissing Gavin Stone. This was insanity.

And then she noticed Alec's shoes at the edge of the couch.

"What the hell?" She jumped up, the light in the bedroom finally registering with her. "Alec?" she called, hurrying into the bedroom. Sure enough, he was at the edge of their dresser, folding clothes into his suitcase.

"Hey," he said, looking up at her. There was a calm neutrality to his expression that was more alarming than any anger.

"Hi! When did you get here? I thought you weren't coming back until Sunday." She resisted the urge to throw her arms around him.

"Kendall got called to New York, so I wrapped things up there sooner than planned."

Mallory couldn't help but feel a surge of jealousy at the casual familiarity in the way he called the starlet just Kendall, not Kendall James.

"Oh. How did the interview go?"

"It went well. She's not jaded enough to stonewall every question, which was lucky for me." He stood up and closed the suitcase.

"Are you packing, or unpacking?" Mallory asked. Suddenly, the kiss with Gavin seemed as trivial as a prolonged glance exchanged with a stranger on the subway platform.

Alec didn't answer her, but carried his suitcase to the living room. She followed him, swallowing a lump of despair in her throat.

"Sit down for a minute," he finally said, after he had already taken a seat on the couch. She sat next to him, both in the same places they had been in when she raced home from the Plaza to find him. But this time he took her hand. "I was thinking a lot while I was gone. I missed you," he said. She sensed a "but," and didn't want to hear it.

"I missed you, too." Unable to hold back another minute, she put her arms around him. When his circled around her, she started to cry. It felt so good to be close to him, she almost couldn't breathe.

"Mallory, the thing is, as much as I missed you, at the same time, it was a relief to be away from the constant tension between us."

"What tension?" she said lamely.

He looked at her as if to say, *Come on.* "I don't know why you did what you did the night of the Plaza, but I know you're not a reckless or promiscuous person. There's something going on in our relationship that led us to that point, and maybe it's my fault. Maybe in the past I challenged you to push your boundaries, and now you reflexively do that to get my attention. Or maybe I pushed you to open your view of your own sexuality, and now it's more open than I can handle and it's my own fault. Either way, I just don't know what else to do but take a step back. Spend some more time apart. And maybe then we'll get the answers."

Mallory reflexively wanted to argue with him, to tell him that was ridiculous, that she didn't want time apart. But she knew how wrong that would be considering where, how, and with whom she had just spent the last hour. She was scared to admit it, but Alec was right. They needed to step back and see what they really wanted, if they were capable of being in a relationship that didn't make both of them crazy. So all she said was, "I'm scared."

"Me too," he said. He hugged her again, and she breathed him in deeply. She wished she could stay like that forever. But after a minute, Alec patted her leg.

"I've got to go," he said.

"I don't want you to leave."

"I have to, Mallory."

"Where are you going to stay?"

"Billy said I can use the *Gruff* corporate apartment for a few weeks."

Of course he did. And she was sure Billy just loved hearing about their drama. She wondered if Billy Barton knew what it was like to feel such anxiety and uncertainty. Had he ever cared about someone enough to make him or her the center of his world? She doubted it. He seemed emotionally bulletproof. It must be nice.

Mallory walked Alec to the door. She wasn't going to stop him from leaving, but she couldn't help but cry when he stepped into the hall. He hugged her one more time, and then there was nothing left to do but watch him go.

16

Billy Barton stepped out of the Lincoln Town Car on the corner of Eighteenth Street and Ninth Avenue. He held a cup of coffee in one hand and the prescription of Ativan he'd just refilled in the other. It was going to be that kind of day.

"Wait for me here or go around the block a few times if you have to. I should be back in less than an hour," he told the driver.

He walked half a block west to the male grooming salon, Sugar, which was owned and operated by his first male lover, Harvey Hixenbaugh. Harvey was twenty years his senior. They'd met when Billy and some friends had ended up at the legendary restaurant Florent after a night of clubbing senior year in high school. Billy's buddies liked Florent for the twenty-four-hour food and supermodel sightings; Billy loved it for the clientele of drag queens, burlesque dancers, writers, actors, and bon vivants who ruled Manhattan by night and slept all day. Even though Billy had months left to go at Riverdale Country School and a four-year stretch ahead of him at Penn, he knew already the life he wanted to live. If he had to jump through a few conventional hoops in order to get there, so be it. That first night, Harvey had surreptitiously slipped him his number. Billy had planned to wait until he was safely at college to act on his homosexuality, but he quickly revised his plan when Harvey appeared to be a perfect partner in exploring the side of himself he could share with nobody in his "real" life—not his billionaire, Wall Street father, not his socialite mother, not his older brother who was in Washington working for a Republican senator who had eyes on the White House.

It was a glorious six-month affair, a blur of drugs and sex and an endless loop of nightlife that introduced him to the artists and tastemakers who set the pace that the fashion, music, and film industries would follow. This crowd validated his desire to live a "big" life—showed him it was possible.

Now he owned *Gruff*, had his pick of the hot male—and occasionally female—models and hipsters who roamed the underbelly of Manhattan after dark. And Harvey was clean and sober, running a successful business, and married to a painter named Oliver. Life was good.

And now this mess with Violet.

When he'd met the Burberry model Tyler Rand at a photo shoot for *Gruff*, he'd referred him to Harvey. All the top male models, actors, porn stars, prostitutes, and successful, closeted "straight" guys came to Harvey for "sugaring"—it was like waxing, but used a warm sugar mix that worked in the direction of the hair growth, not opposite the growth like waxing. When it was done right, it could eventually lead to permanent hair removal. Some salons just added sugar to their waxing mix and called it sugaring, but getting the actual sugar-based paste exactly right was a skill, and Harvey charged an arm and a leg—no pun intended—for his expertise and services. Despite the cost, it was still impossible to get an appointment without a referral. And today at 11a.m. was Tyler's standing appointment.

Billy knew he should maybe deal with this catastrophe in

private, but he hoped that Harvey would be a solid, calm voice in the crisis. As far as he was concerned, Tyler's appointment this morning was perfect timing.

"Hi, Billy," the receptionist, Daniel, greeted him. Daniel was prettier than most of the female models Billy booked in *Gruff*. "Harvey's in with a client."

"Tyler, right? I'm sure it's okay if I go in. Can you ring him for me?"

"Okay—let me check."

Billy looked through the magazines fanned out on a side table and picked up an issue of *Gruff* from two months ago. He was excited about their upcoming March issue. Alec had done a good job with the Kendall James interview. Having her on the cover was a great way to start the New Year. He could feel the magazine gaining clout on the newsstands, with advertisers, and with the A-list celebrities he needed to fill the pages. He was getting better writers, photographers.... He could really see himself taking on Graydon Carter and *Vanity Fair* in a year or two. This was no time for a scandal.

After consulting with Harvey, Daniel gave Billy a flirtatious wink and showed him upstairs. He paused outside one of the service room doors, knocking gently.

Harvey opened it quickly, mid-sentence, shooing Daniel away and closing the door behind Billy when he entered the small room.

"You couldn't stay away from him, eh? Oh, young love. I miss it," Harvey said, washing his hands. "But if you were hoping for a show, you're a few minutes too late. We're all finished."

"What are you doing here?" Tyler asked, smiling. But his gleeful anticipation faded when he noticed the expression on Billy's face.

"I have a problem. Actually, we have a problem."

"Uh-oh. That doesn't sound good."

"It's not. Can we go somewhere and talk?"

"Does this involve me? Good Lord, what could it be this time? I'm finally clean and sober, so I think I'd remember if I'd done something to merit a 'Talk'," Harvey said.

"No—it has nothing to do with you, but I'm thinking you might be the voice of reason. Because I have a serious decision to make."

Harvey sighed, pressed an intercom button, and told Daniel to tell his next appointment he was running a half hour late.

"This way, kids."

Billy and Tyler followed him to his office and took seats on his couch under a Jackson Pollock—a gift from one of Harvey's clients. Harvey closed the door and sat behind his immaculate glass desk.

"What's going on?"

"I told you that I spent some time at the Cellar...."

"Sure. Didn't Roger turn you on to that place?"

"Yeah. And I went for a while and got really hooked on this one dom who eventually slipped me her cell number and said she does house calls. I was getting paranoid about someone's recognizing me there, so I started having her to my place. She's incredible."

At this point, Tyler was looking very nervous. Billy took his hand.

"I wanted to bring Tyler into it—he said he was game because it was important to me. So she came over last week and did a session with the two of us."

"Sounds good to me." Harvey smiled.

"It was good. Until she insisted on meeting up with me last night—and showed me this."

Billy slid one of the photos across the desk to Harvey.

"What is it?" Tyler said.

Harvey looked at it for less than a beat and shook his head. "What does she want?"

"What is it?" Tyler repeated. Harvey handed him the photo. "Jesus, Billy! What the fuck is this? I can't have this floating around. My agent just renewed the Burberry contract!"

"I know, I know," Billy said, squeezing his hand. "I'm going to deal with this." To Harvey, he explained. "She wants me to bankroll a club for her."

"She wants cash?"

"No. She wants me to be a partner in a club with her—she wants my money to back it, but she also wants me involved to use my connections to get the right people to the club."

"What kind of club? Like Tenjune?"

"No. A burlesque club. Like the Slit."

The three men sat silently.

"That photo cannot get out," Tyler said. "It will ruin my career. Not to mention my life—my parents . . . oh, my God."

"First of all, it won't ruin your career," Harvey said. "Homosexuality doesn't ruin models' careers. It might jeopardize your relationship with Burberry, but your editorial work won't dry up. You, on the other hand—" He looked at Billy. "You are on the cusp of being a major player. Being gay is one thing, but this is not the most flattering expression of your sexuality."

"I know."

"I suggest you play ball. At least for a while. In a year or so, you might be able to risk shaking her off. Or maybe you'll find something to twist her arm with. Either way, get the money together, hire someone to deal with the logistics, and buy some time until the day when Billy Barton is a media mogul too big to be pushed from the throne."

"It's not the money I care about—it's being played like this. Who the fuck does she think she is? I want to kill her."

"You need to be coolheaded about this."

"I know. That's why I wanted to talk to you. I needed the voice of reason. Because my impulse is to tell her to fuck off and then find a way to squash her."

Tyler pulled his hand away and looked at him beseechingly, his big, heavily lashed brown eyes turned into pools of anxiety. And Billy knew that there was nothing to do but give Violet what she wanted. He could risk having his reputation take a hit. But he couldn't endure his relationship with Tyler taking one.

"There's no other way, is there?" Billy said with resignation.

"Not right now."

He looked at Tyler, reached for his hand again, and winked.

"I'll take care of it."

Tyler seemed to exhale for the first time since he'd seen the picture.

"Well, then—my work here is done. I have to get back to business. The client I have waiting is a nasty bitch, and I'm sure I have hell to pay already. Feel free to stay here as long as you like and talk strategy. Don't fret, boys. Everyone playing in the big leagues takes a hit every once in a while."

Harvey closed the door. Billy looked at Tyler, who was staring at the floor.

"Hey," he said, putting his hand under Tyler's chin so he had to face him. "It's going to be fine."

Clearly, Tyler didn't agree. Billy felt terrible as he realized he was experiencing perhaps his first taste of failure in life. He was astute enough to realize that Tyler was attracted to him for the same reasons he, as a teenager, had been attracted to Harvey: Tyler saw him as someone to look up to, as a guide to the inner workings of the upper echelon of New York nightlife. And now, instead of being the buoy that Tyler needed and wanted, Billy threatened to be an anchor around his neck.

"I'll make it up to you," he said, dropping to his knees on the floor. "I'm going to suck your cock so good you'll forget all about this." He unzipped Tyler's jeans, reaching into his underwear to find his erection. He knew how much Tyler loved the way Billy fucked him—he was just his second male lover—and usually a little verbal foreplay was enough to get him hard as a rock. But, to his dismay, Billy found that Tyler was unresponsive to him.

Not one to be easily deterred, Billy pulled down Tyler's pants and underwear. He pressed his face to Tyler's balls, inhaling their slightly sweet smell and licking them softly. He stroked Tyler's flaccid cock until it swelled in his hand. Tyler shifted in his seat, and Billy cupped both hands under his ass, taking his increasingly engorged cock fully in his mouth. He massaged the outside of Tyler's anus with his index finger, rubbing in small, firm circles until he elicited a moan. Then he used his free hand to once again work Tyler's shaft, up and down in tandem with his lips and tongue. Tyler had told him he gave the best blow jobs he'd ever had—better than all the girls in his high school and better than the one boyfriend he'd had his first six months in New York. This was interesting to Billy, because what Tyler didn't know was that he was the first man Billy had ever sucked off. Since his first encounter with Harvey all those years ago, Billy had only received oral and anal sex, never given it. But Tyler's beauty moved him to do things he'd never wanted to do before. Billy took great pride in the new sexual dimensions he had discovered with his young lover, and every time Tyler shot a load in his mouth it was sweet validation.

He pressed his finger inside Tyler's ass, just enough to tease him toward coming. Tyler moaned, and Billy probed deeper.

No matter how stressed out and angry Tyler was about the Violet problem, Billy was determined to get him off. He needed Tyler to know he could take care of him—in the bedroom and out. Finally, Billy felt all the muscles in Tyler's upper thighs and pelvis tighten, and he quickened the strokes of his hand and tongue accordingly. Tyler shouted and bucked against Billy's mouth, coming in warm spurts that Billy greedily swallowed.

When Tyler was still, Billy climbed back next to him on the couch.

"Do you trust me to take care of things?" Billy said. His

cock was so hard in his pants, he knew he wouldn't be able to leave the room before getting off himself.

"Yes," Tyler said.

"Good," said Billy. "Now take care of me."

He unzipped his pants.

Mallory could barely sit still at her desk. She'd slept only a few hours all night, her mind running an endless loop of kissing Gavin and the breakup with Alec. Now she was jacked up on three cups of coffee, her emotional pendulum swinging from the excitement of new attraction to the pain of letting go of her four-year relationship.

Gavin had popped his head into her office first thing in the morning. Mindful of the legal secretaries right outside her door, he was all business, talking about a motion he needed to file for one of his clients. But his eyes locked with hers in a way that was anything but professional. Her heart pounded as she listened to him, and although she nodded, in truth she barely heard a word he said. She kept looking at his mouth, wanting to feel it on her skin.

And then when he left the room, she could think of nothing but Alec. *Can you say 'head case'?*

Her cell phone rang.

"What was that little freak-out of yours last night?" Bette said. No hello, no how are you. Usually, Mallory liked Bette's straight-to-the-point conversational style. But that morning she knew it would be exhausting.

"I don't know. I guess I just wasn't in the headspace to perform."

"Don't give me that shit. This is me you're talking to. Is this about your problems with Alec?"

"No," Mallory said.

"Then what?"

"I don't know. And I can't really talk now. And I have to get some work done." *Or think about doing someone at work.*

"Meet me later today. I'm getting a new tattoo. You can keep me company and share your emotional pain to take my mind off of my physical pain."

"What design are you getting?" She thought of her short-lived painted burlesque angel.

"The word *freedom* in Russian. On the underside of my wrist."

Last year, during Mallory's mini-identity crisis as she evolved from budding corporate lawyer to burlesque dancer, Bette had taught her the Russian word for freedom, *svoboda*. She supposed Bette was now trying to remind herself of that as she nursed her heartache over the break-up with Zebra.

"Text me where and when, and I'll see you there." She looked up to see Gavin in the doorway. "Gotta run. Later."

He came in and closed the door.

"Hey," he said.

"Hey."

"I wanted to apologize for last night," he said.

"No need to apologize," she said. "It was...I enjoyed spending the time with you."

"I know, I know. I did, too. But it was inappropriate. And as much as I'm attracted to you, it really shouldn't happen again."

"Oh. Okay," she said, fighting a sinking disappointment.

"Plus, you have a boyfriend."

"We're broken up. For now."

"For now?"

"It's complicated...."

"It's okay. I get it. It's like that with Susan and me, too."

"Gavin, really. No problem. Enough said." She worked hard to keep her expression neutral.

"Okay. Well, thanks for making that conversation easy. If

you had debated me I don't know if I would have been strong enough to resist." He smiled his gorgeous dimpled smile.

Gotta love those mixed messages. She didn't know what to say in response, so she stayed quiet.

He sat down on the chair across from her desk. "But I have been thinking about you. A lot. And I was wondering if you'd given more thought to what I said yesterday at lunch—about your retaking the bar exam."

"Actually, yes. I have thought about it. I'm going to register this week. I will have to cram to get prepared by February, but I'm going to do it."

Gavin slapped her desk. "That is excellent news."

"Wow. You're more excited about it than I am. Not sure that's a good thing."

"It's all good, Mallory. I'm really happy to hear this. You know I'll support you in any way I can."

They locked eyes, and Mallory felt how much he wanted her.

"Thanks, Gavin. I appreciate that."

She couldn't wait to run this insanity by Bette.

Rising Dragon Tattoo was located on Fourteenth Street between Fifth and Sixth Avenues. Bette was waiting for her outside, dressed in a black, faux fur coat, leopard miniskirt, black tights, and four-inch platform clogs. But her trademark black bob was hidden under a knit cap, and oversized Kate Spade sunglasses obscured her face.

"Did you dodge the paparazzi?" Mallory asked.

"Since *Us* broke the news of my split with Zebra, they've left me alone somewhat. Ironically, now I miss them."

"Ah, paparazzi. Can't live with 'em, can't live without 'em."

"You're teasing me but this sucks. I'm almost famous. Do you have any idea how frustrating that is? But I think that's going to change. My agent landed me an audition for the new Ben Affleck movie."

The parlor buzzed them in, and they climbed two flights of stairs. They checked in with the receptionist, a tiny woman with a mop of Raggedy Ann-doll red hair and tattoos covering every inch of her chest and neck.

"I'm here to see Wendy," said Bette.

"Hey, Bette," said a woman peeking around a corner. She waved them over. "I'm just setting up." She was surprisingly "normal" looking—only a small tattoo of a mermaid snaked around her right bicep. Other than that, she was tattoo and piercing-free. She wore jeans and a sweatshirt, and her plain brown hair was pulled back in a ponytail.

"Hey. This is my friend, Moxie."

"Hi, Moxie. You can sit right here." She pulled a stool over next to her station, a shelf filled with a rainbow of ink bottles.

"So, Alec and I officially ended things last night."

"Why?"

"We're taking a 'time-out.' "

"Oh yeah? What's his name?"

Mallory could feel herself blush.

The tattoo artist pressed a stencil of the design against Bette's wrist and peeled it back, leaving the black-and-white outline on her skin.

"That's so cool," Mallory said. "And, to answer your question: no one. This isn't about anyone else."

"Yeah, right. Mallory, you're insanely in love with Alec. There's no way you'd be doing this if someone else hadn't turned your head."

"Did I tell you the story of how we went to that party at the Plaza and that woman painted a fake tattoo on me?"

The tattoo artist turned on her instrument and pressed it to Bette's skin. Bette grimaced slightly, but continued talking.

"Nice change of subject, but yes, I remember. When Violet finger-fucked you, right?"

"Shh! God, Bette. Yes. Thanks for reminding me. Anyway, it started me thinking that I'd like a tattoo. But it just seems like a huge commitment."

"It's not that big a deal. You overthink the wrong things. What would you get?"

"I was thinking of a burlesque dancer in a blue angel costume. But that's not really appropriate anymore since I'm going to quit."

"What? Jesus, don't hit me with that while I'm stuck in this chair and subdued with pain. Why are you quitting?"

Mallory shrugged. "I don't know what the endgame is. I'm barely paying the bills in this city as it is. I'll never make money doing it, and, like you said the other night, if I'm not going to do whatever it takes to get famous and really be in the game for high stakes, why do it at all?"

"I know I said that, but the truth is you have to do the thing you love in life or else you'll be miserable."

"Well, that's a nice sentiment. But this isn't a movie."

"Again, who's the new guy? Because this so isn't Moxie talking."

"Okay, I'll admit I have a slight crush on my boss. And part of what I like about him is that when I'm around him, I feel grounded. He's calm. He talks to me about my work and life with this confidence and belief in me that I never heard from Alec. I mean, Alec told me I shouldn't stop practicing law, but he said it more like I shouldn't do something impulsive like quit—not that I should continue with it because it's what I'm good at. I don't know. And maybe some of the problems with Alec were because we were in this crazy burlesque universe."

"So you're quitting the Blue Angel to have a more stable relationship, but you've ended your relationship?"

"Yes."

"Brilliant."

"I'm doing the best I can." Mallory watched the needle working the ink into Bette's wrist, the loud humming of the instrument filling the room. "That looks really painful."

"I'm willing to suffer for art," Bette said. "But since you're not, you better tell Agnes soon. Like, today."

"I will."

Three days later, Mallory worked up the nerve to talk to Agnes. She went to the club late one afternoon, carrying a bag filled with clothes she needed to return and the law books she had taken out of the library. Her bar exam studies started tonight—no more lost time.

"Agnes?" Mallory called out, to no response. She walked down the short flight of stairs to the office and caught sight of herself in the heavy-framed mirror on the wall along the staircase. She looked pale and bland, and she was startled because she wasn't used to seeing herself that way in the setting of the Blue Angel. She felt it was a bit of a sacrilege even to walk in the door without wearing at least some lipstick. Even the mascara she'd applied first thing that morning seemed to have disappeared, her eyelashes wilting like week-old tulips.

The office door was open, and Agnes was sewing in front of her ancient desktop computer that looked like it still operated on DOS.

"Come in. No need to close the door. The only one here is Kitty, but she's busy rehearsing."

"Yeah. Well, thanks for seeing me. I'm sorry about leaving the other night."

"Are you sick?"

"No."

"I should fire you for that."

"I wouldn't have left if I hadn't known, on some level, that I didn't plan to come back. Something just changed in me, Agnes. I don't want to do this anymore."

"You're talented, so that is a tragedy. But life is full of tragedy," Agnes said, her Polish accent thick, maybe thicker than usual.

"I don't mean to leave you in a bad position. I know you just fired Violet, but I think Bette will do some more shows to fill in."

"Everything is changing," Agnes said, as if Mallory had not spoken. Mallory decided just to keep her mouth shut. Agnes seemed to be deep in thought that had little to do with Mallory's resignation. She supposed she wasn't the only person dealing with problems. Lately, she was so self-absorbed. It was kind of disgusting. And so, although she had come to the club to talk, she was happy to listen.

"There was a time when women came to burlesque because they had nothing else—no means to support themselves. I remember watching little children in the dressing room while their mothers performed to make twenty dollars. And it was their lifeblood, their community. Now...nothing. Every one for herself. I think you'd all be happier on a reality show."

"No, Agnes. That's not it...."

"Bette's fame brought a lot of attention to the Blue Angel."

"I know. That's a good thing, right?"

Agnes shrugged. "Now, so many decisions to be made; someone has offered to buy the club from me."

"Who?"

"I don't know. A lawyer contacted me."

"But you're not going to sell, are you?"

"It might be the right thing. Burlesque has lost its meaning. And I'm tired."

"Who's the buyer? The new owner might change the club— fire everyone. It could turn into someplace trashy."

"The girls will all leave eventually anyway. Just as you are."
Agnes looked at her. "Are you returning things to me?" She
looked at the bag.

And Mallory knew the conversation was over.

Late that night, Mallory woke up to the doorbell ringing.
And then a sharp knock on the door.

She was asleep on the couch, all the lights on, a law book
open on her chest. She checked the time: close to eleven.

Her legs were stiff from the awkward position she'd fallen
asleep in. So much for studying. And yes, that was just how
compelling she'd found studying for the bar the last time
around. What had possessed her to try the thing again? Away
from Gavin's sexy smile and the lure of a corner office, the notion of actually taking the exam was terrifying.

She put the book on the floor and padded over to the front
door, pulling closed the long cardigan she was wearing. Peering
out the peephole, she saw Alec.

She quickly checked her reflection in the mosaic-framed
mirror by the door. She looked ashen.

Her hands fumbled with the lock.

"Hey," she said. "What are you doing here?"

"I wanted to talk to you. Not on the phone." He closed the
distance between them and pulled her close. Despite herself,
she breathed him in, and, even after all the time together, all the
fights, it was enough to make her nearly swoon.

"I heard you quit the Blue Angel."

"You did?"

"Yeah. Bad news travels fast. For the record, I think it's a
mistake."

"I thought you'd think it was a move in the right direction
for me."

"I never thought burlesque was bad for you. And you love

it. I don't think you should quit as some knee-jerk reaction to what's going on with us."

"It's not about you or us, Alec. You can be so egocentric, you know that?"

"Yes, I'm aware of that. But that's beside the point." He sat her down on the couch, then sat on the opposite end. "You know, they tell people who get divorced not to make any major decision for a year—not to sell anything or change jobs."

"We weren't married."

"You know what I'm saying."

"Yeah, well. I appreciate your concern, but this is about my job, not you. I think you were right last year when you told me not to be so quick to give up a legal career. My boss thinks I should take the bar again. He says I'd be a great divorce lawyer."

"Oh really? What else does he say you'd be good at?"

Mallory looked away. "Nothing. I'm just saying, you were right, okay? So this is what I need to do. The burlesque thing was a diversion. It was fun, and I'm glad I did it, but what's the future, right?"

"This doesn't sound like you."

"Yeah, well. It's me. And besides, Agnes told me someone wants to buy the club."

"Is she considering selling it?"

"I think so. She seemed really cynical and down. Maybe you can talk her out of it."

"I can't even talk you out of your craziness. You think I can influence Agnes?"

"Maybe you can find out through your connections who it is and what they plan to do with the club?"

"Why do you care? You just quit."

She shrugged. "I don't know. It still means something to me. And I'd hate to see that stupid Penelope Lowe getting all the business Agnes gets now."

"I'll ask Justin Baxter, see what he knows."

"Good idea."

He shook his head. "I really don't get you sometimes, Mallory."

"I know."

And then he stood up and moved to sit right next to her. She felt her heart race. She had the urge to throw her arms around him, but she held back. But when he reached out to stroke her hair, then leaned in to kiss her, she didn't resist. The feeling of his mouth against hers was as natural as breathing. His hand reached into her cardigan and traced her nipple over her camisole top. As always, the nerve endings that seemed to connect her breasts to her crotch made her pussy throb, and when he slipped his hand inside her jeans, she wanted his fingers inside of her so badly, she shamelessly began unzipping her pants and pulling them down to her thighs. He turned her around so her back was to him, his arm encircling her, his hand between her legs. She moaned and leaned against him, holding his arm. He skimmed her clit with his finger before pressing it inside of her, then out again, rubbing her outer lips with her own wetness.

"God, Alec," she said softly. She lay back, pushing aside a heavy law book. She saw him glance at it, but he chose not to remark on it. He pulled off her panties, and she spread her legs, the thought *this is a bad idea* colliding with *lick my pussy*.

As if reading her mind, he moved his mouth between her legs. She let him tongue her clit for a minute, then said, "Alec, wait—this is a bad idea." She sat up and reached for her underwear.

"It's nothing. Let me make you come. At least one last time."

It sounded outrageous to her—how could it be the last time? But that's what a breakup meant. And she had to stick with her decision even when it was difficult. It was the right thing to do—wasn't it? Who could think straight with her pussy throbbing like a second pulse?

She lay back again, closing her eyes, letting the ripples of pleasure move through her as Alec lapped at her cunt. Then, while his tongue flicked her clit with fast, repeated motions, he pressed a finger deep inside, locating her G-spot right away. It felt so good it almost hurt.

"Alec!" she cried out. He eased off, moving his finger in and out of her slowly and rhythmically. Her pussy shuddered against his fingers, and she grabbed his wrist, clenching her legs, fucking his hand.

"It feels so good," she moaned. This would usually be the time when he would take off his pants, his cock throbbing and ready for her, and she would come again as he entered her.

But not tonight.

He pulled his hand out of her, wet with her juice. She wanted to throw herself against him, to tell him to stay, to sleep there so they could wake up in the middle of the night and mindlessly make love. But she reminded herself that they were broken up for a reason. She loved him, but that didn't mean everything was okay. They needed time apart.

They stared at each other, the weight of their entire relationship between them. She remembered a lawyer from her first job telling her that whoever speaks first during a negotiation reveals the truth of the situation.

"I should go," he said.

She nodded as he got up from the couch and walked out the door without another word. She wondered if someone had once told him the same thing.

17

"**K**nock knock," Gavin said, standing in the doorway of her office. Mallory hadn't even had her second cup of coffee yet, but the sight of him gave her a jolt, and she was suddenly very wide-awake.

"Hey. Come in. I was just doing some research on *Faye v. Doughty.*"

"Great. Listen, I have Marcy Klein coming in this afternoon. I'd like for you to sit in on the meeting with her, but I just want to see where you're at with...the situation we discussed."

"What?" She blushed, thinking of Alec's hands on her last night, the ways she wanted him. And now, the attraction she felt to Gavin. What was wrong with her?

"The little moonlighting situation." He smiled, embarrassed. God, he was so cute. She couldn't even imagine how freaked out he would be if he actually saw a show. He could barely reference burlesque in conversation.

"Oh! That. It's taken care of. I quit."

"Really?" His face lit up, dimples like mini-smiles.

"Yes. It's done."

"Are you okay with it? Again, I don't mean to tell you how to live your life. It's just that for the purposes here..."

"Gavin, seriously, it's not a problem. I get it. I understand."

"Well, I'm impressed. I'm sure it wasn't easy. This calls for a celebration. Are you free tonight? I'll make a reservation for dinner. And I promise only to talk about work eighty percent of the time. Okay, ninety percent."

How could she turn down an invitation like that?

"Sure."

"I think we should try Per Se. Have you been?"

She had read about the restaurant Per Se. There was a lot of fanfare when it opened, and the waiting list to get in that first year was legendary. The bribes and favors pulled to get a table rivaled the backdoor politics that used to be reserved for getting a kid accepted into the 92nd Street Y preschool. And she'd heard if a table for two got out of there with a check for under one thousand dollars, they were lucky.

"Are you sure that's where you want to go?" she said.

"Absolutely. Tom's an old friend. It's a great place. You'll love it."

She knew he was referring to Thomas Keller, the owner, who was famous for his California restaurant, the French Laundry, which the press had anointed as the best restaurant in the country.

"I feel bad I'm not wearing something more...." She looked down at her gray skirt, red and gray argyle tights, and black boots.

"You look perfect. As always. Seriously, you look absolutely appropriate. So here's the plan: I have a hectic day—court later this morning, then meetings all afternoon. Plan to meet me in the lobby at 7:15. The car will be waiting."

"Okay," she said, because really, what else was there to say? She felt slightly off-kilter, like the universe had shifted in some seismic way and she was experiencing the aftershock.

* * *

Violet let herself into Billy Barton's loft with her key. She found him sitting in the living room, looking through magazine mock-ups spread out on the glass coffee table.

"Jesus! What the hell are you doing here?"

"It's 10 a.m. Our standing weekly appointment."

"You can't be serious."

"Did you leave me a message to cancel?"

"I thought that would be redundant, given the fact that you are blackmailing me."

"Don't be melodramatic," Violet said, taking off her coat. "This is just a simple business negotiation. And frankly, I thought you'd show a little more appreciation. I'm handing you a great idea. What are you going to do—publish that stupid rag forever? Magazines are so 1997."

Billy took a deep breath, as if he were counting to ten before scolding a child. He seemed about to say something, stopped, and then, in a measured tone, said, "Okay, just give me my apartment keys."

"Don't be ridiculous."

"I accept our new business relationship. But that means our old one is over. So give me the keys."

They locked eyes, and without breaking her stare, she handed over the keys.

"Fine. I'll accept the redefinition of our working relationship. Did you talk to Agnes?"

He nodded, packing his magazine spreads into a leather portfolio. She sat across from him.

"So don't keep me in suspense. What did the old bat say?"

"She's considering it."

"You're not dicking around with some lowball offer, are you? Why didn't she agree on the spot?"

"First of all, you don't understand human nature, Violet. At least, most human nature—I can't speak for whatever system you're operating on."

"I'll take that as a compliment. So go on—enlighten me."

"Agnes has been running that club for twenty-five years. If she weren't open to cashing out for her own reasons, no amount of money would budge her. She's not in it for the money."

"Okay, Freud. So you think she's ready to bail on the club anyway?"

"She didn't seem offended or surprised or any of the other reactions that might come from someone who had never considered selling out."

"That's good news. What's the time frame on hearing from her?"

"She said she's thinking about it."

"Tell her she has a week and then you pull the offer. You'll go to her competitor and infuse them with a cash flow that will help them become the only club worthwhile in the city. She might not sell for money, but she'll sell not to see her business die a slow death."

"I'll put some pressure on the situation."

"Good. Because while you give Agnes a week, I'm giving you a week. Get the sale done, or I'm calling Page Six and Fleshbot offering a bombshell pictorial."

She stood up. "I'll see myself out...partner."

The stiff formality of the dining room made Mallory uncomfortable.

She had plenty of experience in fancy restaurants, not only in New York City, but from growing up in a wealthy Philadelphia suburb where her parents took her to dine in Center City a few times a month. But something about this room put her off—the muted gray and brown tones, the oversized arrangements of foxtail lilies, and the view of Central Park that made her feel like she wasn't so much a part of the city anymore but an observer in box seats. Even the dark suits and ties of the waitstaff seemed less elegant to her than imposing.

Or maybe it was the company.

Gavin seemed to inhabit the room with a complete lack of irony. Had she been there with Alec, they would have been giggling over the vibe and feigning heart attacks over the prices. But when Gavin ordered for both of them—the prix fixe menu at $235 a pop—he didn't bat an eye. He didn't consult her about the wine, but when he ordered the bottle, their waiter flushed with pleasure.

"This is quite a place," she said, after the waiter collected the menus and left them alone.

"It's a subtle room, right? I like it here a lot."

"Yes. Very subtle."

She shifted in her seat, wishing she had worn a longer skirt. Of course, when she had left for work that morning she hadn't had any idea she would end up on a date with Gavin Stone. If that's what this was. But no—that's not what this was; this was just a celebration of her returning to the law after a brief detour. A break from Alec and the drama of their relationship. A return to sanity.

"So you told me you quit the club that you've been performing at. But have you given any more thought to what I was saying about getting back into law? I mean, as a lawyer, not just the paralegal stuff you've been doing this past year."

Mallory nodded, wishing she had her wine. And just like that, the waiter appeared. He made a big show of opening the bottle, pouring some into a wide glass for Gavin and then pausing for his approval to pour more.

"Excellent," Gavin said. The waiter seemed visibly relieved, as if he had been waiting for a jury verdict.

When their glasses were poured and the waiter had returned to the shadows, Gavin raised his glass.

"To a very bright future." He smiled.

She imagined them as a power couple in the legal world. Of course burlesque wouldn't fit into that life. She'd thought she and Alec could somehow be a creative couple living a more inspired life than the one her parents had led, or the ones her friends would lead if they worked in jobs that alternately stressed them out and bored them. If they forgot the passion for life they'd had when they started college, when anything seemed possible. But where had all that passion gotten her? A year of pursuing it had just led to a chaotic relationship.

"To the future," she said, touching her glass to his.

They sipped their wine. She could tell it was very good; the better the wine, the easier it was for her to drink. And this wine went down like nothing she'd ever tasted before. With wine like this, she could understand how people became obsessive oenophiles.

She imagined that everything in Gavin's life was like this: only the best. While he didn't talk very much about his personal life, she knew he'd grown up in Manhattan, gone to the private school Horace Mann, and then to Princeton. He was great looking; he was smart—she imagined he could have pretty much anything he wanted out of life. And from the way he was looking at her, it seemed at that moment, what he wanted was her.

18

Poppy poured soy sauce, olive oil, lemon juice, and Worcester-shire sauce into a blender. She doubled-checked the recipe for the steak marinade. It said mix for thirty seconds. She hit the On button, confident that the way to inspire passion in her girlfriend was through her stomach.

With the buzz of the machine, she didn't hear her phone ring, but by the time she poured the marinade into a bowl, she realized she had two new messages. She hoped it wasn't Patricia saying she was going to be working late after all; Poppy had been shopping and prepping all day to make a romantic dinner for the two of them. Partly, it was out of guilt for what she'd been doing with Violet. But it was more an attempt to rekindle the spark in their relationship. Ideally, she would love to go somewhere exotic to try to get their sex life back on track. But even if she could finesse a week off from the Blue Angel, Patricia's legal job was too demanding. Poppy couldn't remember the last time she took a vacation, and maybe that was part of the problem.

Poppy dialed into her voice mail, extending one toned leg

and thinking she had to get to the gym. Before she could reach her messages, her phone rang again.

"Why the hell aren't you picking up your phone?" Violet snapped.

"I just did," Poppy said.

"Meet me at the Cellar in a half hour."

"Not going to happen," Poppy said.

"I just want to talk to you. It's business."

"I can't see you right now, Violet. I'm busy." There—she had said no! And she felt better already.

"Doing what?"

Poppy sighed. "If you must know, making dinner."

"So you're at your apartment?"

"Yes," she said impatiently.

"Meet me at the Cellar, or I'm showing up there."

"Violet, I can't do this anymore, okay?"

"I'll see you in a half hour—in midtown, or at your place. It's your decision."

Poppy looked at her watch. It was seven o'clock. An hour before Patricia was due home.

"Jesus, Violet. Fine. I'll be there in a half hour. But I can only stay for a few minutes."

She hung up her phone, scribbled a note saying she'd run out for some ingredients, and left to see Violet for what she planned to be the last time.

Gavin's driver let them off in front of a building on Bond Street.

"I know I shouldn't keep you out late on a work night, so just one drink," he said.

"Yeah, my boss is a tyrant." Mallory laughed, already extremely buzzed. The last thing she needed was another drink. Then she noticed the unmistakable, art deco front gate of 40 Bond.

"You live here?"

"Why do you seem so surprised?"

"I have friends who live here," she said, wondering if she would run into Justin Baxter and Martha Pike, and this gave her a pang for the loss of her burlesque world. But then she looked at Gavin, thought of the incredible dinner they had just shared—and about what lay ahead. "They have one of the townhouses."

"I live in the residential tower. I never thought I'd move from the Upper East Side, but I couldn't resist this place. Everything Ian Schrager does is pretty top-notch."

Gavin's apartment was similar to the Baxters' place, with floor to ceiling windows, oak floors, eleven-foot ceilings, and a wood-burning fireplace. Gavin's décor was very masculine, but not as aggressively modern as that of the Baxter residence. This place was more Ralph Lauren chic, with comfortable couches and rugs in earth tones, and lots of wood with some accents of chrome.

"I have heat lamps outside if you want to sit on the roof garden," he said, leading her through large glass doors. Sure enough, the garden deck held two towering heaters like the kind they had at outdoor restaurant spaces in LA.

"This is amazing," she said, looking at the view of Bond Street below.

"I'll be right back with the wine. I figured we should stick with the reds. I have a bottle of Silver Oak I've been waiting to open."

"Sounds good," she said. She folded herself into a comfortable chair under one of the heaters. When Gavin returned with the wine, he handed her a cashmere blanket.

"Just in case the heaters aren't doing the trick," he said. She thanked him and pulled the blanket around her like a wrap. She was perfectly warm, and with her first sip of the Napa Valley

Cabernet, she felt a sense of luxury and well-being that was completely foreign to her.

"It's amazing to be having wine outside at this time of year," she said.

"I know. Some nights it's just too cold even with the heaters, but we got lucky tonight. It helps get me through the winters, though what I'd really like to do is get a place in California and travel more during January and February if I could swing it with the workload at the office."

"Can I ask you a personal question?" Mallory said, emboldened by the wine and the seeping tiredness she was beginning to feel.

"Sure. Ask me anything."

"How do you live like this? I mean, even with the office being busy—it can't bring in enough for this place. And your car. And another place in California? You're not that much older than me, and my friends are all living in glorified studios."

He laughed. "I did my time in glorified studios—believe me. But I got tired of it, and the truth is, my family has a lot of money. I didn't rush to tap into it, but once I hit thirty I felt ready to start living a more...adult lifestyle. I used to look down on my parents for their extravagances, but now I realize that when you get older, it feels good to have nice things. Especially when you work as hard as we do. No matter how stressful a day I have in court, when I walk in the door here, I feel calm."

She looked up at the sky, took another sip of wine, and exhaled.

"I feel calm, too," she said. And she did—except for the thing that neither one of them had mentioned since last Friday night: their unfinished business that she found herself wanting, more and more, to finish.

"So how does Alec feel about your decision to return to law?"

"I don't really know. We aren't speaking right now."

"Oh—I'm sorry, Mallory."

"Are you?" she said, suddenly feeling remarkably sober.

He looked at her, and their eye lock was turbo-charged.

"No. Actually, I'm not."

She shivered.

"It's getting cold out here. I guess modern technology has its limits." He held his hand out and helped her stand, arranging the blanket around her shoulders so it didn't fall off. She had an overwhelming sense of being taken care of. It felt different— and it felt nice.

He opened a different set of glass doors than the ones they had used to get to the roof garden, and instead of returning to the living room, she found herself in his spacious master bedroom.

"This is beautiful," she said, because really, what else was there to say? Maybe nothing. But she was too nervous to be silent.

He stood behind her and helped her off with her coat.

"Mallory," he said quietly.

She turned to face him.

"I have to admit I still feel weird about this because you work for me."

Mallory nodded to convey that she heard him, but also because she had an epiphany: She realized she should be more proactive so he didn't feel that he was the one hitting on her or taking advantage of someone who worked for him. She would have to put her nervousness aside, and take charge; he could be her boss in the boardroom, but she had to call the shots in the bedroom. It was the only way this relationship would work.

She put her arms around him and kissed him the way she

had the other night in the office. He pulled her close and ran his hands up and down her body, eagerly cupping her breasts under her light sweater. His hands were cold but his touch was gentle, and as his fingers played with her nipples his kiss became more ardent.

He was shorter than Alec—most guys were—and this threw her off slightly. She decided it might be better to sit. She moved to the edge of the bed, and he followed her, his hands never leaving her body. It was a good thing he didn't stop touching her—she hadn't had sex with any guy aside from Alec in four years, and being on the verge of it made her nervous. Mallory was an overthinker, and the only thing that turned off her mind was turning on her body.

Gavin stretched out on the bed and took her hand, pulling her next to him. She lay down on her side and propped herself up on an elbow. Heart pounding, she undid his belt, and he helped her slide his pants down. He had great legs—long, lean, and muscular. She imagined them wrapped around her waist, then had a fleeting thought that she might not be able to go through with it. She wondered if he would think she was a tease if she just wanted to fool around a little, not have actual sex. Thinking of sex made her feel like she would be cheating on Alec, which was crazy for so many reasons, she knew. Or maybe once she and Gavin were fully in the moment, she would want to sleep with him.

Gavin pulled her close, and she felt him hard against her. She ran her hand lightly over his boxers, feeling his cock hard underneath the fabric. She slipped her fingers inside the opening and touched his bare flesh, his penis so warm against her hand it was practically throbbing. She couldn't believe she was touching Gavin Stone like this.

He lifted her sweater to kiss her breasts, and she pulled the sweater off to give him quicker access to her body. His tongue ran over her nipples, followed by his hands. She moaned and unzipped her skirt, tugging it down along with her argyle-patterned tights. She could barely remember what underwear she had put on that morning, and could hardly believe that she'd gotten dressed earlier that day having no idea that she'd be getting undressed in Gavin's bed.

She glanced down at the lacy, pale coral Belabumbum boy shorts she was wearing. Thank God she'd done laundry on Sunday and wasn't stuck with the dregs of her underwear drawer that morning.

Gavin looked at her.

"God, you're flawless," he said, his hand trailing from her breasts to her belly to the top of her underwear. From her vantage point, he was pretty damn perfect, too. She reached over and unbuttoned his shirt, then slid it off to reveal his magnificently proportioned shoulders, his muscled, nearly hairless chest, and his taut stomach. She knew he could have any woman in New York, and for some reason he wanted her. She was flattered, and her nerves slipped away. The perfectionist in her kicked in, and she wanted to impress him. She wanted to be worthy of his interest, to seduce him as much as she was being seduced.

He kissed her, his hand in her hair, then cradling the base of her head while his arms brought her closer to him. Their bodies pressed together, only their underwear between them. She could feel his cock so hard and defined between her legs; it was as if they weren't wearing anything at all. But somehow the fact that there was still something left to remove made the press of their bodies all the more thrilling.

She pulled back slightly, adjusting herself so she had leverage to get on top of him. She straddled him, and he looked up at her with a sort of awe that she used to get from Alec. To be fair, sometimes she still got looks of passion and reverence from Alec, but they were more rare. Maybe guys could only look at women like that when things were new and exciting. When a relationship gelled into love and domesticity, it was hard to maintain that level of intensity. Maybe that was why Alec wanted other women sometimes; he missed looking at someone that way as much as she missed being looked at.

Mallory shook thoughts of Alec from her mind and, slipped off her panties one leg at a time. She tossed them aside, and Gavin immediately pressed his hand to the wetness between her legs. He touched her gingerly, his finger slow and almost uncertain inside the folds of her pussy lips. His hands weren't as big as Alec's, and she knew she wouldn't be able to come as easily as she could from her lover's touch, which was so practiced and perfect it was as if she were a Stradivarius in the hands of a master musician.

Stop thinking about Alec!

Again, she thought maybe Gavin was afraid to be too assertive because he didn't want to do anything to offend her. He could only be sure she was okay with what was going on if she initiated everything.

Then she had an idea to unleash Gavin's reserve once and for all.

She gently pressed his hand away—it wasn't doing anything for her yet, and she'd rather just wait a minute and lower herself onto his gorgeous cock. She knew they would click. But first...

She leaned forward and grabbed her paper-thin cashmere sweater from the corner of the bed.

"Come back here," Gavin said, smiling and pulling her gently back into place. Still holding her sweater, she leaned down and kissed him, then quickly wrapped the sweater around his eyes, a loose, bulky blindfold. She reached down to touch his cock—

"What the hell are you doing?" he snapped, pulling the sweater off his face and throwing it across the room.

"What's wrong?" she said, jumping off him.

He looked at her like she'd just kicked his dog.

"What's *wrong?* What do you think is wrong? Why don't you tell me what you think you're doing?"

"I'm, um, blindfolding you."

"Yeah, I gathered that, Mallory." His voice softened, but he spoke to her as if she were a child. "I can only overlook so much. It's one thing to act slutty on a stage, but I don't want these S&M antics in my home."

Mallory sat back on her heels. She couldn't have been more shocked if he had struck her.

Then she thought no, he must be joking. *Please let him be joking.*

"Very funny," she said, though she was sure her face was drained of all color.

Gavin sat up. She couldn't help peeking to see if he was still hard.

He wasn't.

"I'm serious, Mallory. Maybe in your line of work you're used to sleeping with guys who expect a show in the bedroom, but I'm not one of them. I like women who have a little class."

Mallory couldn't, in that moment, think of any reply to that—other than to tell him to fuck off. But considering he signed her paycheck, that probably wasn't the best response. Although, was she really going to be able to work for him after this?

"I should go," she said, fumbling around for her clothes. She felt more naked than she ever had on stage.

Poppy walked into the Cellar steeling herself against whatever Violet had in mind for her; no matter what she was offered, Poppy wasn't buying.

The same girl sat behind the reception desk.

"Can I help you?" she said.

"I'm here to see Violet."

Poppy took a seat on one of the red velvet couches. She wasn't going through those double doors no matter what. If Violet wanted to speak with her, she could meet her in the reception area. Fortunately, she didn't have to argue this point; Violet appeared from behind the doors, swinging a long, black trench coat over a purple and green old-fashioned barmaid frock, gartered white stockings, and five-inch, black patent leather Mary Janes.

"I'm checking out," Violet said to the receptionist.

"*Auf wiedersehen,*" the girl said. Poppy smiled. Nothing like a little dominatrix humor.

"Where are we going? I don't have a lot of time," Poppy said, as Violet hustled her out the door.

"Will you stop bitching and moaning. This won't take long."

They rode the elevator in silence. Poppy felt she could hear the cables squeaking and straining, and she was relieved when the doors opened into the dark lobby.

Outside, midtown bustled with the after-work and theater crowd. Poppy pulled her coat closed more tightly and thought about her marinade. She wished she'd never heard the name Violet Offender.

Violet steered her into a small Irish pub. She ordered two scotches and commandeered a booth in the corner. Two stockbroker types eyed them, and Violet gave them the finger.

"I don't want this," Poppy said, pushing the drink away. Violet shrugged, downed her drink, and then started on Poppy's.

"So, I was having some thoughts. Big picture ideas. Since you seem pressed for time—though I can't imagine what could be so interesting in your apartment—I'll get right to it: I suggest you quit the Blue Angel."

Poppy shook her head. "I don't even want to *know* what is going on in that head of yours, but you're out of your mind.

I'm not leaving the Blue Angel. Agnes gave me my start, and it's the best club in the city."

Violet sighed and took Poppy's hand. Poppy tried to pull it away, but Violet turned her wrist and put her thumb on her pulse. The odd gesture distracted Poppy from withdrawing from her touch.

"Agnes's day is over. She just doesn't realize it yet." Violet said. "I'm going to make her realize it: I expect you to quit."

Poppy laughed. "Why should I care what you expect?"

"If you don't, I'll cut you off. And I don't think you'd last very long without what I'm giving you. That ugly dyke you have at home is certainly not taking care of business."

"That so-called 'ugly dyke' is twenty times the person you are. You make me come—so what? My vibrator does the same thing."

Violet had an odd smile on her face.

"Do you know that every time I fucked you I was pretending you were Mallory?"

The remark was so out of context, so out of the blue, Poppy couldn't reply. She knew her silence was giving the comment more power than it deserved, but for the life of her she couldn't think of a retort.

"And the next time I see you, you will be answering to me. That is, if you really mean what you said about wanting to work at the Blue Angel."

19

Mallory's office door was closed, but she kept glancing at it as if it might open at any moment. She had yet to see Gavin, thank God, but she couldn't hide in her office all day. For one thing, it was almost lunchtime, and she was hungry. Even if she ordered in from Guy & Gallard she'd have to go out to the reception desk.

The more she thought about it, the more last night's episode struck her as funny—humorous bordering on the absurd. Unfortunately, the person who would most appreciate the hilarity of the story was the one person she couldn't talk to about it: Alec. She was even thinking that the botched hookup would make a great burlesque skit. But that, too, was no longer an outlet for her. Which led her to the obvious question: what the hell had she done?

Her cell phone rang. She didn't recognize the incoming number.

"Hello?"

"It's Poppy. Sorry to bother you at work. And I know you

probably don't want to deal with everyone else's drama anymore. But it would be great if you could talk."

"Sure. I can talk." It would be a relief to deal with someone else's problems. "What's going on?"

"It's about the Blue Angel. Can you meet me for coffee or something?"

"Meet me at City Bakery in a half hour."

Mallory found Poppy at a table on the upper level. Amidst the Flatiron lunch crowd—the publishing types and the stray tourist—she stood out with her razor sharp blond bob and hipster, vintage clothes. Mallory, on the other hand, dressed for work at the law firm, blended right in.

"I hardly recognized you," Poppy said.

"I spotted you right away," said Mallory. They half hugged hello, and it was awkward. "So what's going on?"

Poppy sighed. "Do you want to get food first?"

Mallory looked over the railing to the first floor buffet. She was tempted by the macaroni and cheese—her favorite in the city—but she was too stressed out to eat. "I'm okay," she said.

Poppy was already picking at a piece of chocolate zucchini cake. "Okay, so this is the deal. Remember when I asked you if you ever got bored with sex because you and Alec have been together for so long?"

Mallory tried not to visibly wince. It wasn't Poppy's fault. Maybe some people still didn't know about their split.

"Yeah, I remember."

"And I told you I was attracted to other people sometimes?"

"And I told you that was normal."

"Okay, but what I did about it wasn't that normal. I started hooking up with someone else."

"It happens all the time, Poppy. Did Patricia find out?"

Poppy shook her head vigorously. "No."

"Did you end it?"

"Yes."

"Okay, then what are you worried about?"

"You don't understand. I wasn't just cheating on her with a normal person. I was cheating on her with ... Violet."

Mallory put her head in her hand. "Oh, Poppy. Why her?"

"I wasn't looking for it. It just ... happened. And she's so hot, and she just started telling me what to do, and it was thrilling, and I got addicted to it—to her. She really is like a drug. But I decided I was done with it—I am done with it."

"Okay. Good. Stick with that decision."

"I'm trying to. She called me last night, and I told her I didn't want to see her anymore. But I was wondering.... Are you involved with her, too? Or were you?"

"What? No—absolutely not. Why would you think that?"

"We got into sort of an argument last night, and maybe she was just trying to piss me off. She said every time we had sex she pretended I was you."

Mallory's eyes widened. "She was ... probably just, like you said, trying to upset you."

"Except I really think she meant it. She was very calm when she said it, very matter-of-fact."

Mallory considered this bit of information. If she accepted it as true, then it put that night at the Plaza in an entirely new light. Violet was a manipulative person. If she wanted to get to Mallory, she would be smart enough to first remove any obstacles in her path—an obstacle like Alec. And apparently, she'd succeeded.

"But the thing that really bothered me was a comment she made about the Blue Angel. She told me I should quit. So I started asking around. And I think Agnes is selling it."

"Yes, Agnes mentioned something like that to me."

"What did she say?"

Mallory relayed the conversation she'd had the day she quit.

"This is not cool, because Violet said one more thing: she said the next time I saw her, I'd be answering to her if I still wanted to work at the Blue Angel."

"That doesn't make any sense."

"I know. That's why I wanted to talk to you about it."

"Violet doesn't have the money or the connections to buy the club. The ambition, maybe. But she's nobody. It's not possible."

They sat in silence for a minute.

"Who else can we talk to about this?" Poppy said. Again, Mallory wanted to call Alec. But she would have to go with plan B.

"I'll call Bette," she said, already pressing the numbers on her phone.

Billy Barton stopped by the front desk of the Maritime Hotel and picked up the room key.

"Can I have bags taken to your room, Mr. Barton?" said the concierge.

"No bags. Just point me in the direction of the Hiro Ballroom."

Billy walked into the dramatic space to find a flurry of activity and the photo shoot already well under way. When his art director had suggested using this space, with its enormous paper lanterns hanging from the twenty-foot ceilings, he'd thought it was a great idea. Maybe dressing Kendall James as a modern-day geisha wasn't the most inspired fashion direction, but she did look great in the black wig. But he wasn't here to admire Kendall in her faux-Japanese salon. He was there to see her beautiful cohort, sidekick, and editorial prop, Tyler.

Billy was the one who'd suggested Tyler for the job. He was biased, of course, but who better to set off Kendall's exotic, French-Irish–Cherokee beauty than the all-American, corn-fed boy from Kansas? It was going to be a gorgeous spread—those assholes at *W* could eat their hearts out. Of course, Tyler's Burberry contract required him to wear Burberry in the editorial, which didn't quite fit with the Japanese vibe—but the art director was being a good enough sport about it. What Billy wanted, Billy got—at least when it came to *Gruff*.

"Hi, Mr. Barton." An editorial assistant showed him to a banquette. "Do you want something to drink?"

He looked at his watch. 11 a.m.

"A mojito," he said. "Are they breaking soon?"

"Any minute," the girl told him.

The drink calmed his nerves, and he settled back into the red banquette, watching his hot boyfriend work it, counting the minutes until he could get Tyler's cock in his mouth.

The photographer started setting up a shot with a topless Kendall covering her breasts with a sushi tray while Tyler held a live koi.

"This looks like it might take a while. Maybe we can take a break?" Billy called out.

"You want to break now?" the photographer said.

"If it's not a huge problem," said Billy.

"I can wrap for lunch, but I need everyone back in an hour."

"Perfect."

Everyone whipped out their cell phones. Kendall's publicist, an aggressively well-groomed older woman with a questionable British accent, rushed to her side. The assistants started taking lunch orders.

Billy waved Tyler over, and he had to admit that his boyfriend didn't seem overjoyed to see him.

"Hey—the shoot looks great," Billy said.

"Yeah," said Tyler.

"What's wrong?" Billy said. Tyler shrugged. "Follow me—I have something to cheer you up. Let's go."

* * *

The room he'd reserved was a penthouse suite. Billy loved the nautical theme of the room, with the round, oversized "cabin" windows and the outdoor deck with a shower which, unfortunately, it was currently too cold outside to use.

He'd arranged for room service to set up a lunch spread, and it was waiting for them.

"Are you hungry?" he asked Tyler.

"No. I'm too stressed out to eat."

"What are you stressed about? The shoot is going great."

"It's not that."

"What, then? Burberry is renewing your contract; your agent said she's getting requests for you to host a male model reality show.... I'm fucking crazy about you. It's all good."

"What about that other stuff? The ... situation?"

"I told you not to worry about that. I'm taking care of it. Agnes is selling. The lawyers drew up the paperwork yesterday. By the end of the week, this will be a done deal. Violet's not going to do anything stupid."

"How do you know?"

"She's not going to mess with her golden goose, Tyler. She's all jazzed up about a spring opening. She's renaming the club "Violet's Blue Angel." We're going to do a piece about it in *Gruff*. I'm keeping her happy, okay?"

"Okay."

"Now why don't you keep me happy."

After watching Tyler strut around with Kendall James for an hour, he was already hard. If he really had his way, he'd have her up here, too, for a little creativity. Ideally, he'd watch Tyler fuck her, and then Billy would lick his cock until he was ready for Tyler to put it in his ass. But he could tell Kendall didn't roll like that. He didn't know how that guy Justin Baxter always managed to get people to do the craziest things at his parties. Like the time he somehow convinced Poppy LaRue to masturbate for them in a private room. He could never pull off things like that without paying for it, and look where that had gotten him.

Tyler poured himself a glass of champagne, and Billy unzipped his jeans. Tyler stood a few feet away, watching as Billy took his cock out of his boxers, stroking it. Tyler's eyes locked on Billy's cock, and Billy could tell that despite his bad mood, Tyler still wanted him.

Tyler walked over to Billy in quick strides, knelt, and licked the tip of his cock, then trailed his tongue down to his balls. He took them into his mouth one at a time, tonguing them, his hand working Billy's shaft in hard, fast strokes. Billy moaned, wanting to feel his cock hit the base of Tyler's throat, wanting to hear him gag.

"Open your mouth," Billy said, grabbing his hair. Tyler took Billy's cock in his mouth, letting Billy fuck his throat, knowing Billy would only come when it seemed like it was too much for Tyler to take. Billy thrust so hard and fast, it only took a few minutes for Tyler to almost retch, triggering Billy's orgasm deep in his mouth. Tyler swallowed, clutching Billy's ass, pulling him deeper. Billy's moan trailed off, and he was still. He slumped back against the wall.

Tyler pushed him to turn around, and Billy smiled, bracing himself against the wall. He heard Tyler undoing his belt, the sound of his jeans hitting the hardwood floor. Tyler spit into his hand, and although Billy couldn't see behind himself, he knew Tyler was rubbing his saliva on his cock, and that it might or might not be enough to help get his cock into Billy's ass, which was all Billy had been thinking about since the minute he woke up that morning.

Tyler pulled Billy to the couch, standing behind it so he could bend Billy over the back of it. Tyler spit on his ass, using his thumb to rub the wetness into Billy's asshole until Billy felt the head of Tyler's cock breaking against any resistance his ass

might have held. The club, the magazine, the photo shoot—
none of it mattered. The entire universe revolved around the
feeling he had at this moment as Tyler inched his flesh inside
Billy's, with agonizing slowness, until Billy felt himself fill up.
And then the exquisite pain as Tyler pulled out and then in
again, over and over. Tyler smacked his buttock, hard, and
called him a bitch. Billy, to his surprise, felt himself cresting
again, and then felt his release that made the room fade to black,
and he didn't recognize his own voice as he cried out. Even as
Billy finished, Tyler continued to work his ass, pumping away
until Billy heard him call out, too, coming with such aggression
and volume that Billy felt it spill onto his legs.

They dropped to the floor, lying against each other, panting
for breath.

"You know what?" Billy said.

"What?" said Tyler.

"I know you feel like Violet has us by the balls right now,
and maybe she does. But I promise you, by this time next year,
I will find a way to fuck her in the ass harder than you just
fucked me."

"You want to have sex with her?" Tyler said.

"No! I'm speaking metaphorically."

"Well, speak un-meta whatever you call it. What are you
gonna do?"

Billy rolled over and kissed him on the cheek. "Let me surprise you."

20

When Bette arrived at the restaurant in less than a half hour, she wasn't alone: she had Alec with her.

He looked more handsome than Mallory had ever seen him, with a few days' worth of stubble and his hair longer than he usually allowed it to grow. All in all, he looked in need of a good fuck, and she found herself dying to deliver one to him.

Regardless of how embarrassing last night had been, she was thankful things had played out the way they had. Looking at Alec cross the restaurant toward their table, it was unthinkable that she had almost slept with someone else.

He acknowledged her with a smile, sitting down next to Poppy while Bette took the empty seat next to her. Alec leaned in to put his coat next to her on the bench, and she caught his scent and almost swooned.

"I hope you don't mind my bringing Alec into this conversation, but he has more info than I do."

Mallory and Alec locked eyes. She looked away first. And only then did he start talking.

"I knew that Agnes was selling the club," he said. "Mallory

knows that because she and I talked about it a couple days ago. Then I told Bette just yesterday that I heard rumors around the *Gruff* offices that Billy was buying a club. I wasn't sure if it was the Blue Angel, and I figured he didn't want to talk to me about it since he knows my relationship to the club. Then I was thinking if it's not Billy, it would be great if the buyer were someone we knew, someone who loved the Blue Angel and would want to retain its character. So I told Justin Baxter that Agnes was selling it, thinking maybe he would want to throw his hat into the ring."

"Great idea," said Mallory.

"Yeah, but it's too late. Justin's lawyers found out that the Blue Angel has already been sold...to Billy Barton and someone named Gina Offinici."

"Who is Gina Offinici?" said Bette.

Poppy turned white. "I have a feeling I know."

Mallory looked at her, then reached for Alec's iPhone. "Can I use this for a second?" She opened the browser and went to Google images for Gina Offinici.

"Fuck," she said, and passed around the photo.

"Violet?" Alec said. "Why would Billy team up with her? Why wouldn't he come to you and me?" he said to Mallory. "You're a bigger name in burlesque than Violet. And we're friends with him."

"I don't know," Mallory said. "But none of the girls are going to want to work for her."

"That's the end of the Blue Angel right there," Poppy said.

"There's always a new crop of girls. It's just the end of the show we've been doing, the show that Scarlett and Kitty and everyone else have made their names doing. They'll just have to find other clubs. It won't be the same."

"Where? Lavender Lounge? The Fan Club? Those places have their regular girls, and places like the Slit just suck—it's not even real burlesque." Poppy said.

"I don't know, but I'm glad I don't have to worry about it," Bette said. "I hope by the time this all shakes out I'll be on a film set in Boston."

Mallory and Alec looked at each other. She barely heard anything Poppy and Bette were saying. All she could think about was getting him alone so they could talk. And she knew Alec well enough to know he was thinking the same thing.

"Do you want to get out of here?" Alec said to her, and it was like being in a movie where the action freezes for all but two characters.

Outside, Alec steered her toward Sixth Avenue, and they caught a cab a block away. The air between them was so thick with tension she could hardly breathe. She thought he would want to talk—usually he had a hard time leaving things unsaid. But he just stared straight ahead at the plastic barrier between them and the driver.

"We can get out here," he said when they reached West Twenty-fourth Street—which made no sense since they lived on East Eighty-third Street. They weren't even near a subway to switch over to.

He paid the driver and took her by the hand.

"What are you doing? I thought we were going back to the apartment."

"I can't wait that long."

They crossed the street and walked east. In the middle of the block was a nondescript building with a wooden doorframe and a placard that read, simply, HOTEL.

Alec held the door for her. Inside, the front room was more a vestibule than a lobby, with a few small chairs and a guy behind a glass window that made him appear more like a bank teller than a hotel receptionist.

Mallory listened to Alec ask for a room, and he forked over eighty dollars in cash. The guy slid him a key through the glass window, and Alec gestured for Mallory to follow him. He opened a door to the left of the front desk, and she started walking up a narrow set of stairs.

Alec stopped her at the first landing and checked the number on the green plastic keychain. It was a flat oval of plastic with the number seven on it and a single key dangling. It almost looked like the type of thing she had carried as a hall pass in high school.

He opened the door to a small room dominated by a queen-size bed covered with an ugly, art deco bedspread circa 1991. There was a small desk, and in the corner—freestanding—a shower.

"What is this place?" Mallory said, half-laughing, half-appalled. "And how do you know about it?"

"We did a piece for the magazine about the top ten hotels you need to know—and not for family vacations, if you get what I'm saying."

"I think I'm getting it," she said, opening the bedside drawer. Instead of a Bible, she found two condoms. "You're crazy," she smiled. "Why did you bring me here?"

He walked to her, taking her face in his hands.

"It was just an impulse. Thinking maybe if it could be just us for an hour, away from everyone and everything else, we could find our way back. That, and the fact that I can't wait another second to make love to you."

He kissed her, and the world fell away—Violet, the Blue Angel, the bar exam. Even that night with Gavin was like a tiny flickering star in an infinite universe. The rightness of that moment, of being held by him in that shitty little hotel room, told her on a visceral level that no matter what was going on externally, they were the center of the world. He was her gravity. She could look for that in other places, but she would never find it.

She helped him pull off her coat. The room was freezing, and he found a space heater near the dresser.

"I think that's a fire hazard," she said, eying it.

"We won't need it to get warm," he said. The seriousness in his eyes quieted her, and she didn't say another word as he undressed her. She lay back on the bed and watched him take off his own clothes. Her heart pounded, and she wondered how she could have considered what she felt for Gavin as attraction. It was nothing compared to this primal state of arousal. Every one of her senses felt heightened.

He moved on top of her, and she spread her legs, already wet for him. She reached down to hold his cock, to guide it inside of her, but he held her hand away, pushing his way into her in a way that was as rough as it was satisfying, making her close to coming almost instantly. She clutched his back, kissing his neck and rubbing her face against the rough stubble of his cheek.

She knew, of course, that he could read her body—probably knew it almost as well as she knew it herself—and could sense that she was close to coming. For that reason, probably to prolong their buildup, he pulled out of her. He stood up, at the edge of the bed, and she sat up, slightly lightheaded as she moved her legs on either side of his. She placed her hands on his hips and traced her tongue along his cock before closing the warmth of her mouth over as much of him as she could. She didn't think there was anything more intimate than tasting yourself on a man's cock, and she knew that few things turned Alec on more than her willingness to lick her own pussy juice.

While she worked her mouth on his cock, she stretched her hand up to his chest, and sure enough, she could feel his heart racing. He wound his hands through her hair and pulled her head back, off of himself so that he didn't get too close to coming.

He knelt down in front of her and kissed her so hard she knew her mouth would feel bruised in the morning. She took his face in her hands and kissed his fluttering eyelids, the bridge of his nose, his stubble-sharp jawline.

He leaned back to get something off of the floor, and she saw he was holding the long argyle socks she wore under her boots. He scooped one arm under her and lifted her toward the top of the bed, where he proceeded to tie her hands to the rickety iron headboard. He knotted each sock just tightly enough to make it impossible for her to get her hands free but not so tightly that it would hurt her or distract her.

Now it was her heart that was pounding, and she couldn't help thinking of the contrast between the way Alec was fucking her and Gavin's freak-out last night.

Alec trailed his hands down her arms, over her breasts, down her belly, to her pussy, where he stroked her clit before putting his face between her legs. He pressed his tongue inside her, his finger and mouth working in tandem, building the pressure in her cunt to an unbearable degree, making her dig her heels into the bed, wanting to grab him and pull him on top of her but not being able to because of the restraints. She moaned as he stopped touching her, using just his tongue to lick the outside of her pussy. The feeling of air on her abandoned flesh just heightened her arousal, and each warm stroke of his tongue brought her teasingly close to coming.

"Alec," she said.

"Tell me what you want," he said.

"You know what I want." Now his finger moved inside of her, and she couldn't speak at all. She spread her legs wider and moaned.

"Say it," he said. Even after all this time, and everything they did with one another, it was hard for her to verbalize what she wanted.

"I want you to..." She couldn't finish the sentence—he had reached the spot inside her that felt so good it almost hurt.

"Tell me," he said softly.

"Fuck me," she said.

"I am fucking you."

"With your cock," she said.

He moved on top of her but still not inside of her. First, he reached up and untied her wrists. She immediately grabbed him, pulling him so hard she knew her nails were digging into his back. She couldn't stop herself, and he didn't complain. She felt she had never needed or wanted anything more than the simplicity of his cock inside her at that moment. But Alec buried his face in the crook of her neck, his hand stroking her breast. She felt him hard against her leg.

"What are you waiting for?" she said, her voice so breathless she barely recognized it.

"I'm afraid when we're done you're going to leave and I won't see you again for weeks."

She stroked his hair, kissing the top of his head. "I'm not leaving."

Then, from somewhere in the room, his phone rang.

"I forgot to turn that off...."

"Do you need to get it?"

"Why would I need to answer it? You're here with me."

And then she felt his cock nudge inside of her, very slowly despite how wet and ready she was. She kissed the underside of his jaw, and he bent his head to bury it in the crook of her neck. Her pussy throbbed around him as he stroked in and out, and when the pulsing of his cock changed to quick, hard thrusts, her body clicked into that mindless place where she was just one vibrating nerve of pleasure. The ripples of her orgasm washed through her

Alec cried out, and she was vaguely aware—considering that she was barely conscious of anything but the physical sensations taking her over like a possession—that he was feeling the same, that they were, in that moment, almost a single physical entity, because one could not exist without the other.

He pulled out and collapsed by her side. She turned toward him, placing one hand on his heaving chest.

They looked at each other and smiled. He kissed the top of her head.

And she thought about last night and felt guilty. She knew she had to tell him about it, but he spoke before she could.

"I'm sorry about not handling what happened with Violet better," he said. "I know I've given you mixed messages in the past about what I've wanted. But I never wanted that."

"It's my fault. I'm insecure. When I moved to New York to be with you, I felt like you could have anyone in the world and wondered if you still really wanted me, the girl you'd been with since college. I guess that's part of what drove me into burlesque—to be someone more than just Mallory Dale from Penn. Because you're already so much more than the boy I met there. I want to be the one you want and not just someone you're keeping along for the ride—out of comfort or habit when you've outgrown me."

"I never, ever felt that way about you," he said, pulling her close. "Mallory, I know I've made mistakes. And yeah, part of it is because we've been together since college, and maybe for a brief moment I thought I wanted you and more, but I know and have always known that all I really want is more of you."

She smiled. "Wow. The perks of dating a writer."

"I'm pouring my heart out and you're making jokes?"

"I'm not joking. I couldn't be more serious." She bent over toward the floor and pulled her shirt to her chest as a cover. "Listen: for the record, I've messed up more than you, and I'm really sorry."

"No, you haven't."

She swallowed hard. "Yeah, I have."

"Like what?"

"I hooked up with Gavin."

Alec sat up so abruptly the bed shook.

"You slept with him?"

She shook her head vigorously. "No."

"What, then?"

"We just, you know, hooked up a little. But we did not have sex—I swear."

"When did this happen?"

"Recently," she said—understatement of the year. But really, honesty had its limits. "While we've been apart."

"How many times?"

"Just once," she said, telling herself the incident in the office didn't count.

"Do you have feelings for him?"

"No," she said. "It was more that I wanted to know that I could be physical with someone else—that my relationship with you didn't define me. I really felt lost—and I still do. Am I Mallory or Moxie? Whose future do I want? Because there is no way to have both or be both."

"You are both. And I love that about you."

She again thought of Gavin, and how guys like him could be titillated by her Moxie persona, but could never truly accept or live with her. And most people—even her own friends—thought she had to make a choice. When she'd met Julie and Allison for breakfast that morning a few weeks ago, they'd made it clear they saw her foray into burlesque as a detour, a distraction that took her further from herself and from the future she was meant to have. But she knew, and Alec knew, that it brought her closer to the right answer about her life.

"You know you can't work for that guy anymore. That is, if you want for us to be together. And I hope you do, Mallory."

"I do," she said.

"You'll quit?"

"Yes. But I don't know what I'm going to do. My life is so chaotic."

"No, it's not," he said. "We have the most important thing right."

"How about you?" she said. "I'm so mad at Billy. Why wouldn't he come to us if he was interested in getting into the burlesque business? How does he even know Violet? It feels like such a slap in the face. And I can't stand her, Alec. I partly blame her for our breakup. She came between us—and you let her, to some degree—but after talking to Poppy I have no doubt she intended for that to happen. What if she's getting involved in the magazine, too? Maybe they're sleeping together or something."

"I doubt they're sleeping together. I'm pretty sure Billy is gay."

Mallory thought about Violet's sexual relationship with Poppy, and Poppy's theory that she was obsessed with Mallory.

"And Violet isn't into guys."

"So what's going on there?" Alec said.

"Who knows? We should just stay as far away as possible."

His phone rang again, and he ignored it.

"Maybe you should check your messages," Mallory said. Alec nodded and retrieved his coat. He waited to make sure the call went to voice mail, then dialed into his phone.

"It's Justin Baxter," he said.

"What does he want?"

"He said that he and Martha feel bad they didn't get to Agnes in time to buy the Blue Angel, and they can't stop thinking about it. He wants me to go to their place tonight for a drink."

"Do you think they have an idea of how to get the club after all?"

"No. If it's sold, it's sold. I don't know what they have in mind. But I guess we'll find out."

"We?"

"Aren't you coming with me?"

"Yes," she said, kissing him. "I'm going with you."

"Well, I guess our work here is done," Poppy said after Alec and Mallory absconded from City Bakery like two lovesick teenagers.

"I feel so used," Bette joked.

"Really? I don't feel used enough," Poppy mumbled, barely daring to say it.

Bette laughed, then rifled through her Vuitton handbag. "God, I wish I could smoke in here. After being in Paris and Milan I realize how uncivilized this damn city is."

"I'll walk outside with you," Poppy said.

"Do you smoke?" Bette said.

"No. I would just... I don't mind walking outside," Poppy said.

Bette raised an eyebrow. "Are you flirting with me?" she said, in that unnerving, direct way she had.

"What? No! Not at all," Poppy said, flustered. The truth was, she wouldn't dare flirt with Bette. She could barely think straight sitting across the table from her, could barely take her eyes off of her matte red, pillowy bottom lip. But that was different than flirting.

"Well, that's a shame," Bette said.

"What?" Had she heard her correctly?

"I said that's a shame. You've never looked better, my dear." Bette smiled faintly, then looked off across the room as if thinking about something else entirely.

"Oh, well, thanks."

"I noticed it that day we ran into each other at M&J Trimming. You're hotter now than you were when you first came to the Blue Angel. But that happens to girls, you know. It's an inner confidence thing. It shows through. People think that's bullshit, but it's absolutely not. And that show you did the other night? Inspired. Who's been teaching you? Mallory?" She smiled a devilish smile, her eyes a smoky mix of blue and gray against her dark silk blouse.

"No, not really."

"Not that cunt Violet, I hope."

Poppy turned bright red—she could feel it. "No."

"Are you still seeing that dowdy lawyer?"

"Patricia? Yes."

"Well, that's nice. Relationships are a good thing if you can swing it. I, apparently, cannot."

"You're not with Zebra anymore?" Poppy said, although she had already bought the *Us*, *Life & Style*, and *OK!* issues detailing their breakup.

"No," Bette said. She poked her straw in and out of her can of Diet Coke as if fishing for something at the bottom.

Poppy had the urge to confess that she wished she had the nerve to break up with Patricia, but that she was afraid no one would ever love her the same way again. She was sure Bette would never stay with someone for such a stupid reason. She had no idea why Bette and Zebra had split up—every magazine cited a different implausible scenario—but she was sure Bette had been the one who initiated it. She couldn't imagine Bette ever not being in control.

"Are you and Patricia monogamous?" Bette said.

"Yes," Poppy said, thinking regretfully of Violet.

"Well, that's unfortunate," Bette said.

"What?"

"For me, that is. Unfortunate for me."

"How do you figure?" Poppy said, her pulse racing. She braced herself. *No matter what she says, I won't do anything!*

Bette shrugged. Poppy resisted the urge to push the issue. There was something so maddeningly remote about the woman! But she had finally gotten away from Violet, and she didn't need another complication, no matter how tempting it was. No matter that the woman she had a crush on—or was maybe the tiniest bit in love with—seemed to be opening the door to the possibility of the two of them fooling around.

"Well, I should get going," Bette finally said, pulling a cigarette out of a silver case. Poppy noticed the large monogrammed Z on it. "Catch you later," she said.

Poppy watched her leave.

21

The cab pulled up to the gates of 40 Bond, and Mallory tried not to think of the fact that she had been there just last night. What were the odds of her ending up back there in less than twenty-four hours? It was as if the universe was mocking her. But she wasn't going to mention it to Alec. She just prayed she didn't run into Gavin.

Fortunately, the Baxter townhouse was in a different area of the complex than the high-rise where Justin had his apartment, and as soon as they turned into it she felt safely ensconced in the world of her and Alec, no one else.

"Glad you two could make it on such short notice," Justin said as the butler took her coat. She knew from past experience that she had to remove her shoes—Martha was obsessive about her oak floors imported from Austria. "Mallory, we've missed seeing you at the Blue Angel."

"Oh, yeah, I took a little...leave of absence," she said.

"Mental health break?" Justin said.

"Something like that."

Martha Pike lounged in the corner. She looked as unkempt and overweight as usual, her feet stuffed into unattractive but serviceable shoes. In her right hand, she clutched an elegant wooden cane.

"Forgive me for not getting up," she said.

"Martha's having some problems with her hip," Justin said. Mallory knew she should be used to them by now, but she always marveled at the incongruous couple.

Mallory and Alec sat side by side on one of the low, pale couches. A white-gloved cocktail waitress offered them champagne and chilled vodka. Mallory took the vodka. Ever since Bette had gotten her started drinking it last year, she recognized it as the best balm for her nerves.

"So as I mentioned in my voice mail, I find it terribly frustrating that we were too late to get in on the Blue Angel deal."

"Yes, Justin and I have a real soft spot for that place," Martha said wistfully. "But if the deal is done, the deal is done."

"But since we started thinking about the possibility of owning a burlesque club, we haven't been able to get off that track. And we realized over breakfast this morning—if we can't buy the Blue Angel, why not just start our own?"

Alec and Mallory exchanged a look.

"I don't have time to mastermind the whole thing. I'm about to launch Honeymoon Two in the market, and I think it's going to really take off. I have to be there for my new baby. And, of course, Justin isn't very business-minded. Don't get me wrong—we all know he's a genius when it comes to aesthetics, and that's important in this game. But we would need someone to be on the ground every step of the way with this. And we thought of you two," she said, looking at Alec and Mallory.

"To . . . run the place?"

"Yes. You're a lawyer by training; you both went to Penn. Not Wharton, we know, but Penn is still Penn. You both know this world, you get what makes a club work, and you have the relationships to get girls on the stage—as do we— and people in the seats. I think we would make an unbeatable team."

"This is an amazing idea," Alec said. "And I'm flattered. But there's a lot to think about. It's a huge commitment. And it might not earn back your investment for years."

"I don't get the sense Agnes spent her life running that place because it was such a moneymaker. She did it because she loved it. And you know how Martha and I feel about art and beautiful women. And we are certainly in a better position to take the financial hits than Agnes is. There's really no downside. We just need operational partners to get it going. Will you consider it?"

"It's incredibly tempting," Mallory said. "But Alec is busy writing for the magazine, and I..." And she what? She had to quit yet another law job. She didn't have a burlesque gig anymore. "Actually, I could do it. But I don't know if it's the right thing for Alec."

"Mallory and I don't have the money to effectively not work for the year it will take to get this off the ground," he said.

"We didn't imagine you did," said Martha. "I propose we put you both on payroll until the club gains momentum. Then you have the option of staying on salary or buying in as partners to share in the profit of the club."

Mallory looked at Alec. She knew they should talk about it in private, but also that there was little doubt they would do it. If the way Martha and Justin paid their fish tank girl was any indication, the Baxters were generous with their employees.

"It's an incredible opportunity. We are flattered and thrilled that you guys thought of us. Let us talk about it and call you in the morning?" Alec said.

"Of course. In the meantime, we're having people over if you care to stay for a few hours. It should be an interesting group."

It was always an "interesting group" at the Baxter parties—
movie moguls mingled with rap stars, politicians talked to porn
stars, Academy Award-winning actors were entertained by
street performers. The atmosphere was always sexually charged,
and the sense that anything could—and often did—happen
made the evenings "must" events. Mallory had made her performing debut at a Baxter party in LA, and so she had a soft
spot for their festivities. But she didn't have the energy for a
party that night and only wanted to go back to the apartment
she shared with Alec. They'd been apart for too long.

"Another night," Alec said.

Mallory curled up against Alec in the dark and quiet of her
own bedroom. It felt so good to be home.

She rubbed her leg against his thigh.

"You're such a horndog," he said. "You want to go again?"

"Sort of," she said.

He nudged her over onto her back and slipped his hand into
her underwear.

"Jeez, you're already wet. You really are the horniest girl
I've ever known."

"Is that a problem?" she said, kissing him.

"Only when I can't keep up with you any longer. But I
think I've still got a few good years left in me."

He stroked her softly, and she slipped her hand inside his
boxers to find him already hard.

"I guess I'm not the only horndog in the room."

She moved on top of him and pulled off her shirt. He looked
up at her with great intensity, and she was moved by the expression in his blue-gray eyes.

He ran his hands over her breasts and down her shoulders.

"That night you got that painting on your arm...it looked
so beautiful. You know, I came to that room looking for you so
we could go home. I didn't want to be out with Violet or at

some crazy party. Were you taking me out with Violet to test me?"

"Maybe. I don't know. I'm sorry. And I loved the painting. You know I've been thinking about getting a tattoo, but I'm not sure what image I can really live with long-term."

"Yeah. I know. And I've thought about it since that night. I'm thinking about a new image you can play around with."

She looked down at him. "If you've got a new tattoo, it must be somewhere really interesting because I thought I saw every inch of you earlier today."

"I don't—not yet. But I have an idea for one."

"It must be contagious. Bette just got a new one."

"I know. She told me you went with her and you said you could never go through with it, that it's too permanent."

"That's right," she said.

"I'm ready for something permanent," he said. "Will you come with me?"

"You're seriously going to get a new tattoo?"

"Yeah. I'm not afraid of commitment," he teased.

"What are you going to get?"

"You'll have to wait and see," he said. "In the meantime, I'm going to keep looking for inspiration." He pulled down her underwear.

22

Wendy the tattoo artist was waiting for them.

"I recognize you," she said to Mallory. "Moxie, right?"

"Yes," Mallory said, and she could feel herself blushing. Alec laughed.

They sat on a black couch with Wendy, and she pulled out a sketch book.

"I made the changes you asked for after I e-mailed you the preliminary sketch. You wanted her hair to be longer, right? And the feather fan to be bigger?"

"Yeah," he said, looking at the piece of paper she passed him. He smiled, then handed it to Mallory.

"It's my girl!" she said with delight, looking at an image very similar to the one that had been painted on her arm that night that seemed so long ago. Except... "But she looks just like me," she said.

"Yeah—it's *my* girl," Alec said. She looked more closely and smiled.

"You're getting a tattoo of me on your arm?" she said.

"Yes. If it's okay with you. I'd hate to get something permanent if you didn't plan to be around for a while. It's a big commitment, you know."

She kissed him. "It is."

"Alec e-mailed me a picture of you," Wendy said. "I recognized you from the day you were here with Bette Noir. And Alec told me you're a performer, too."

"Yeah. I've taken a break the past few weeks but...I'm going to get back into it."

"I really need to get to a show," Wendy said, gesturing for them to follow her into the main part of the parlor. "I went to a late show one night at the Slit, but I was too drunk to remember anything about it."

"That's not real burlesque, anyway," Mallory said. She was already thinking of the Slit as her competition—not as a performer at the Blue Angel, but as a club owner herself.

Of course, she and Alec had agreed they should do it. She would quit her job effective immediately, and Alec would finish his final article for *Gruff* and resign before announcing that he was going to be running a club to compete with Billy's. Justin and Martha were thrilled.

"Where should we throw the launch party?" Justin had asked.

"Let's find a space for the actual club first," Alec had told him.

Wendy sat him in the chair at her station, and again Mallory marveled at the little tubes of color, the instruments, and the sketches all around the room.

Wendy snapped on her blue rubber gloves, then shaved the area of Alec's arm where the tattoo would go. She pressed the stenciled image against the spot, peeling it away, leaving an outline of the girl. Alec checked the placement in the mirror.

"What do you think, Mal?"

"It looks amazing," she said. "Are you really doing this?"

"Of course," he said, winking at her.

He sat in the chair. Across the room, another tattoo artist, a thin guy with a ZZ Top beard, cranked up the Metallica.

"How long do you think this will take?" Mallory asked Wendy.

"Maybe two hours."

She couldn't imagine being in pain for two straight hours, but Alec seemed unfazed by this estimate.

Wendy touched the needle to his arm, starting one of the girl's legs.

"I do the outline first, then the shading and colors," she said. "What color do you want the corset?"

"Blue," Alec and Mallory said in unison.

Mallory was surprised by the blood. Lots of it, beading through his skin like it would never stop. She hadn't noticed it with Bette because she hadn't stuck around long enough. But she was noticing it now.

"Is that normal?" she asked Wendy.

"Yes," she said.

The Blue Angel girl was almost complete. Wendy was just adding details to the long plumes of feathers in her fan.

"Are you read to finish it off for me?" Wendy said to her suddenly.

"What?"

Alec squeezed her hand. "I asked Wendy if you could do the last mark of the tattoo."

"You guys are crazy," Mallory said with a nervous laugh.

"I really want you to do it—to know that you marked me outside as permanently as you marked me inside."

"You are such a romantic!" she said. "But I don't know if I can."

"Here, I'll show you the part that has to be filled in," Wendy said. Mallory leaned down close to look over her shoulder.

"Just this dot at the top of the plume. It's a circle—you won't mess it up."

"Am I allowed to do this?"

"Not really," Alec said.

"No," said Wendy. "Rihanna's tattoo artist lost his license for letting her tattoo him. Paparazzi snapped a photo of it. So don't tell anyone. But your boyfriend told me your whole story, and you're right—he is a romantic. You'd be surprised how many people come in here and get tattoos with barely any thought about it. It means nothing but getting some perceived hipster cred. And it's not often I get to design something from scratch like this. So I'm excited about it, and I'm happy to let you be a part of the process."

"Just think, Mal—how many times have you wanted to inflict pain on me? Now's your chance."

If Wendy was willing to let her do it, and Alec trusted her to take a needle to his arm, who was she to say no?

"Okay. What do I do?"

Wendy gave her blue gloves, and Mallory pulled them on. She felt as serious as if she was about to perform surgery. Wendy stood up to give Mallory the stool. She put the tool in her hand, and it was surprisingly heavy.

"Put your foot on this pedal—press it to start the needle."

"Oh, my God," Mallory said. She looked at Alec. He winked at her. She pressed the pedal toward the floor, and it started a whirring sound. Slowly, she lowered the needle to the spot on the design that needed the final mark. She was afraid to press too hard and hurt him, and ink sprayed off the surface making it hard for her to tell if she was making contact with his skin or not. She released the petal and pulled the needle back and looked at her handiwork. Sure enough, there was a small dot. With a deep breath, she restarted the tool and pressed it to Alec's arm again, this time making a conscious effort to move the needle in a circular motion. After a few seconds, she pulled back again. Wendy wiped the area of the mark, and, there was a small blue circle completing the design of the feather.

"Is it done?" she asked, as amazed as if she had just witnessed a birth.

"It's done," Wendy said.

"Thanks," Mallory said. "That was something I'll never forget."

"Damn right," Alec said. "You'll be looking at it for the rest of your life."

"Oh, you think?" she said to him.

"I can only hope."

She leaned over and kissed him.

23

Mallory stretched her leg up on the barre, bending into a deep plié. She wore a pair of black Hard Tail workout pants, a black tank top, and her pink ballet slippers. Black leg warmers stretched from her ankles to mid-thigh. She remembered how her childhood ballet academy had required them to wear black leotards, pink tights, and pink ballet slippers. No deviation from that, and hair always pulled into a low ponytail.

She wondered what her old instructor would think of her now—rolling the dice and gambling everything on making her way as a performer. It wasn't ballet, or even jazz, but burlesque performance *was* dancing—her former practice space partner, Nadia, had assured her of that. Now Nadia had a spot with the Pennsylvania Ballet, and Mallory was on her way to running the club she herself would perform in. If they ever found a location for the club—or thought of a name.

They'd tossed around plenty of ideas and rejected them all. For a while, the front-runner was "Moxie," but Mallory told them it would turn off some of the more ambitious girls who would want to imagine they could become headliners or the top girl there, an impossible goal when the club was named after another performer. They had thought about calling it Ivy's, in homage to the university where Alec and Mallory had met; they considered the Pike, after Martha's sensational Kegel aid. They considered random names like the Revue, Gloss, and Stilettos. But they still hadn't found something worthy of the club they envisioned.

She cued up the old CD player at the ballet studio, and the opening of Marilyn Manson's "Heart-Shaped Glasses" filled the room. The night she had abruptly walked out of the Blue Angel before the start of a show three months ago was the night she had planned to perform to the song. In the days that followed, she thought she might never again be in front of an audience, and that meant the "Heart-Shaped Glasses" choreography, probably her best routine aside from the one Bette had taught her the first night she ever performed, would never be seen by anyone. It was a waste, but at the time, she'd felt it was what she had to do.

She still wasn't sure when she would get to unveil "Heart-Shaped Glasses"; once the Blue Angel closed for remodeling by its new owners, she had no place to perform. A few of the girls were picking up gigs at other clubs, but she knew that when she performed, it would be on the stage that she would help design, in a show she would conceptualize and direct—Martha and Justin had made it clear they wanted her and Alec to be as involved with the creative direction of the club as possible. The thought was thrilling.

She sat in the center of the room as the song kicked in, languidly unfolding her body, seducing the "audience" with her slow, purposeful movements. She rolled onto her side, experimenting with changing her position on the "bed" to start out half propped up instead of on her back, when a rap on the rehearsal room window interrupted her. Alec waved. She jumped up off of the floor and let him in. He kissed her perspiring forehead.

"Hey," she said. "I still have twenty minutes left."

"I couldn't wait to pick you up; I have to show you something."

"Okay, show me."

"You have to come somewhere with me."

"Alec! I have to practice. I can't let myself get rusty. Bette said when she took four months off it was really hard to feel confident on stage afterward."

"I wouldn't interrupt you if it wasn't important," he said. She tried to read from his expression if he was being serious or was just messing around with her, but she couldn't tell. His eyes looked bright and excited and playful, but there was something focused and determined in the set of his jaw.

"Okay, okay. I'll meet you out front in five minutes. Just let me change."

"Don't change. Just put your coat on over that."

"I'll be quick."

"No—I'm serious. Don't change."

"Fine. I'll meet you out front."

She was learning not to waste time debating Alec when he was determined. Maybe that was the way relationships survive—constantly learning how to coexist with someone. Picking your battles. Only putting your foot down when it was a deal breaker. Fortunately, she hadn't been confronted with any of those lately. She was starting to feel confident she wouldn't ever again.

Alec told the cab to let them off on the corner of Elizabeth Street and Houston. He took Mallory by the hand and led her to the center of the block. She wondered if he was taking her shopping for an early Valentine's Day present. Two of her favorite stores were on Elizabeth, the jewelry store Me & Ro and the Tory Burch boutique. Even though Tory Burch clothes tended to be a bit on the conservative side, Mallory had a soft spot for the designer because she had grown up in the same town as Mallory. Alec was amused that Main Line Philadelphia was the birthplace of Princess Grace Kelly, designer Tory Burch, and burlesque dancer Moxie.

"And one day you'll be more famous than the other two," Alec had said.

"I don't need to be famous," Mallory had said.

"Oh no? What do you need to be?"

"Loved," she had replied.

Now he stopped her four storefronts before Tory Burch. It looked to be a former restaurant. She could have sworn she'd been there before, but she couldn't remember exactly what used to occupy that space.

Alec pulled a key from his wallet and began opening the door.

"What is this?" she said.

"It's your club."

"No way."

"Yeah. Justin and I found it a few weeks ago."

Mallory's heart started to beat faster. It was a perfect location—not too out of the way, but not as overrun and crazy at night as the Meatpacking District or the Village. And they had all talked about creating a more intimate venue than the Blue Angel, and certainly more intimate than the circus-like atmosphere of the Slit. From what she could tell from the outside, this space was exactly what she had in mind.

"Why didn't you tell me you found something?" she said, following him into the darkness. He locked the door behind them and flipped a wall switch so the room was lit by a few bare bulbs hanging from the ceiling. The walls had been stripped down, and there were construction directions and markings all over them. Exposed wires ran along the wall and some from the ceiling. An empty bar lined the right side of the space, covered with a few discarded jackets and equipment left by construction workers. The room widened toward the back, with slightly higher ceilings and a corridor that she assumed led to the former restaurant's kitchen.

"The layout could work like this: tables here, a few rows of non-table seating along the sides and back. Keep the bar where it is. And this space back here"—he led her by the hand to where the room widened—"will be the stage. Behind this spot is a kitchen, but we're going to take it out and build a really good dressing room."

Mallory hugged him. "It's perfect! Oh, my God, I'm so excited. I can't believe this is really happening."

Alec picked up what appeared to be a large poster board propped against the back wall. He turned it around to show her, and she saw that it was painted with a large replicated image of the dancer that Alec had tattooed on his arm—the Mallory burlesque angel. Next to it, in bold script, were the words *The Painted Lady.*

"What is that?" she said, looking at his smile.

"I'm thinking it's the name of the club. What do you think?"

"It's perfect. It's just all...perfect. I'm at a loss. You're the writer—how do I express how amazing this is? I don't know where to start."

"Maybe we should christen the stage," he said.

She looked at the floor. "You want to have sex in here?"

"I was thinking maybe the next best thing. Want to do a little inaugural performance?"

She smiled. Now she knew why he hadn't wanted her to change out of her workout clothes. "There's one problem: I need music."

He walked over to the bar and picked up an iDock that was still plugged into an outlet. "Luckily for us, the construction workers feel the same way." He set his iPhone between the speakers. "What do you want to hear?"

"You really think I'm going to do this?"

He walked over to the sign and held it up. "You are my muse, baby. Gotta keep the inspiration flowing."

She smiled. "Fine. You win. As usual! Do you have Marilyn Manson on there?"

"Of course."

"Play 'Heart-Shaped Glasses.'"

She took her coat and his coat and spread them out on the floor to make a "bed." Without props, tassels, and schoolgirl clothes, the routine wouldn't work. But she knew that piece had to be her inaugural dance. It hadn't made it to the Blue Angel stage for a reason—it was meant for this space, hers and Alec's.

She pulled two hairclips from her bag and put them on the floor next to the bed. Quickly, before she could change her mind, she shed her clothes, leaving on only her black lace thong from the Gap. Not the most inspired undergarment, but she hadn't planned to be on display when she woke up that morning. Of course, living with Alec, she should know to always be at the ready. And she loved it that way.

She stretched out on the coats, rearranging them so a zipper didn't dig into her bare back. When she felt comfortable enough to begin, she told him to start the music.

The song filled the room, its rhythmic opening slightly tinny in the wide open space, and Alec sat on the floor in front of her. The opening built to a swell, and then the lyrics kicked in. At the first sound of Manson's low, growling voice, she extended her body out, raising her arms in an exaggerated morning stretch. She turned away from the "audience," giving a view of her ass. In the actual show, she planned to use stuffed animals to tease the crowd with only a partial view. She would make sure the color scheme was mostly pink with a few accents of red, and when she was fully dressed at the end, her final accessory would be an oversized pair of red, heart-shaped glasses.

With practiced slowness, she sat up in bed, giving a final stretch. She shimmied her breasts, wondering if she should cover her nipples with tassels during the performance or maybe just heart-shaped pasties. As she considered the finer points of how the performance should debut when The Painted Lady was open for business, Alec jumped up from his perch at the edge of the "stage" and practically tackled her on the coats.

"What are you doing?" She laughed.

"I heard this was an audience-participation show."

"No! Go back to your seat. I'm just getting started."

"You're getting me started, I can tell you that. And I've changed my mind."

He pulled her against him, his hand running down her back, cupping her ass.

"About what?"

"Your original idea about how to christen the stage was much better. I defer to your wisdom."

He kissed her, and she threw her arms around him, knowing that as long as they were together, the whole world was their stage.